The World's
Most Evil Cults

The World's Most Evil Cults

Peter Haining

This edition published by Parragon Books Ltd in 2006

Parragon
Queen Street House
4 Queen Street
Bath BA1 1HE, UK

Produced by Magpie Books,
an imprint of Constable & Robinson Ltd
www.constablerobinson.com

A copy of the British Library Cataloguing in Publication Data
is available from the British Library

ISBN-13: 978-1-4054-8825-9

Printed and bound in the EU

1 3 5 7 9 10 8 6 4 2

Contents

Foreword

In 1964, while I was working as a journalist in Fleet Street, I wrote one of the first exposures of modern cults, *Devil Worship in Britain*, in conjunction with Bill Sellwood, a *Daily Mirror* reporter. The book led us to some strange groups and some even stranger people. Often working undercover, we infiltrated several witchcraft covens and were provided with eyewitness accounts of black magic and satanic rituals. As our enquiries went deeper, we also began receiving anonymous and often menacing telephone calls – as did our publishers. Despite these threats, publication went ahead and there was a lot of interest shown by the media in *Devil Worship in Britain*'s detailed exposure of a mysterious underworld just beneath the surface of the 'swinging sixties'. The experience of writing the book, though, was something that neither Bill nor I would ever forget.

The investigation produced a number of leads about other strange cults operating in Britain at that time. I continued researching and planned a sequel, *Strange Cults*, which would focus on a number of secretive groups whose members had an attitude towards religion, morality and behaviour that was very bizarre and often quite dangerous. Yet although *Devil Worship in Britain* had sold well and none of the threats had materialized, I could find no one to commit to publishing the book. Although I had written seven chapters, I decided to seek another avenue of publication. I turned to magazines and at last found an editor willing to print my reports as a seven-part series. The publication was *Fiesta* – 'A Magazine for Men' – which was one of the leading 'girlie mags' that had established themselves in the fifties including Hugh

Heffner's *Playboy* and Bob Guccione's *Penthouse*. Vic Briggs was trying to emulate them by running serious articles and features alongside the photographs of beautiful naked girls. It was in publications such as these, in fact, that the boundaries of controversy were then being pushed back more resolutely than anywhere else.

Briggs ran my articles under the somewhat sensational title of 'Slaves of Lust' through the summer months of 1965. They, too, prompted a number of phone calls and letters – but with words of encouragement rather than abuse. However, the demands of book publishing, into which I had just moved, prevented me from pursuing the theme any further – although my interest in cults never ceased. Those original seven articles have remained in magazine form until I was asked to write this book. I have therefore decided to include them here because, although the activities of the cultists half a century ago may have seemed tame by some of today's extreme standards, their obsessions have contiued to inspire cults during the rest of the twentieth century – namely religion, satanism and, inevitably, sex. In that watershed era can be seen the origins of many of the world's most evil cults and their extraordinary leaders who have emerged, briefly flourished and – almost without exception – destroyed themselves.

When Bill Sellwood and I wrote *Devil Worship in Britain* we optimistically hoped it might serve as a warning to the unwary about joining dangerous cults. The evidence of these pages is that a great many did not heed the message at all.

Part One

Satan in the Sixties

The Sisters of Wicca

Eleanor Bone is a witch. She is not a gnarled, snag-toothed old harridan reminiscent of the Middle Ages, but an attractive, well-dressed suburban housewife who belongs to a cult which is, in fact, older than Christianity.

She is a woman prepared – indeed stubbornly prepared – to accept ridicule from the general public for holding views which most people regard with suspicion, even fear.

To those who belong to Mrs Bone's coven – the witch term for a group of believers – she is a High Priestess called Artemis; to others who know her she is just a friendly neighbour; but to some she is a crank, a woman to be treated with care. The fear of the 'evil eye' supposedly possessed by all witches was not dead in the swinging sixties, it would seem . . .

Mrs Bone is, in fact, a 'white' witch, and, as I shall show, there is a whole world of difference between 'white' magic and the highly publicized, scarcely understood 'black' magic. The aims and practices of these two groups are in no way similar – they seek different ends for different purposes. One is as dedicated to good as the other is to evil.

However, we shall also see how the two cults do overlap and how some 'white' witches drift into black magic mistakenly thinking it is just an extension – a dark and mysterious extension, perhaps – of what they are already practising. Their mistake can cost them very dearly financially, physically and certainly in human dignity.

Witchcraft – the ancient religion of Wicca, which venerates fertility – is worthy of more serious study than most people give it; just as those who belong to the cult should not be dismissed as weak-minded fools, charlatans or sex maniacs. It is people like

3

Eleanor Bone who are trying to set the record straight after centuries of suspicion and persecution.

Her own example helps to demonstrate that the modern witch is an ordinary person, living among us but forced to confine his or her beliefs just below the veneer of society, behind high walls and in conditions of privacy. A person cautious of publicizing their views *too* freely for fear of the sensational newspaper stories which the word 'witch' always attracts.

Mrs Bone's home in busy Tooting is a neat, three-storeyed building, kept with the kind of meticulous care that any woman would be proud of. She runs it to a strict timetable and looks after her husband with considerable devotion – strangely he is not a witch and treats the cult with a kind of wry amusement. An ordinary enough woman, certainly; the kind whose neighbours stop for a chat with her in the street and wave greetings as they pass in the supermarket or hurry for a bus.

But it is this woman – this typical housewife – who also holds the position of 'liaison officer for witch covens'. It is she who has answered frankly and fearlessly questions concerning her religion and her fellow witches.

She admits to holding witch meetings in her house; once every month, in fact, in her spacious, well-furnished lounge. These gatherings are conducted on the Saturday night nearest to the full moon, and the group consists of Mrs Bone – the High Priestess – and twelve 'disciples', thirteen being the ancient specified number for a coven.

There is nothing to chill the blood or send a shiver up the spine about the meetings. In fact they are rather homely: an electric fire burns in one corner, and that symbol of the modern age – a television set – is turned to face the wall in another. A chalk circle is drawn on the carpet, nine foot in circumference, and inside it a small altar is placed bearing incense, salt and water, and a number of 'holy' vessels. The ritual which follows is the same as those performed all over the country – from secluded Scottish valleys to spacious grounds in rolling Oxfordshire countryside.

Stripped completely naked – 'clothes stifle the emanations from our bodies and they are also a reminder of external influences' the witches contend – they chant the old-as-time prayers of the religion designed to produce fertility and conjure up powers to do good.

4

The rites undoubtedly act as a stimulant on those taking part, and the witches in fact contend that joy can only be experienced when the senses have been satisfied. To this end they use herbs with purifying and stimulating powers – like sandalwood, juniper and myrrh – to arouse themselves. Each part of the ceremony – which is still cloaked in considerable secrecy and even those who have witnessed gatherings have not learned the true meaning of many of the actions – has its own special significance.

In its early stages the participants are brought gradually to a pitch; they dance around the circle, slowly to start with, clasping hands. As the High Priestess invokes the ancient powers, *'Eko Eko Azerak, Eko Eko Zomelak, Eko Eko Gananas, Eko Eko Arada,'* the dancers whirl ever faster, their bodies sending swirls of incense up to the ceiling and making the candles – the only lights in the room – flicker eerily.

The witches appeal for fertility and good health. They implore the ancient gods to watch over them and prepare them for the day they will die. They ask, too, that they may learn about reincarnation – for all witches believe that they will return to earth after death in different guises.

If any spells are to be cast, they will be made at this point as a general rule. Much has been said and written about witch spells – some claim a witch can 'wish' illness and death on anyone, while others believe their power is restricted to simple cures. The witches themselves say they only use their power for good, but they can 'spell' a person simply by mind transmission. However, they maintain they will only do so when 'attacked by someone really wicked'. (To me the simple explanation of this 'power' seems to lie in auto-suggestion, if a person really believes someone else is trying to help them – or indeed cursing them – the power of the mind can make it an actuality.)

At the height of the ceremony, the Priestess holds a small knife, the Athame, up before her, pointing it to the ceiling, and prays that the coven may better understand the life force which motivates them all. Her final request is that the coven may be strengthened in its resolve to do good – and the members perform their last ritual dance, hands linked.

And what about after it is all over? When the naked witches

have reached a pitch of frenzy? Do they – as has frequently been claimed – take part in unbridled sex orgies? Do the men and women have promiscuous sexual intercourse until they finally collapse exhausted? Or do they – as the believers themselves contend – just rest quietly and sip wine as genteely as orthodox Christians at a vicarage tea party?

On this score Mrs Bone is very forthcoming – and very definite. 'There are certainly no orgies in our covens. I cannot speak for every coven in Britain today, of course, and I don't think there is much doubt that some do dabble in black magic with sex rites, but our only purpose is to invoke good.

'As I have told people before, why should we go to all the trouble of holding such a complicated ritual if we simply wanted to go to bed with someone?'

All the evidence I have amassed during my enquiries into the witchcraft sects leads me to confirm this view. In the highly charged atmosphere of a room heavy with incense and sticky with heat, obviously sometimes control does become difficult for certain witches but in the main the ceremonies are observed with the care and reverence of a Church of England service or a Roman Catholic Mass.

Make no mistake, the belief in witchcraft is widespread today – far more widespread than it has been for many centuries. And the way Mrs Bone came to enter the ranks of the witches is typical of many of her fellows.

She was brought up by strict Anglican parents who compelled her to attend Sunday school and later the full church services. As soon as she was able to weigh the matter up for herself, she found many questions unanswered and particularly rebelled against the 'stuffiness' of the church.

'It was just boring, so I decided to study the occult instead. There were answers there in plenty to my questions . . . and gradually the path of discovery led me to witchcraft,' she says.

This self-same urge to rebel is leading more people to witch-craft every day. An estimate was given recently that over two dozen people apply to gain admission to the covens every week.

So just how many practising witches are there in Great Britain today? That was the question I set out to answer. And even with my already considerable knowledge of the cult, the answer still came as something of a shock.

*   *   *

At a carefully reasoned estimate there are approximately 30,000 active witches in the British Isles today. Their covens are to be found in provincial cities as well as rural towns; practically every county can boast at least one – several, like Bedfordshire and Sussex, have dozens. The largest number of witches are to be found in London, Bedfordshire, Sussex, Lancashire, Warwickshire and Perthshire in Scotland. Even Northern Ireland can claim its own flourishing groups.

One of the most startling aspects of witchcraft that I have noted is that the followers – almost to a man (and woman) – are people in responsible jobs demanding a reasonably high degree of intelligence and earning above average salaries. During my enquiries I learned of witches who are psychologists, company directors, secretaries, researchers, lecturers, and even doctors. A few are afraid that exposure would prejudice their jobs, but most believe the public is slowly – painfully slowly, they say – beginning to understand Wicca and refrain from persecuting those who follow it. It is reasoned that as we tolerate homosexuality, lesbianism and other deviations in human relations, it is sheer hypocrisy to condemn what is in essence a private practice which does not attempt to influence or corrupt outsiders.

I have also discovered that there is a complicated but efficient system of communication linking the major covens. This enables the groups to get in touch with each other over activities and rituals. Precautions have been taken, however, in case one should be broken up or disbanded leaving the consequent possibility of information about other covens leaking out. To prevent this, each coven in the underground cell system has a letter of identification; while members are known simply by numbers. In this way few witches know who their colleagues are, unless they choose to reveal their identity.

The covens are quite small units, never more than thirteen witches in each. A High Priest rules over each group and will probably adopt the witch name of Loic. The only other member liable to be addressed by name is the Witch Maiden who may be called variously 'Olwin', 'Tanith', or 'Dayonis'. The highest witch strata of all are the High Priestesses, like Mrs Bone, and these matriarchs usually control three covens each.

The covens meet at least eight times a year, sometimes far more frequently. The most important dates on their calendar are May Eve, Hallowe'en and Christmas. Witches prefer to gather as often as possible in the open air – secluded woods or the grounds of spacious, well-wooded private estates being ideal. When they are forced to meet indoors, they restrict the rites to one sparsely furnished room with a carpet on the floor and the windows blanketed. The centrepiece is invariably the knee-high altar which is placed so that the traditional nine-foot circle – made either of tape or chalk – can encircle it and leave room for the followers to dance around its edge.

* * *

During the actual ritual, the naked witches worship two ancient gods – one male and one female. The admiration of the female – the Great Mother – predominates, as the witches believe she personifies fertility and the life force.

The Book of Shadows is the witches' bible. Its pages contain details of how the ceremonies are to be conducted, how initiation is performed and instruction of how to work the spells of witch-craft. Quite what age this work is, no one is really sure – or, come to that, who wrote it. Every witch possesses a copy – having laboriously copied it by hand from an original 'loaned' to them after the initiation ceremony.

This highly secret manual is as important a tool to the cult as the swords which are brandished by members during the worship. These implements – called Athame – are remnants of the days of sacrificial offerings when live animals were offered to the gods. They are held aloft by the members while they are being blessed by the High Priestess – who is the only one at the altar during the early stages of the ceremony. When she had completed this act of 'purification' the twelve 'disciples' can then enter the circle, and having done so link hands and dance frenziedly around to conjure up the life force.

To those people who have heard of this ritual it appears as fairly harmless but rather pointless. What is it supposed to mean? And what has it to do with the witches' claim that they do good for people?

According to one witch, a blonde attractive housewife from Sheffield, Mrs Patricia Crowther, the ceremony is needed to abjure the ancient gods to heal the sick and help the needy. Prayer is not merely enough, the ritual along with special prescribed devotions must be used.

Mrs Crowther has appeared on television several times talking about witchcraft and its power to do good. After every appearance, she says, she receives an enormous number of letters.

'The majority of the writers,' she explains, 'want me to help them win the football pools, or else get money some other way for their own selfish ends. But there are a few genuinely seeking our aid for deserving causes and these we try to help.'

Mrs Crowther's coven – and others to my knowledge – claim that they have actually restored people to health with witch prayers . . . some from quite serious illnesses.

At about the time I was investigating this particular aspect of Wicca, I heard of a case where a farmer appealed to a coven for help because his crops were being ruined by torrential rain. He said a few days uninterrupted sunshine were essential to save them. As a result a special service was held at which the witches danced and chanted the specified prayers. The following day the sun shone and continued to do so for several days afterwards. It could have been sheer coincidence rather than witchcraft that brought about the weather change, but it was pointed out to me by the witch who recounted the case that the rain continued unabated on farms no more than ten miles away from where the farmer had sunshine.

In another case witches were said to be responsible for curing a herd of cattle in Dorset of some deadly diseases including redwater and loor.

In yet another, they supplied lucky talismans to a rural family dogged by ill-luck and allegedly halted their string of misfortunes.

There are appeals made to them to remove spells, too. Mrs Crowther received one such letter from a woman who claimed that a neighbour must have put a jinx on her as she could never win at bingo!

Recently this outspoken modern witch wrote a lucid and entertaining article in a magazine describing the kind of wishes witches are expected to grant. They include: to have triplets; to gain power over others; to marry Elizabeth Taylor; to be loved by Cliff Richard; to be an astronaut . . .

'But the greatest desire of all,' Mrs Crowther summarized, 'is for money. Happiness and good health are right at the bottom of the list.'

One of the most interesting facts I learned from Mrs Crowther was that she had had quite a considerable amount of correspondence from clergymen. This confirmed my own findings that the Church is slowly – and not without considerable suspicion – looking into the revival of witchcraft.

I had myself already been in touch with a minister in a northern industrial town who had actually joined a coven of witches. He talked freely enough about his associations with the coven, but asked that I did not reveal his name as he felt his parishioners were not yet sympathetic enough to accept that a minister of the Church could also be a disciple of ancient, pre-Christian gods.

'Witches are really most tolerant of other beliefs – more so than most of us who call ourselves Christians. They find nothing odd in a man being able to worship both Christ and the old gods,' he said.

This man is typical of those who have written to Patricia Crowther.

'I have one letter from a minister who favours the witches and thinks it is high time a clergyman spoke up for them. He says the church should state publicly that witchcraft is not evil,' she claims.

On the other hand there have been cases where the motives of clergymen – if they were clergymen – could at best be described as dubious. One vicar wrote asking for a book of witchcraft rites 'so that I can try them out', and another offered a coven a guinea for a tape-recording of their secret rites.

Ordinary members of the public likewise pester the witches with suspicious requests.

'Some write to us thinking they can join a secret cult . . . their letters are of the "cloak and dagger" type signed with some mysterious name or sign and very suggestive in content,' explained Mrs Crowther.

She has also had appeals from people to send them love potions, details of how to turn their mothers-in-law to frogs and even requests to be put in touch with vampires and werewolves!

'These letters would be laughable if it wasn't that the people really believed such things do exist,' she added, not without some concern in her voice for human gullibility.

Mrs Crowther – like me – believes that such evidence also shows how the kinky are now preying on witchcraft in their search for fresh diversions.

'Of all the hundreds of letters I receive, I doubt if there are more than a handful of real seekers after the truth. Most of them are the "what can I get out of it" type,' she says.

The witches would very much like to be able to sort the genuine applicant from the phoney – believing that if they could their numbers would increase dramatically.

'I think there are probably many hundreds of people at this very moment who would like to join us if they could do so without the risk of possible embarrassment,' says Mrs Crowther. 'These are the kind of people who just don't write letters for fear of them getting into the wrong hands – you know, the mail order specialists – and having themselves immediately classified as kinky.

'Why, if we could only organize some kind of body to promote a better understanding of witchcraft and effect introductions to covens, I feel sure we would get several thousand new members in no time at all . . .'

And from this intriguing statement arises the much more urgent question: how has it all come about? Why should witchcraft suddenly rear its head again after lying dormant for so long? What has it to offer in this permissive and enlightened age?

The answer is not without surprises.

* * *

The resurgence of witchcraft in Britain has only taken place during the past half-century. Before that it had been secreted away for over two centuries, practised by only a few devotees, and thought by most people to be defunct. And there was good reason – plus plentiful evidence – for thinking so . . .

The last witch had been executed in Britain at Exeter in 1684 – an unfortunate old woman called Alice Molland who was convicted and sentenced to death for supposed dealings with the Devil. She had been put to death in the manner prescribed by law – hanging. This form of capital punishment was reserved especially for witches, while their sisters who committed either treason or heresy were burned.

The execution of Alice Molland was not the last time a witch was hauled up before the justices, however. Trials of suspected practitioners continued until as late as 1711. During the later years those found guilty were sent to prison and the pillory.

Nevertheless, public feeling was growing all the time about the inhumanity of the witch trials and finally it reached the ears of Parliament. In 1735 the Witchcraft Act was tabled and passed, and it decreed that witchcraft was no longer a statutory or ecclesiastical offence. Although this brought to a close a black period in England's history when any harmless old scold could be accused of being a witch and have her life cut short on the gallows, it could not wipe out the fact that in the previous 70 years witches had been hanged in the country at the rate of 23 every year.

Many people tried to push from their minds the fact that there had ever been such a thing as witchcraft – and developed an attitude of supposed sophistication which refused to believe that such a 'primitive' practice could ever develop again. The authorities were inclined to take this view, too, and so witchcraft – the real witchcraft which venerated the Goddesss of Fertility – was left to its own devices.

The last statute about witchcraft was finally removed from the law books in 1951 by the confident authorities who now felt it was just a ridiculous relic from the past. The occasional report of witchcraft again being practised which did come to the ears of the police was rebuffed by them with the comment that the law was no longer interested in the cult so long as any ceremonies or rites did not step outside the law.

It was not surprising, therefore, that when it finally became patently obvious in the early 1950s that the old cult was on the upsurge again, several scholars and supposed authorities were quick to rush into print with statements that what was being practised was a modern hotch-potch and 'bore no resemblance to the old Wicca of bygone eras'.

But it is just not so.

* * *

A highly strung, one-time rubber planter and customs officer, Gerald Brosseau Gardner, was the man mainly responsible for the revival of witchcraft in the twentieth century. For years he had stealthily practised the 'white arts', gathering around him an élite group of men and women handpicked to follow in his footsteps. He had striven especially to uncover the hidden secrets of Wicca, and there was every good reason in later life for him to declare himself a master of witchcraft. His pupils were not slow to give their support to his claims, either.

In his childhood, Gerald Gardner travelled extensively around the world seeking to cure the asthma which blighted his life. It was in Africa – and later India – that he came into contact with the power of witchcraft – both black and white – and formed an interest in the subject which was to last all his life. A well-educated man – he won for himself degrees in philosophy and literature during his schooling in England – Dr Gardner pitted his intelligence against all the claims of witchcraft . . . and emerged from his enquiries firmly convinced of both the power and the good of the ancient cult.

After working for a while as a rubber planter in Malaya, he changed his job and moved to Singapore where he became a customs officer. In his spare time he continued to press on with his research into the occult, and then in 1939, on a rare visit to England, he was put in touch with one of the very few covens of witches in the country at that time, in Hampshire. His immediate reaction, he admitted to later, was not to get involved, but the witches convinced him that destiny had brought him to the coven.

In that same year Dr. Gerald Gardner became a witch . . . and unknowingly set into motion the chain of events which led to today's big revival.

This small man with his thin, almost emaciated body, haunting eyes and goatee beard, found little difficulty in understanding and appreciating the secrets of witchcraft. By the end of the Second World War his name was familiar among most witches and he had assumed a position of authority which no one questioned. He had, in fact, been instrumental, during the days when the Nazi invasion of Britain was imminent, in arranging the meetings of witches in the New Forest to 'send' the idea to the minds of the German High Command that any plans to land in this country were doomed to failure from the start.

After peace was declared he settled at Castletown on the Isle of Man, finding there the right kind of atmosphere in which to attempt his big ambition . . . the promotion of witchcraft as a serious religion.

He bought an old mill on the outskirts of the town, renovated it, and renamed it 'Witch Mill'. There he amassed a huge collection of witch paraphernalia including cauldrons, broomsticks, 'tool' sets, the apparatus of the ceremonial rituals, bones, charms, instruments of torture from the great witch purges of the past and all manner of other items. This museum was soon drawing hundreds of visitors – at a shilling per head. Many people came to jeer, a few came to puzzle, but even fewer came to try and understand. However, with a steady supply of money, Dr Gardner was able to dedicate himself to his work and after lecturing tourists by day could settle down to experiment by night.

From his island seat the master continued to guide the covens across the water in Great Britain. Under his influence new ones sprung up with increasing regularity and he was frequently asked to attend secret meetings and settle disputes. He also made himself approachable to both the public and the press and would argue for hours on the virtues of the 'old faith' in which he believed so strongly. He wrote extensively on witchcraft and several of his books are considered the most authoritative in the field.

In February, 1964, having reached the venerable age of 80, Dr Gardner died while returning from a winter holiday in Lebanon. He died seemingly well pleased with his work; the witch covens had multiplied a hundred-fold during his years of 'leadership' and the public were showing more sympathy towards the religion

The Sisters of Wicca

than at any other time in history. Perhaps even as he died he uttered a simple prayer of thanks to the ancient gods he revered.

In Great Britain his death came as a considerable shock. Several of the covens even got together and took the unprecedented step of issuing a statement to the press expressing their grief at Dr Gardner's passing. To them it was also a great tragedy that he took to the grave a number of the secrets he had painstakingly uncovered during his lifetime.

Soon after his death his will revealed that witchcraft had helped him accumulate a considerable fortune. The bulk of his £25,000 estate and 'all my equipment for making magic' he left to one of his protéges, the High Priestess of the Scottish covens, Mrs Monique Wilson of Perth. Another £3,000 was also alloted to Mrs Patricia Crowther of Sheffield.

Big money, people thought, for a man who seemed to be just a dabbler in old, pagan practices. What they didn't realize – and probably still don't – was that Dr Gardner's wealth illustrated the biggest change of all in twentieth-century witchcraft. It has 'gone commercial'.

Strange as it may seem – and there is so much that is stranger than fiction about witchcraft – the sect now supports an industry which nets thousands of pounds a year . . . perhaps more.

A couple of hundred people in this country are earning their living making equipment and materials for witches. They certainly don't all know it, as quite a few of the items they produce don't usually go to witches. In fact the range of goods manufactured for the devotees extends from 'holy' vessels, and occult symbols on the one hand, to special suits to be worn at ceremonies when the weather is cold, on the other!

Much of the equipment bought by the witches comes from addresses passed around the covens; while some of it is supplied by members setting themselves up as 'wholesalers'. Quite a considerable percentage, however, is advertised in the columns of the dozens of small magazines and leaflets which circulate among those interested in the occult. One or two of these publications like *Fate* and *New Dimensions* – are on sale to the general public as well.

The wares are offered with all the salesmanship that the big soap combines or motor manufacturers employ for their products.

15

'Special Offers' are proclaimed in the very best tub-thumping tradition, and 'speedy delivery' plus guarantees of 'money back if not satisfied' can also be spotted.

Take these few examples chosen at random from the dozens of advertisements which I have collected over the last few years:

MYSTIC INCENSE. This fine slow-burning incense powder is especially blended for the development of your highest spiritual powers. 40 *pence a canister.*

DRAGON'S BLOOD 25 *pence per oz. Magical list 6 pence stamps.*

GENUINE and Rare Occult Supplies. Lists free. Photos 15 pence (refundable).

'COVEN LEADERS – when the weather is extra cold, track-suits would be ideal for your members. All sizes most colours, quantity discounts . . .'

And, for the ladies, what better offer than:
MOON MAGIC Beauty Balm. The secret way to beautiful skin. Secretly made for you 'where two streams meet' from genuine old magic formula. In plain wrapper fifty pence.

There are details, too, about 'best quality' bat's blood, 'finely ground, high quality' rhinoceros horn, and 'carefully bottled' deadly nightshade.

Perhaps, though, the printed word is the most profitable line of all. Pirate versions of the famous *Book of Shadows* – printed in America – are offered at 'a bargain price', as is the *Book of Forbidden Knowledge* which purports to contain secret formulas 'as practised by the ancient wise men'. But the really big money is secured for titles like *Magic in Theory and Practice* by Aleister Crowley, a sinister, perverted man who was as much responsible for the rise of modern black magic as Dr Gardner was for white: you will read of him in a later chapter. And for works like *The Book of Ceremonial Magic, The Gospel of the Witches* and *The*

Ancient's Book of Magic. All these sell – and sell well – at over £2 each.

Possibly the most unusual 'literary work' available to the curious is *Witchcraft* a gaudy, profusely illustrated booklet produced by Dumblecott Magick Productions of Charlwood, Surrey. It treats the subject of witchcraft quite light-heartedly and proclaims its policy as *Magick with a smile*. Edited by 'Dr Othney Rib' – described as 'one of the most extraordinary witches of England' – the publication debunks some of the witches' spells in one article and reveals in another that the secret of the 'Magic Wand of the Wishans' had been discovered and can now be obtained from the publishers – 'although it should only be used by the true devotee'.

The same publishers have also produced *Witch*, *a* work claimed to be 'the secrets of modern witchcraft revealed'. The book, subtitled glowingly 'the complete witchcraft rituals as taught and practised by Gerald Brossean Gardner', is by Rex Nemorensis, a practising witch who lives in Surrey.

Going hand in glove with 'bargains' such as these are other adverts which represent to me a most amazing trend in witchcraft today. For they imply – and imply with considerable emphasis – that certain of the rapidly expanding witch covens are now actually touting for new members!

Such a development would have been completely out of the question a few years back. Magazines – even the most 'way-out' and adventurous – would not have considered opening their columns for appeals from or for witches. Now, however, the recruiting campaign is being carried out both in small publications and national-circulation journals with readerships running into many thousands. There is no attempt to conceal the purposes of the advertisers, either. They are blunt and to the point.

WITCHCRAFT. Ceremonial Magick. London Occultists invite sincere seekers to join activities. Either sex. Confidence respected . . .

WICCA. Dianic, Aradian Society, Cardiff; enquiries welcomed. Box number . . .

WICCA PERTHSHIRE CIRCLE welcomes sincere seekers. Fullest details. Confidence respected ...

And let me assure you that these are quite genuine. I have written to several of the 'advertisers' myself – and although not all replied (some, I suspect, sensed that my purpose was not that of a person seeking initiation), those that did wrote from bonafide addresses and were not opposed to discussing the matter further face to face.

In case anyone intrigued by the announcements should care to know a little of 'what he can expect of witchcraft' before replying, a further advertisement in a recent issue of *Fate* has a suggestion to make: take a correspondence course in the craft!

BREAKTHROUGH in the new conception! Witchcraft – invaluable new correspondence course available to approved applicants. Be first! Literature five pence.

In the words of the well-known phrase: you pays your money and takes your choice. Surely, though, even in this day and age, this is 'do-it-yourself' gone mad!

But if this particular insertion can be treated with amusement and not taken too seriously, there are also to be found in the self-same columns 'wanted ads' which are anything but funny. For there is nothing funny about the sinister ... and these other advertisements have very definite sinister undertones.

They are appeals by people anxious to get into witchcraft covens – any witchcraft covens.

I do not doubt that some of these notices are genuine, that the people who have placed them want to make a sincere contact with witches. But think for a moment of the history of witchcraft and all the ugly connotations that go with it, whether deservedly or not. Sex orgies and unspeakable perversions. Torture and evil practices. It is unreasonable, then, to think that some of the advertisers could be perverts hopefully trying to contact other perverts?

Is there not, for example, something slightly strange about this 'request' taken from the 'smalls' column of one occult journal:

WITCHCRAFT Young man seeks genuine female assistant. Manchester.

Now as we've already seen, witchcraft is not practised in ones and twos – it is a group activity. So why should this young man – always assuming that it is a young man – want to contact just one young girl? And to be an assistant for what?

Equally odd, take these ominous few lines from another monthly magazine:

WITCHCRAFT. White Magic or similar circle. Details of centre in Newport/Cardiff area sought.

It is the word 'similar' which strikes a note of discord in my mind. It somehow does not tie up with everything I have learned during my investigations into 'white' witchcraft.

And it is here, at this point, that we enter the twilight world of modern witchcraft where the 'white' begins to turn a murky shade of grey. Where we find people who can no longer restrain themselves to obey the rules of 'good' witchcraft and seek darker pleasures. Where the 'devotees' no longer wish to hold the urges in their bodies in check . . . *Where white magic overlaps with the degraded, dedicated-to-evil black magic . . .*

The Brotherhood of Evil

In the early hours of a January morning a tall, blonde, terrified girl staggered into a police station on the outskirts of London. Her clothes were dishevelled and torn and her face bore the marks of a severe beating: a cut above the left eye was bleeding and her lips were swollen and puffed. Tears had smeared what little was left of her make-up and bruising was already beginning to discolour her cheeks.

The girl took a further step forward and collapsed into the arms of the desk sergeant who had moved to her aid as soon as she appeared in the doorway. The sergeant shouted instructions to the young constable seated at the switchboard behind the desk and made a pillow for the girl's head with his lap. As the young policeman began to summon an ambulance and alert the officers on duty, the girl forced a few painful words through her lips: 'The Master will come . . .'

The sergeant leaned closer to the damaged face, a little of its beauty still evident despite the beating, and strained to hear anything else she might say.

'The Master will punish . . .' the voice faded and the girl's eyes closed as this time she mercifully lapsed into unconsciousness.

In a moment or two the constable had completed his telephone calls and hurried to his sergeant's side with a cushion. The two men gently lifted the girl on to the wall seat, placed the cushion beneath her head and prepared to wait for their colleagues.

Later, the girl was to be taken to a local hospital and watched over by a team of detectives for almost twenty-four hours before she regained consciousness. Only once during that period was she to speak again, a half-scream born out of nightmare and terror: 'The Devil!'

The girl – we now know – had been unwittingly lured to a gathering of satanists, had been forced to endure their terrible rites and then savagely beaten as she struggled to escape, still half insensible from the 'spiked' drink she had been given. Acting on the information she eventually gave them, the detectives raided a semi-detached house not half a mile away from the police station where she had first appeared. In the nondescript little house they found cabbalistic symbols on the walls, a crudely constructed altar complete with obscene ritual implements, a sheep's heart in a plastic bowl full of blood, and the very evident signs of a hasty departure.

To this day the satanists in the suburbs who perpetrated that dreadful outrage on the young girl are still free . . .

* * *

A chill winter breeze blustered noisily among the tombstones and plucked at the coats of the vicar and his three assistants. The sky was overcast and threatened rain at any moment and had already caused one of the men to glance apprehensively upwards at the piling clouds. In fact the grimness of the weather was matched only by the stony, drawn faces of the four men who had stood silently around one of the graves for some minutes.

Behind the unmoving group, the old church loomed dark and massive, its calm seeming to have remained unchanged since it was built back in the twelfth century. But the calm was deceptive – just as was the silence of the four men. Their purpose, as they stood in quiet reverence, was to rid the church of the most bestial and evil slur which had ever been cast on it.

The vicar and his assistants were holding a service to exorcize the marks of a black mass.

In silence, the vicar lifted his right arm to make the sign of the Cross over the weather-beaten, moss-encrusted tomb where three nights before – on Hallowe'en – unknown hands had slit the throat of a rabbit and then ripped out its entrails, laying them out to form a cabbalistic symbol. The eyes of the three assistants – they were church wardens – followed the sweep of their minister's arm as it crossed the tomb and they saw again the bloodstains which had caused such horror when they were first

21

discovered. No amount of cleaning would ever completely erase the marks, just as no amount of time would ever completely remove the dreadful sacrilege which had been perpetrated on the church. The service – the ancient service of exorcism – was the least, and the most, the church officials could do.

There was another pause and then the clergyman spoke loudly and defiantly, the harshness of his tone coming as a surprise to the three men grouped round him. It was the first time they had ever heard such emotion from their normally quietly spoken vicar.

'Evil Spirits,' his voice commanded, 'go back to your place and never return to trouble us again.'

Another silence fell and the four men bowed their heads to make their own quiet prayers. In a little while, they turned together from the grave and walked slowly back towards the church. As they reached the porch, a few spots of rain were starting to fall.

* * *

That ceremony is not – as you might think – a piece of history culled from a fading and dust-covered tome of medieval life. It happened in England – not three miles from one of our biggest and most modern coastal resorts – in November 1968.

The vicar was the Rev. John Clemenston, a quietly spoken, dignified man whose record of service to his parish could hardly be bettered by any other clergyman. And the rite was his way of answering the curse which he believed was laid on his church – the twelfth century building of St Leonard's at Beaumont-cum-Moze near Clacton – by a group of people who held a black mass there on the night of Hallowe'en.

When the news of the discovery of the rabbit's remains on the tombstone had first been brought to the Rev. Clemenston he was openly sceptical and suspected a prank. When he actually went to the scene of the outrage, however, he quickly changed his mind. The way the small animal had been slaughtered and left on the granite stone pointed to something more sinister than the handiwork of young children or even teenagers with a perverted sense of humour. His trusted church wardens who were called to the scene also felt inclined to agree.

The incident soon spread far beyond the bounds of Beaumont-cum-Moze. In the ultra-modernity of Clacton the story was greeted with surprise and a certain amusement. Many people felt that progress must have completely passed the village by if the parishioners still believed in nonsense about black magic and midnight rituals.

Further afield, reactions were even more mixed. Not surprisingly, the national press took up the incident with open scepticism – while other opinions were voiced which ranged from outright rejection to a distinct sense of apprehension.

As we know now, those who were apprehensive were the nearest to the truth – just as was the Rev. Clemenston in his on-the-spot diagnosis. For there seems little doubt that Beaumont-cum-Moze *was* visited by a group of devil worshippers who defiled the churchyard for their own evil ends. Neither was it the only place that has been – and is being – subjected to the handiwork of these perverted minds.

*　*　*

In the space of just a few years black magic has become a widespread evil throughout the length and breadth of Great Britain. From being the preserve of a few isolated cranks and sexual perverts, it has grown with alarming speed into a nationwide network with members in all stratas of society. And it is not just an occasional activity – the practice of the cult's sacrificial and sexual rites occur as frequently as church services: the twentieth century devotees of the Devil are disciplined and regular in their observance of black magic's depraved ceremonies.

The presence in the land of this evil cult is, however, still unacknowledged by the vast majority of people. Many are inclined to ridicule the very idea of black magic. Others may accept that it exists but denounce all its practitioners as sexual perverts. The few who treat it seriously as a growing evil have watched it slowly emerge from the underground in recent years; for as little as ten years ago the Devil and his disciples concealed themselves very carefully. Today they are less reticent.

*　*　*

Investigating black magic is no easy matter if it is to be done properly. The sketchy, beat-the-deadline stories served up by sensation-seeking newspapers usually confuse the genuine black magic with witchcraft – an entirely different religion dating from antiquity.

When enquiring about black magic one has to take considerable care not to become enmeshed in the web of fear and blackmail which surrounds it. For this is a web which binds people in the brotherhood of Satan and demands the dedication of their lives to glorifying evil and debasing Christianity.

It is also a web which, once it has trapped its victims, rarely allows them to go free.

Black magic in twentieth century Britain attracts people from all walks of life. It is no longer the preserve of the degenerate wealthy classes as it was in the past – although there is little doubt that some devotees do come from among the idle rich searching for fresh perversions and amusement to satisfy their jaded palates. Clerks, office workers, factory hands, labourers – all are also known to belong to the ranks of this black art.

The satanists in the suburbs are not – as is often being said in newspapers and magazines – just students, young people or cranks attempting to get perverted pleasure by reviving an old ritual. These people know precisely what they want to perpetrate and for what ends.

The sects of black magicians recruit many of their members from among the weak-minded, the unfortunates who think it is a harmless relic of the past . . . and learn their mistake when it is too late. For once the 'disciple' has been initiated into the secrets of the cult, there is no intention that he should ever be allowed to pass on this information to others.

In many cases, the simple hint of a beating-up is enough to quell any ideas of leaving the sect. In others the threat of violence to family and relatives is required. While in extreme circumstances – where a man holds a position of trust and authority – blackmail may also have to be employed.

To a movement which rejects all that is good and honourable, any ends justify the means whereby they can prevent their numbers being depleted, or their dark mysteries exposed.

Much that has been rumoured about black magic is true. And much more that has not been said.

The covens *do* meet at dead of night and dance abandonedly in the nude.

They *do* carry out blood-sacrifices using live animals.

They *do* perform diabolical acts of sacrilege, desecrating graves and wrecking churches.

They even carry out terrible rituals with human beings . . . women being brutally raped and men flogged to the point of collapse. They are no strangers to death, either, and there are very good reasons for suspecting that black magic has taken its toll of several lives within the last few years.

*   *   *

Selected people are, of course, approached quite openly to join the black magic covens and do so after undergoing a series of exhaustive enquires into their lives and motives. They are mostly known perverts, whose degraded lives have come to the attention of the leaders of the black cults. But when they join what do they and those who have been tricked into 'membership' find?

Firstly they enter the most publicized, most attacked, most bestial, yet most secret sect in the country. More words have been written about black magic than probably any other subject, apart from Vietnam, politics, and the royal family. It is regarded by newspapers as a circulation booster, though few of them ever put it in its right perspective and usually confuse it with a variety of other practices. It is also without doubt the most thoroughly evil organization flourishing in Britain today.

Secondly they enter a cult which imposes the strictest vows of silence on members – and metes out the most terrible punishments on those who disobey. It strips a man of his dignity and may frequently demand he debase himself in the most sickening ways. It deprives a woman of her honour and allows her no morals whatsoever. It has even been known to force small children – boys and girls who have barely reached puberty – to take part in barbaric acts which most people believe ended in the fourteenth and fifteenth centuries.

Thirdly they enter an organization dedicated to undermining the Church, outraging society and exploring any means for corrupting the authorities and government.

The covens of black magicians are known as the Fraternity of the Goat. Like the witches, they often foregather in groups of thirteen, though it is not unusual for the number to be much larger than this. Unlike witchcraft, however, the women do not play the leading part in black magic, instead their role is very limited, being frequently reduced to that of an unpaid prostitute for the use of the men taking part. Each sect is administered by 'the Goat' or High Priest, usually an elderly man who takes little part in the physical side of the ceremonies and sometimes keeps his identity secret beneath the grotesque goat mask.

There are a few set dates upon which these Devil worshippers meet – they are usually governed by the availability of somewhere secluded and the chances of discovery. The 'meetings' are called Sabats, and it is at them that the notorious 'black mass' is performed.

There are, however, four dates on the 'black' calendar which the devotees observe come what may. They are: 2 February, 23 June, 1 August and 21 December. Each of these dates marks the start of the Sabats-in-chief, black magic festivals that could be equated in importance to the Christian Easter and Christmas festivals. And mention of these religious festivals reminds one that there is a link – however slender and unwanted – between the good and the evil. For a number of Church ministers who once knelt humbly before the Cross now lead those who defile it. In every case these unfrocked clergy deserved their expulsion, but in their fury they have become the Church's most fervent antagonists.

How well established are the sects? There is documented evidence of their existence in no less than sixteen counties – and I believe that is barely scratching the surface. My own estimate is that the number of devotees runs into many thousands, the majority of whom have managed so far to keep their nefarious activities secret from the police and the authorities.

Although outsiders find it extremely difficult – in fact almost impossible – to identify these people in everyday life, black magic practitioners from one end of the country to another *can* make contact with each other if the need arises. Not surprisingly, the cult does not encourage communication between members of different sects – reasoning rightly enough that if a person decided to try and expose the whole business he could reveal the names of more people, the more sects he had been in contact with.

Should one group need to seek out another, however, adequate provision has been made through a complicated system of 'fronts'. These test the urgency of the matter – and the advisability of a contact. Individual members can, nevertheless, side track the 'middle' men – recognizing other practitioners by finger signs not unlike those used in freemasonry.

With secrecy being of the utmost importance, the hierarchy of the sects watch their followers very closely. Any member inspected of breaking his ritual oath of silence will be put under constant surveillance. His every move will be observed by fellow devotees and regular reports on his conduct, those he meets and where he goes, supplied to the leaders. Members are even encouraged to inform on each other and are promised 'rewards' – usually sexual in nature – for their work.

As I have already said, no one – even the most degenerate – gets into the cult easily. It is not just enough to be 'kinky' or searching for bestial pleasure: a potential member must be capable of defying all that is good and prepared to waive any standards of decency he may have. He must be ready and willing to desecrate the most holy symbols of the Church and disqualify his soul from any chance of an afterlife.

But it is the final test before initiation that demands more than all the others. For the weak it is a sickening task that many flinch from: even for the strong it can be a trial which leaves them vomiting and ill.

The neophite is called upon to ritually kill a small animal – a bird or a cat, perhaps – and then drink its still-warm blood. Finally, in full view of the members of the brotherhood, he must have intercourse with a selected woman. Young girl, or elderly degenerate, he has no choice.

From that moment on he learns that the 'commands' which govern the black magic sects are harsh and exacting, permitting no weakness.

To serve his 'apprenticeship', for example, they demand that he desecrate a churchyard.

He is required to defile a grave and leave on it the mark of Satan – either an animal's heart pierced by thorns or one of the cabbalistic symbols of the cult. He does not necessarily have to perform this act alone – he may take along with him as many as three fellow satanists. And a few have the stomach for such a dreadful act on their own.

The most important commands of all govern the Sabats, the spine-chilling acts of profanity which affirms the members' devotion to evil.

While compiling this report I travelled extensively throughout the country, investigating reported incidents of black magic 'Sabats'. Some turned out to be nothing of the sort – while others left very real doubts in my mind. Gradually, however, I was able to get to the centre of the whole ghastly business. And finally I learned the secrets of the midnight rituals where the old evils and the new mix together in a ceremony which reminds one of inquisitions, of torture and terror in the night.

* * *

Gaining admission to a coven of satanists is by no means an easy task and, in fact, the groups usually tend to recruit their own new members from the fringes of the occult world – the areas of grey around 'white' witchcraft and spiritualism when certain members have become dissatisfied with the controlled sensuality and seek more positive 'rewards'. One such person was introduced to me while I was researching and subsequently prepared a statement about her experiences which I shall now reproduce. It is not a pleasant report and underlines the dangers inherent in black magic.

The 'victim', a woman now in her middle thirties was, before her experience, a gay and lively person, attractive and popular in the Midland business circles in which she moved after office hours. She delighted in parties and through meeting a practitioner of Wicca at one such gathering, decided to join a coven. At first, she says, her interest was sincere and she was eventually admitted into a coven based in Manchester. Not troubled by inhibitions, she enjoyed the sexual side both with her chosen partner and, separately, with others from the group at secret rendezvous.

'I suppose,' she recalls, 'I got a reputation for being promiscuous, although in fact I only went with two other men. When I expressed a desire to one of them for a bit more excitement he asked what I knew about black magic. Of course all I knew was what I'd read in books and it seemed to be just a bit more advanced than Wicca with a lot of extra thrills thrown in. I couldn't have been more wrong.'

The supposed witch to whom she had confided her secret was, in fact, a contact man for a group of satanists and the next thing she knew she was being carefully screened for admission. This is her story:

'The introduction was not hurried. I was told that there was a way to have all the things I longed for in life. And the bait worked. Foolishly I agreed to be initiated.

'Then, late in the evening of one August bank holiday Monday, shortly after I had gone to bed, there was a knock at the door. I pulled on a dressing gown over my nightdress, went downstairs, and found a car waiting.

"In this car, with a driver, was my "instructor" from the coven and another man. It was pouring with rain. We drove into the centre of the city where we left the car and changed into a plain van. A little later we picked up another passenger, a short, stout man wearing a trenchcoat and cap. Then, after passing through two big wrought-iron gates, the van stopped. One of the men looked at me and said: "Ought she to have her blinkers on?" My acquaintance replied that he could vouch for me, but the others appeared nervous.

'We walked about fifteen yards from the van to a house. It was still raining. Inside the house, in a large dimly lit foyer a man was standing waiting for us. Someone else touched my arm almost immediately and I went through a side door into another room where there was a strong smell of flowers, and of incense. Facing me, in the middle of the opposite wall, were drawn curtains. They were parted by a woman in dark maroon robes. A long veil was pinned over the centre of her head and draped over her face. She said: "You're late." Then: "Oh, you've already robed." I had not, of course; she had mistaken the dressing gown. "Well," she went on, "you'd better come behind the curtains."

'This led into another, brighter, room. I remember getting the impression there were a lot of people there before the woman pushed me back again behind the curtain while she fetched a robe for me, and a veil. She told me to let my long hair fall.

'I slipped the robe over the top of the things I was already wearing. It was a choirboy's kind of robe with long, wide sleeves and a round neck. After pinning on the veil I felt a little queer and I leaned against the wall until someone called for me. I could hear drums beating, quietly.

'I went into the other room, only now it seemed to be full of a pink glow. I could just distinguish people and that was all. It seemed very large. It couldn't have had carpets, because there were markings on the floor. I turned left through the curtains, and walked between two lines drawn for the initiated to follow. Three other women walked behind me. They joined me inside the door and had walked from the other, right-hand, end of the room.

'In the top left-hand corner, facing me, was a semi-circle of twelve men – hooded, masked and robed. One woman from the three behind me took up position with them to form a coven of thirteen. I turned right, and with the drums still beating, walked to the middle of the wall, where three men making a triangle were standing – the triad, three-in-one. Behind them against the wall, was a two-feet-high statue of the Mother Mary on a stand. I approached this point as I had been told, walking slowly with hands held as if in prayer but pointing fingers to the floor. Stopping at the statue, I brought my hands slowly up and opened them out with fingertips touching, a sign of sexual obeisance.

'I continued walking to the other corner now facing me, while the second of the women behind me fell out and took her place in the centre of the triangle.

'In the top right-hand corner of the room which I now approached was an altar. On the wall itself was a mirror and the symbol of the goat – the Devil. A small wall light was over the symbol and on the altar, below it, five unlighted black candles with gold symbols. There was a tray in the centre of the candles and a tall cross standing in the centre of the tray reaching up almost to the centre of the mirror. I stopped at the front of the altar and the remaining woman still following me walked past me to the other side. In the centre of the room were drawn a large and a small circle, one within the other, with nine triangles set out from the outer circle. Facing the room now I noticed quite a number of people standing at the bottom, and behind them angled across the

30

corner (left-hand, facing me) curtaining from the back of which seemed to come the drumming.

'Suddenly, from the curtained doorway by which I had entered the room, came three men with a young girl. They walked forward with her to the Mother Mary statue. The men were cowled and masked, but I am certain one was my "instructor".

'The woman from the group in the corner at the right-hand side of me (as I faced the room) walked slowly between the lines towards the door, meeting another man in robes who was carrying a live black fowl. He had his finger and thumb securely on the bird's neck and was also holding its feet. He walked between the lines to the triangle and held the fowl towards the statue, then bowed to it. After that he walked to the altar. He knelt, still holding the bird, in front of the altar star.

'One of the men who had escorted the girl left her and made to the statue a sign with hands together pointing downwards and touching the front of his trousers. He took up a position beside the man with the fowl, turned his back on the altar and slowly recited the Lord's Prayer backwards. After this he called on the covens and told them a sacrifice was about to take place "and tonight we have a virgin in our midst who is to be initiated".

"Hanging from the girdle of his robe he had a flat, tapered knife. He took the cockerel and it squawked loudly. He held the bird up in the air by the neck and slit it with the knife from the throat right down across the breast and between the legs. Blood gushed all over his hands and the robes of the other men standing nearby. While this was going on, chanting began.

'Now the young girl, who seemed about fifteen or sixteen and was probably below the age of consent, was brought by her remaining two escorts up to the statue. She seemed to be half fainting, and had to be helped to walk. The triad broke and stood apart. The girl was made to declare aloud that she was giving up all thoughts or rights of prayer to Mother Mary. Afterwards she was brought across, one man holding her, dragging her feet, to the altar star. The members of the triad walked into the centre of the circle and knelt. The coven from the bottom of the room walked forward on to the outer circle. Eight people from the right-hand side of the door took up positions at the points of eight of the altar stars, leaving one point opposite the altar empty. The drums

31

quickened. The eight on the stars swung incense burners and the room was full of the smell, choking.

'The girl, still at the altar star, was told to kneel. As she did so, the man with the cockerel held it up, then placed a bloodied hand on the girl's head and gave a parody of the blessing. The other man at the altar was pouring blood into glasses. He had taken the cockerel and drained the blood from it down its beak. The woman on my left brought forward a small silver tray. We were told that we were to partake of a body that night in honour of the new initiate. Powder and dust were sprinkled on the top of the glasses. The lady from my left took the tray of glasses round the room. As the girl was given a drink she seemed stupefied, probably the result of an injection given to her earlier.

'She tried to push the glass away but she was held and given it forcibly. Some of it spilled on to her open-necked white blouse and ran down her small breasts. Chanting went on all the time.

'The girl, still kneeling, was told to repeat certain words. She promised to give her soul to the Devil, declared that she belonged absolutely to him, and condemned God and His Son. Afterwards, her hands taken by two men, she was brought to the altar and ordered to stand the cross upside down with the head inside the body of the cockerel. Now she was told to look into the mirror, to keep on looking and she remained like this while a parody of the Catholic Mass was carried out. She had to turn round to face the room to repeat her "vows", but just before this she had a hood placed over her head, and was also veiled. At this point the girl fainted. I went forward to help her but was at once told to go back to my place as I had offended. Now the circle began to open up, leaving only the eight points. The girl was taken to the ninth point, slumping between two men. The rest of the eight came up to the altar.

'A long table was brought into the middle of the central ring and they carried the girl and put her upon it. One of the four men in front of me muttered: "I'm afraid they've given her too much." I did not realize at that time what he meant. Now dancing began. Everyone was served with drink. As soon as a glass was empty it was refilled.

'I refused a drink because I was feeling worried and ill and for this I was reprimanded by one of the members. The drums were beating faster now. People began to be intoxicated, stamping their feet, jumping about. It turned into an orgy of sex.

'I walked from the altar to the girl on the table; she still wore her veil and hood, but her hair draped back over the end of the table and touched the floor. I remember stroking her hair. I knew something was really wrong. Everyone was shedding clothes. There seemed to be many more women in the room. I was afraid for the girl. Then the man I thought was my "instructor" came and told me to go back to the altar or to leave the room. I was taken across to the altar and given an injection. Before I began to feel dopey I saw them stripping clothes off the girl. There were a number of them round the table interfering with her body. I tried to speak to someone near me but they said: "Why don't you stop worrying. You can't do anything now. She's beyond it."

'Someone removed the last of the girl's clothing. Her eyes were wide open, staring. Then a naked man climbed on top of her. After he had finished another took his place. I felt awfully ill and had to lean back against the wall for a while. I had to be helped out of the room and sat on a chair in the other room behind the curtains. I remember I asked what would become of the girl and was told it was quite all right, that would be attended to.

'After a bit a veiled woman came to me and said I had been given permission to go home. But first I must return and make my vow of silence. I went back into the big room. The girl, still on the table, had been pushed up in front of the altar. I gave my vow of silence to the full room and was told that black magic was for the strong and not for weaklings. I was to remember in case anything ever went wrong that I was as much responsible as anyone else in the room. After this I had to give my handprint – dipped in blood on a tray and put on a fresh piece of paper. This I had to sign. I was told that the paper would be kept and used if I ever spoke about what had happened.

'I felt numb from the effects of the injection. I know I was put in a car but how I subsequently reached home I just don't know. All I remember is I came to my senses in my hallway. And I was still in my nightdress, slippers and dressing gown . . .'

The story does not end here for my anonymous lady recruit, for she was subsequently approached several times and taken to a number of other satanic meetings, being called on to participate in most of these. She admits that after her first experience she went in constant fear of the man who had first taken her to the group and did not dare to defy his calls although she was revolted at what happened. After a while his interest in her waned and when he was no longer a member of the parties which came to collect her, she decided she could cut herself off from the group. For two years she went to live abroad and, in fact, only returned to this country a few months ago, to settle in a quite different area some hundreds of miles away from the scene of her ordeals. Despite the fact that she has heard nothing further from the original group, my informant does not believe she has truly escaped their clutches.

'I have broken my satanic oath,' she says, almost in a whisper, 'and I know the power of these people is such that they won't rest until they have taken their revenge on me. I don't sleep too well and a knock on the door – any door – always makes me nervous. Do you think I am wrong to worry still?'

I had to tell her, sadly, that I did not.

* * *

The cellar is large and damp; despite the dexterous use of black paint over the walls, water has seeped in at several points and a little film of green mould has developed in one corner.

The air is dank, though there is still the trace of some indefinable incense or perfume in the atmosphere. Two pink bulbs hang from the ceiling – they have no shades – and throw a subdued light into all but one corner; it is partly blocked by the shadow of the altar in the middle of the room.

The altar, which stands about four feet high, is the only piece of furniture in the cellar. Covering it are three black linen cloths, and on top of them – laid carefully lengthwise and with a little overlapping each side – is a strip of black velvet. This is decorated with four obscene frescos, each depicting men and women involved in sexual acts under the eye of a goat-like figure. In the centre stands a twisted and distorted crucifix, the figure of Christ pierced with numerous nails and small wooden stakes.

On either side of this monstrous parody of the Cross are three black candles. Although they have been mass manufactured and purchased at a local hardware shop, they are exactly like the candles made for this same purpose a few hundred years ago of human fat mixed with sulphur and other substances. On the right of the Cross also stands a small black statue of a Devil figure, somewhat crudely carved, and provided with grossly exaggerated features.

To the left of this array is a large hook, bound in expensive, hand-tooled leather. Three hundred years ago an earlier edition of this same work stood on just such an altar . . . bound in human skin. The work is known as the *Paper of Blasphemy* and was copied painstakingly in black ink from a much earlier copy around the beginning of the present century. It is a book of blatant obscenity and sacrilege, a deliberate and vile parody of the Bible.

On top of the book stands a small gold salver containing thin sacramental wafers which evil hands have recently spirited away from a local church. There is also a chalice of wine which has found its way to this cellar from the same source as the wafers. It has been doped before being placed on the altar – now it contains an aphrodisiac brewed to have a violent reaction on all those who drink it.

The scene is almost set now. Only the atmosphere needs attention. And in a matter of moments – as a clock can be heard faintly chiming eleven in the distance – a hooded figure enters the cellar carrying a golden thurible. The incense it is burning has a strong, choking smell and is causing the man's eyes to water. The distinctive aromas of asofoetida, sulphur, alum and other herbs can be detected.

The figure places the container on the altar and quickly withdraws. The incense spirals slowly to the ceiling, making weird patterns as the heat from the light bulbs deflects its course. Even without the presence of human bodies, the air in the cellar is getting noticeably warmer.

It is to get much warmer, however. In fact it will reach fever pitch before midnight – and be as hot and fetid as some satanic Turkish bath before morning.

For it is here in a cellar beneath the now quiet streets of Highgate in north London, that a group of black magic practitioners who model themselves on a notorious eighteenth-century sect of Devil worshippers are to meet and conduct their evil rituals.

The Sons of Midnight.

The eighteen people file slowly into the cellar, taking up their positions around the altar in a half circle. All are wearing black cloaks, and, to an observant eye, nothing underneath.

Five of the figures are women, their white, shapely legs exposed with each step they take. They take up positions interspersed among the men.

There is a short pause before a small, fat man, his head concealed beneath a grotesque goat mask, is suddenly framed in the doorway. He is also wearing a long black cassock and over it a chasuble of red silk decorated with a pentagon of gold thread. Inside this dreaded occult symbol is the tiny figure of a he-goat.

'The Goat!' one of the 'congregation' whispers involuntarily, unable to contain the shudder, half of terror and half of pleasure, which runs through his body whenever the High Priest first appears. 'The Goat' – the classical manifestation of the Devil.

The little man walks into the centre of the circle and turns to face the altar. The hushed assembly watch transfixed as he lifts his gown and steps closer to the altar.

For a second the distorted crucifix glints in the light of the pink bulbs . . . and is then dulled as the man slowly and deliberately urinates over it.

The Mass has begun.

A cry now goes up from the worshippers who have stood silently like statues through the whole bestial scene. But not so much as a muscle twitches when the Priest spins around to face them.

At this 'sign' – for such it obviously is – the unholy congregation set up a weird chant which rises and falls unintelligibly in the cellar. It is the notorious 'black prayer' – the Lord's Prayer said backwards.

In the pause that follows, the oily flames of the black candles – which had been lit by one of the congregation – gutter slightly.

The atmosphere of evil grows more malevolent with each passing second.

As solemn as a churchwarden, one of the worshippers steps forward, carrying before him a silver plate. His fellows strain to see what the offering is this time: it is the still-warm heart of a sheep.

'The Goat' takes the sacrifice in his hands and holds it up before him, offering it to the ceiling. As he mutters beneath his breath, the life-blood runs between his fingers and on to the cuffs of his cloak. But he does not notice.

A minute passes and he lowers his arms over the wine chalice on the altar. And when he squeezes the heart, the blood runs thick and red into the holy cup.

Taking up the vessel, he touches it briefly to his lips, and then beckons to the nearest of the worshippers. The man steps forward and seizes the proffered gift eagerly. Some of the blood trickles down the side of his mouth as he drinks . . .

No sooner have all those present taken part in this dreadful parody of the Holy Communion, than the High Priest picks up the plate of wafers from the altar.

With the reverence of an orthodox priest, the little man then wheels slowly on his heels to face the worshippers. He gives the merest inclination of his head. Immediately, as if galvanized into action by some hidden force, the men and women strip off their gowns and come forward one by one to receive the 'body of the Devil'.

The wafers seem to be the final stimulant to the group; some of the men are now visibly aroused and three of the girls are trembling uncontrollably. Aware only too well of their excitement, the High Priest lets his gaze rove slowly – deliberately slowly – over the rapt faces before him.

His features break into a twisted smile as he savours each second before giving the signal which sends the 'faithful' jostling eagerly to link arms and form a circle with their backs to him around the altar. He is smiling still when he gives the sharp command to begin dancing.

The bodies of the worshippers throw weird shapes around the cellar, and as they whirl faster they are hardly aware of the moment when their 'master' draws a vicious, long-handled whip from beneath his cloak. And they certainly do not see the fleck of saliva which runs across his jowl or the hungry look which flashes in his beady eyes. But they feel the taste of the whip as its long tongue cracks harshly in the still air.

Once, twice, three times the Priest lashes out, but the human chain around him does not break. Spurred on like some avenging demon he flails about himself more wildly still, his breath rasping in his lungs.

In no time at all, several of the men have ugly red weals on their shoulders and one of the women has a deep, bloody slash mark across her buttocks.

Exhausted at last, he lowers his whip, and around him the worshippers slow to a halt, sinking gratefully to their knees. Their arms are still locked firmly together.

Once again all is still in the cellar, save for the laboured breathing of 'the Goat' and the groans of those he has lashed. The respite is only temporary, however. Leaping upright with surprising energy considering his recent exertions and age, the little man begins the second part of the ritual. Again it starts with a chant – stranger still than those which had gone before – and continues with a dance.

At first the naked men and women move sluggishly, their tired bodies performing without enthusiasm. But in an instant all is changed – with just one word from the Goat, 'Acoka!' – 'come together'.

Their motions become violent and jerky – they thrust backwards and forwards in suggestive positions, their hands still linked. And for the first time the women become the centre of attention.

Until this moment they have been anonymous members of the circle. Now they become fiercely female.

Here enacted in a cellar in the suburbs of the greatest metropolis in the world is all the lust and horror portrayed in the works of the fifteenth-century painters. Complete abandon under the watchful eyes of the horned Devil – personified by the little man in his Priest's outfit. A revival of the pagan tradition of glorifying evil for debased personal satisfaction.

* * *

The modern black mass is not performed with the idea of trying to conjure up the Devil in physical form. Today's black magicians do not believe there is such a being as the Devil, just as they no longer believe that the way to see a vision of Lord Satan is to smear one's face with the blood of a goat which has been boiled with vinegar and crushed glass.

They believe in the existence of evil as a *living force*.

That the faithful still pay lip-service to the idea of a Devil by honouring 'the Goat' is a concession to the past. The satanist taking this role represents, in a form they can see, all the many powers of evil.

One man, however, became regarded as a devil in his own right. The man responsible for the spread of black magic today. The man who shaped it lovingly into its present form and whose influences are still strong at this very moment. The sinister figure who has now passed into history as one of the most truly evil men of all time: Aleister Crowley 'the Great Beast'.

Aleister Crowley, a man of satanic features and imposing build, dedicated his life to evil. From his very earliest years his one aim was the perpetration of wickedness.

As a boy of twelve he brutally slaughtered a cat, and then repeated the process again eight times in eight different ways to find out whether it was true that the animal had nine lives.

In his teens he performed his first simple 'black mass' crucifying a small frog and reading some hymns backwards.

And by the time he was nearing his twenties he was steeped in the occult and had delved further into the black arts than many a stout-hearted person twice his age.

But Crowley was no simple young man with a sadistic streak. On the contrary he had had a first-class education at Trinity College, Cambridge, and left with a degree. Nor was he a coward, trying to prove his courage by dangerous and sacrilegious acts. While at university he had never been slow to undertake the most hair-raising 'dares', and had led a mountaineering party to scale Kilimanjaro. What, then, started him on the path that was to earn him the title of 'The Wickedest Man in the World'?

Without a doubt there was a defect in his character, a 'kink' which drove him to plumb the depths of evil searching for the one perversion which could satisfy him. He never found it, however, despite intimate contact with the most vile sexual deviations, drug-taking, homosexuality, masochism and all the worst forms of exhibitionism.

His first meetings with other occultists came shortly after he left university in 1898, when he joined the then most prominent 'strange' society, the Hermetic Order of the Golden Dawn. The restless, probing mind of Crowley was not long satisfied in this austere company, however, and in 1906 – his decision made easier by the inheritance of £30,000 from his brewer father – he broke away and went to live in seclusion in Scotland to explore the mysteries of the occult.

The place he chose to dwell in was a rambling, eerie mansion called Boleskine on the banks of Loch Ness. It has seemed since that this was – as one writer has noted – a case of 'one monster keeping company with another', and indeed it was here that Crowley first undertook the practice of black magic in earnest.

Strange tales grew in local gossip about what the 'laird' was up to. Some residents claimed to have seen demons in the grounds late at night and one terrified farmer even swore he saw the Devil himself gallop across the lawns. Of one thing there was no doubt, however, those close to Crowley found his influence unnerving and quite frightening.

Two workers on the estate committed suicide because they could no longer bear living in an atmosphere of such terror. An unfortunate butcher to whom Crowley sent a cheque covered with demonic names was so shaken that he severed an artery while cutting up a joint and died shortly afterwards. A harmless parish worker became a chronic alcoholic after a brief contact with the self-styled 'Master of Boleskine'.

But the tranquillity of the Scottish mountains did not suit Crowley for long and soon he set off again, this time with his wife, Rose, on a tour of the East to seek out the old magic in its ancient home. His researches proved fruitful, particularly in Egypt where he formulated many of his future plans for the battle with Christianity which he had now come to loathe with an all-consuming hatred. He wrote to friends of his intentions and quoted the stanza which was to be his motto: 'Do what thou wilt shall be the whole of the law.'

And from that moment on Crowley certainly did as he pleased.

His undoubted fascination for women had become very evident at this time and he was soon embroiled in a long sequence of affairs with the 'Scarlet Women' as he called his mistresses. He gave these women strange, degrading names like 'the Ape of Thoth' and 'the Dog', and forced them to submit to the most appalling perversions and ill-treatment while he practised his dark magic.

This delight in strange titles, Crowley extended to himself as well – Prince Chiao Khan, Brother Perdurabo and the Great Beast were just a few of those he conferred on himself during his life.

By now converts were seeking Crowley out with increasing regularity, and he realized that sooner or later he would have to set up a community for them all. His research was not quite complete, however, so he continued to travel awhile and spent some time in the United States where he wrote a long and sickening account of how he had performed a mass and crucified a small animal. There was a trip to Britain, also, but the authorities kept a wary eye on him this time.

It was in 1919 that he finally realized his dreams to start a settlement for himself and his 'black disciples'. He chose a sultry little island just off Sicily called Cefalu. There, in a mountainside villa, he established the 'Abbey of Theleme' which in the next few years was to be the home of almost every known perversion.

Certainly most decent, God-fearing people would have been horrified if they had gone into the Beast's new home. The walls had been decorated with the most obscene paintings, and a lavish altar for the black mass was set up in the lounge. The women who drifted listlessly about, and there seemed to be a surplus of them – attracted immediate attention because of their wide, staring eyes . . . and the 'Mark of the Beast' which Crowley had branded on their breasts.

Local people avoided the 'Abbey' and its 'mad' owner like the plague; they made long detours rather than risk coming into contact with anybody from the villa.

While the leader delved further into the black arts – translating ancient works on satanism which he had somehow obtained, and dosing himself up with opium and hashish – the 'faithful' tried to adhere to the rules he set. They must cut their arms with 'a razor

41

every time they used the word 'I'; they must ritually slaughter, animals and meditate on the glory of the Beast. And so on.

At the height of his 'ministry' on Cefalu, the arch-enemy of Christianity was rumoured to have sacrificed a baby which he had taken from a nearby village while the parents were asleep. (Whatever the truth in this story, Crowley later wrote in one of his books: 'A male child of perfect innocence and high intelligence is the most satisfactory and suitable victim for use in the Mass), He was said, too, to have driven one of his followers to commit suicide and another to have a heart attack, from which the poor man died.

But by 1923 the word of these atrocities had reached the ear of Mussolini – who had recently risen to power in Italy and in the May of that year he ordered the expulsion of Crowley and his unholy band. The Beast returned to England and devoted the last years of his life to writing of his discoveries in the field of black magic. His sight was failing fast and the years of drug-taking were beginning to have their effect on his bloated body.

He worked on, nevertheless, producing *Magic in Theory and Practice*, and a dreadful record of wickedness entitled *Book of the Law*. In them he gave minute details of how the black mass was to be celebrated, how the animals were to be sacrificed and even guidance – if such were needed – on the orgies which followed.

As Crowley drifted slowly towards death, those who remained of his followers were busy propagating his work. They sought out likely converts and showed them how the Beast had revived black magic – given it new application and purpose for the twentieth century. In ever-increasing numbers people seized on the cult and its idea, providing the start of the boom which is now becoming so evident throughout the country.

Crowley himself died in 1944, wracked with pain and tortured in mind and spirit. His wealth had been frittered away and in his last hours he was virtually alone. But his consolation – whatever good it was to him then – was that his efforts to encourage the practising of 'evil for its own sake' were already starting to come to fruition.

The Abode of Love

'The Abode of Love' looks out gauntly on the picturesque Somerset countryside. It is a tall, impressive brownstone building with an air of mystery that seems to exude from every brick in its structure. High walls – over fifteen feet tall – hide the lower half of the house and the windows above stare without seeing into the distance, as if remembering . . .

And there is much to be remembered about this thirty-roomed mansion in the sedate little village of Spaxton. Tales of violence and evil; of degraded activities performed in the spacious grounds. Stories of men howling and dancing in the moonlight and strange love rites. Rumours which spread unanswered about the people who lived in 'The Abode of Love' . . . the Agapemonites.

In February 1962 the last of the inhabitants quit the rambling mansion leaving behind a few scraps of furniture . . . and a number of clues as to what had been happening there during the past half-century. Pieced together with other facts gleaned over the years, they at last enabled the history of the Agapemonites to be unfolded.

The story of the strange mansion, called the Agapemone by its inhabitants (Agapemone being a Greek word meaning 'Abode of Love') goes back nearly a hundred years.

On a bright Sunday morning one spring the Anglican rector of Spaxton, the Reverend Henry James Prince, climbed into his pulpit as usual. He paused to hoist his cassock around his shoulders and then began a sermon much like those he had preached many times before.

In their pews the congregation eased themselves as congregations in their Sunday best are inclined to do. Hardly had any of them settled, however, than the tone of the Reverend Prince's voice changed suddenly and dramatically . . . and his words fell like bombshells in the still church.

'I am,' he proclaimed with conviction, 'the immortal messenger of the Holy Ghost.'

The congregation was stunned, unable to believe their ears. Was this the quiet, dignified rector they *thought* they knew so well? It hardly seemed so!

Prince leaned further out of his pulpit and stared hard at his dumbfounded audience. He continued in a quicker voice, his words becoming more fervent.

'I am the chosen one – the messenger to bring light into the world!'

He said that God himself had revealed his status to him. And the Lord had also told him that a man need not be bound to the system of one wife only.

'Follow me and you can share my privilege,' Prince urged his still wide-eyed male parishioners.

Quick as a flash he turned to the white-faced ladies, their hands pressed to their mouths.

'If you come to me and follow my ways I shall show you how to get closer to your Maker,' he said.

Prince had said enough . . . far too much as far as the shocked congregation were concerned. First one man and then others overcame their amazement.

In a fury they rose from the pews – shaking their fists and denouncing the preacher for his blasphemy.

Seeing the infuriated gathering advancing before him, Prince realized his acceptance as a messiah was not going to be immediate. He hurried down from his pulpit and fled for his life from the church.

For days he secluded himself in his house, deciding what to do next. He could never return to his church. He would probably be hounded wherever he went in public.

But then, out of the blue, he learned that there were people who had taken notice of what he had said.

A group of converts wanted to follow him.

Among those who intimated their willingness to join Prince were a number of wealthy women. Their money – which they freely offered to him – provided the minister with the answer to his problem. He would build a special retreat where he and his followers could live.

Once established in their sanctuary far from prying eyes, the Agapemonites (as Prince had now named his group), practised the 'cardinal virtues' advocated by their leader – brotherly love and *free love*.

For nearly 40 years the sect dwelt in seclusion, believing implicitly in the 'incarnation' who led them.

In the world outside the high walls, the Agapemonites were a constant source of rumour and gossip.

In the local shops, public houses, and even churches, there were stories about midnight ceremonies in the grounds of the mansion. Of sex orgies which would have made even the debased Romans blush. And wild singing and dancing in the grounds.

But not one word of denial came from Prince and his followers. The world – as far as they were concerned – could think what it liked.

What the world thought was coloured by numerous accounts of the sect which appeared in newspapers and magazines.

The reports – many of which claimed to be written by people who had actually witnessed the ceremonies – said that the Agapemonites performed a ritual not unlike that of the church – but everybody was naked 'so that no member could have secrets from any other'.

Prayers would be recited and each man and his 'wives' would be blessed by the leader. The group would then dance on the lawns and sing special songs – often clasping and fondling each other.

According to one report a man was free to seek the favours of another's wife – as long as he asked permission *first* and was prepared to share one of his own spouses!

'The sight of those naked male and female persons cavorting about under the moonlight', says one report 'was certainly enough to inflame any passion.' And indeed did so as I watched.

'Couples with their arms entwined about each other and mumbling what they claimed to be religious chants disappeared into the shadows on all sides.

'What ensued under the cover of darkness, modesty forbids me to record here. But it was carnal lust of the very lowest and animal kind,' added the account.

How accurate this and the other similar stories are is open to conjecture. Undoubtedly they are highly coloured – but many people have felt there is at least an element of truth in them.

It was in 1902 that the next notable event took place in the sect's history. Quite suddenly, and unexpectedly, Prince died.

This was a great blow to the Agapemonites for they firmly believed their leader to be immortal. Hadn't that been what he had said?

. After weeks of mourning the followers were confronted with the problem of who should now lead them.

But they need not have worried, for some miles away in London, an event was about to take place which would bring them a new guiding light.

On a Sunday morning, just as Prince had done, another Anglican preacher, Reverend John Hugh Smyth-Piggott, stood up in the pulpit of his church in north London and announced: 'I am the promised Messiah.'

The reaction of the parishioners on this occasion was quicker than in Prince's time. The vicar was sent scuttling from the church before he could speak another word – and police had to be called to protect him and his house from stone-throwing crowds.

Soon afterwards, Smyth-Piggott, who knew of the Agapemonite community, decided to seek sanctuary with them. He took with him to the high-walled hideaway his wife Kathie, and a young woman, Ruth Preece, who, he explained, was his 'spiritual bride'.

In the early days as Spaxton, Ruth bore her 'spiritual husband' three children – who were named Glory, Hallelujah and Power.

Smyth-Piggott also quickly seized the chance to become the leader of the sect which at that time had about a hundred members of both sexes.

Once he had obtained this position and the news had leaked to the world outside, he was, not surprisingly, defrocked by the Anglican Church for his 'immoral life and habits'.

Once again a furore of whispering and innuendo centred around the 'Abode of Love'. There were more stories – weirder still than the others – of candlelight processions, incense burning and demented love rites.

Still only silence answered the curious.

But now, years later, with more facts available, what really *was* going on behind those walls? Were the sect members as evil as they were painted? Were they all leading lives of sin?

There is little doubt that through the years many people – by far the majority of them women – went to the Abode of Love to live in seclusion. And it is fairly certain the morals under the first leader, Prince, were lax.

But what of the time when Smyth-Piggott was in command?

He died in 1927 at the age of 74 – to the bewilderment of his followers. Like his predecessor he had told the sect: 'I shall never die. I am immortal.'

Kathie, his real wife, then became the owner of the mansion, until her death in 1936. Ownership later passed to Ruth, Smyth-Piggott's 'spiritual wife', who was the matriarch of the sect until she, too, died twenty years later.

The final owners were to be the three children, Glory, Hallelujah and Power – now grown up. They, too, have remained silent about the Agapemonites.

However, during my enquiries, I did manage to contact an old man who belonged to the cult for some years and was prepared to speak a little about his life there.

He denied that free love was practised or that strange rituals were held in the dead of night.

'The most exotic services held in the place in my time consisted of a psalm, a prayer, a sermon and a hymn to conclude,' he said.

Probably we shall never know the truth about the rumours of orgies and love rituals – but all the same they are a fascinating insight into yet another example of a strange cult which flourished in our midst.

The Gospel of Polygamists

'Marriage to one women is nothing more than sheer humbug.' This is the considered view of a sect who have been variously labelled by newspapers as 'crazy crackpots' and 'sex sensation seekers'.

The followers of this creed have a burning desire to sweep away the time-honoured institution of marriage which they maintain is against the teachings of the gospels. The cult is known as 'the Gospel Polygamists'.

In a story published in November, 1961, a national newspaper described the sect as believing in a 'vile creed'. It called the leader, a man who identifies himself only as 'Dr John', a 'religious crank' and said he was running a harem of attractive girls 'which would shock anyone'.

At the time of this story the sect was based on a houseboat in a quiet Essex backwater. But immediately the craft was hit by angry waves of public opinion against the members' advocation of polygamy.

'Dr John' had taken his followers to live on the river because, he said, the world was going to be devastated and only he and his disciples could escape in their twentieth-century 'Ark'.

Instead of fire and flood, however, only enraged local residents darkened the horizon and they threatened to destroy the boat or cut her moorings if the group did not leave.

As far as 'Dr John' was concerned he felt he was being made a martyr because of his views. With as much dignity as he could muster, he and his 'wives' and the rest of his followers left the craft.

The move necessitated him changing his views about the end of the world, the newspaper reported in a further story. They said he had now decided to concentrate on 'converting' the world to the virtues of polygamy.

But the idea of living on a boat was not abandoned altogether. 'We still hope to raise enough money to finance a crusade around the world,' said the leader. 'We still have a boat and may get a larger one.'

The spot where the strange little sect have now settled is a typical charming rural village. Row upon row of neat little houses present a picture of tranquillity which would appear to have been undisturbed for generations.

The setting is ideal for study and meditation, and perhaps it was this atmosphere which attracted 'Dr John' when he began to plan his next project: a book on his life and work.

To house himself – and the other members of the sect – while he works, he had bought a rambling, white-walled cottage strung with wild roses and honeysuckle. Behind the cottage's lace curtains, however, the scene is not quite what one might expect.

For one thing there seems to be more women than men – considerably more. But they still busy themselves in the way women throughout the world do: polishing, cleaning and cooking. All the while their 'master', works on in his study, covering sheets of paper with huge, scrawling handwriting.

The treatise he is writing will be titled *The Case for Polygamy* and he says it will run to well over one thousand pages.

'I expect the book to earn me thousands of pounds in royalties when it is published,' says the self-styled messiah. 'This will provide me with the finances I need to start my campaign among the unenlightened of the world.'

The 'unenlightened' are those who do not see the value of polygamy. And the crusade which is being prepared to 'let light into their darkness' will, according to 'Dr John', surge out from the tranquil cottage at 'practically any time now'.

What do those who plan to carry 'the Gospel Polygamists' message to the public propose to recommend as the best way to overthrow the long-established monogamous society?

'The first step will be to promote a nationwide campaign,' says the leader. 'We shall unite all those who favour polygamy under our banner and organize them as a pressure group.

'Then when we are strong enough we shall petition Parliament to wipe out the existing marriage laws and make it legal for a man to have more than one wife. After all the idea of one woman for one man is perfectly ridiculous isn't it?' says 'Dr John' with almost disarming candour.

Warming to his theme, he goes on: 'When the wedding vows are swept away mankind will realize that the only true way to live happily is for every man to take as many wives as he possibly can. Our lives will be richer and fuller – and there will be no more of that unfortunate species, the spinster.'

When the enquirer gets on to topics like what is to be done to provide for the large numbers of children that will result from the multi-unions and how men are to settle disputes between their womenfolk, 'Dr John' ducks the questions and pleads that he has not yet finalized the plans for his 'utopia'.

Nevertheless, the campaign has already got under way, inspired, no doubt, by the leader's own example. His 'wives' are a nurse, a young shop assistant, a cook and an attractive ex-dancer. Each of the girls idolizes 'Dr John' – and they seem quite content to share the little 'messiah'. One has had a baby by him.

Apart from the cottage, the sect has purchased a number of other pieces of property – including a shop – to serve as administrative bases for the campaign to come. Where the money to buy these buildings came from, 'Dr John' is keeping to himself: but it is known that apart from his own wage-earners he has a number of female admirers who fawn on him like adolescent schoolgirls discovering their first 'pop' star.

Not surprisingly, though, those who admire this man and his Eastern ideas are distinctly in the minority. And some of those who are most strongly opposed to his crusade are those who live closest to him.

A member of the local parish council told me: 'The whole business is absolutely sickening – and if those people didn't confine themselves to private property we should jolly soon try and do something about them.'

A shopkeeper was equally emphatic: 'The sect seems to want to bring Eastern ideas into our midst – you know harems and all that nonsense. This country wouldn't be worth living in if what they proposed actually came true.'

But the number of members *is* getting bigger – as each day's post illustrates with its letters of application for membership of the sect.

For example, take this one in a precise and educated hand from a man in Cambridge: 'I'd love to come and live with you all. And give up my home and job as a security officer.'

Or the one from an insurance agent which was postmarked Aberdare, Glamorgan, and began 'I want to join your crusade and invest my savings in your movement.'

Or even the correspondent from north-west London who scribbled on paper torn from an exercise book: 'I admire people who refuse to conform and take an independent line of conduct.'

But all these 'appeals' were outdone by a woman.

With hasty, nervous flourishes she penned: 'I feel the world now needs diversion from the usual religious themes and I wish you the best of luck. Please let me know about your crusade and whether you would like any more recruits or converts as I am deeply and sincerely interested. I am 37 years of age and without any worldly ties.'

These letters pleased 'Dr John' greatly – for he tends to ignore adverse publicity and give the same comment on all attacks: 'It usually takes most people a long time to see the light.'

Those who 'see the light' with him sleep one man and his 'wives' per room, but eat in a communal lounge. They claim that each wife receives her share of her husband's affections in rota and this prevents any woman becoming a 'favourite'.

The men say they are very satisfied with this arrangement.

But what of the women? One of 'Dr John's' wives admitted cheerfully that the adverse publicity had upset them a little at first – but had done nothing to change either her mind or those of any of the other girls.

'We are just as devoted to the cause and our men and are all very happy together,' she said from the door of the sect's cottage 'headquarters'.

That may very well be so. The only thing I am happy about where 'the Gospel Polygamists' are concerned is that they have precious little chance of ever succeeding in their aim of 'Polyamy for All'.

The Slaves of Lust

To an outsider it would probably have seemed like a fairly wild party: most of the guests were drunk and ties and blouses were being discarded all over the place.

But this was far from being a party in the ordinary sense of the word. It had been arranged by members of a sect, the cult of which is the exchange of wives.

Secrecy cloaks the activities of all these sects as one would expect. There is too much at stake for the members to run the risk of exposure. But what do we know of these cults? Is there any indication as to how widespread the practice of 'wife-swapping' has become? And just what goes on at their gatherings?

To probe, and acquire information about the activities of the 'wife-swapping' cult is, for obvious reasons, not easy. I was not investigating cases of straightforward casual promiscuity where individuals, now and then, lose their sense of values, but an organization that had regular, planned meetings, esoteric in the extreme.

But there is a renegade in every organization – in this case, to disclose the confidences with which he had been entrusted is to be applauded – and I was fortunate enough to find one man who admitted that he had once belonged to one of these sects. The information he gave me stood up to much thorough cross-checking and examination. The group to which he belonged is still active today.

The cult, he says, meets in isolated country houses – usually the property of wealthier members.

'If you saw a "meeting" you could well have imagined you had stepped back in history – because most of them looked like Roman orgies in full spate,' said my informant. 'There was no attempt to be secretive – or show any modesty.'

But, as my contact pointed out, there was little chance of any intruder stumbling on the meetings – or even getting within spying distance, come to that. For nearly all the venues were large mansions standing in their own grounds and shut off from prying eyes by high stone walls. Most were further protected by intricate bell systems which gave early warning of any intrusion to those inside.

He particularly remembers a series of 'meetings' held in the county of Middlesex. 'They were really perverted and wild – but I hadn't got any excuse for allowing myself to get mixed up in them,' he says.

This is part of what he says happened. 'The one gathering that sticks in my mind most vividly took place at an old mansion out past —.The place was hidden by trees and the man who owned it had dogs running loose in the grounds. It was sumptuously furnished, too, full of Georgian antiques and costly drapes.

'When I got there the first thing I saw was a young girl stripping in one of the rooms. There was a circle of men around her.

'When she had finished undressing one man carried her off to a bedroom. Then another girl came in and started the same thing all over again,' he said.

While this was going on, exactly the opposite was taking place in another room further down the passage . . . a man was stripping before a group of women.

'While this pairing-off was taking place, everybody was drinking like mad and quite a few people were drunk. I remember some of the newer members used to get drunk straight away so they didn't have to know what was happening to their wives.'

This particular group was believed to have been started back in the early 1920s with the purpose of giving free rein to every form of sexual expression.

The sect had in its ranks at one time or another, top businessmen, entertainers and – allegedly – some members of the staff of a foreign embassy.

When my contact left the group in early 1965 he said the membership figure was climbing rapidly and the 'hierarchy' were having considerable difficulty in catering for everybody at their gatherings.

'About the time I left, a number of other people also left. They went because some new wife-swap sects had been started and they wanted to get better pickings.

'I decided to quit because my wife said she was leaving me for another man who belonged to the sect. When that happened I started to think about just how low I had got – and it was all my own fault. I was nothing more than a slave to lust – just the way people are slaves to drink and drugs.

'Now I've seen the error of my ways – I only hope some of the others will do, too,' he added.

My contact is fairly convinced that those who 'separated' at the same time as he did were able to get into new 'swapping sects'. Details about these organizations are, naturally enough, extremely hard to come by. How do people join? Word of mouth and personal recommendation are the most frequently used channels.

In recent months, however, one or two of the sects have shown what amounts to incredible – and perhaps time will prove foolhardy – daring by inserting advertisements in big city shop windows and the personal columns of national newspapers, and it takes the 'kinky' to spot them, reading between the lines.

The idea of wife-swapping in this country is nothing new – at least not according to one of our leading social anthropologists, Dr Fernando Henriques, who is a lecturer at Leeds University and author of a famous book on sexual customs, *Love in Action*. He believes it has been practised in isolated areas of the country for generations and still goes on quite openly in some communities today.

It was during an outspoken address to the International Planned Parenthood Federation at their conference in London in June, 1964, that Dr Henriques claimed that it is – and has been for many years – the custom in some remote Welsh valleys for the men to exchange their wives.

He told the gathering that this statement was based on field-work carried out both by himself and a team of researchers. He said the practice had resulted from conditions which existed centuries ago.

The only difference between the wife-swapping of the valley people and those in towns and cities is that one is organized while the other is not. The members of the 'kinky' cult plan their exchanges in secret while the country folk do so on a whim and without prior thought. And of the two categories, one is as perverted in its motives as the other is innocent.

Denials of Dr. Henriques's claims came thick and fast – with Welsh professors and even the president of the Welsh Nationalist Party joining forces to protest that such things did not happen any more and 'anyway there was nothing peculiarly Welsh in the idea of "wife-swapping".'

Controversial though the social scientist's remarks were, the most startling disclosure relating to wife-swapping came from America recently – where police have uncovered a worldwide wife-swapping sect . . . which has one of its largest branches in Great Britain.

The police made the discovery when they investigated a nudist colony in the sultry old jazz-town of New Orleans. They found it was in fact a 'degenerate cult . . . which indulges in perversion and wife-swapping'.

John Grosch, a special investigator for the police, said that they had seized a trunk at the colony containing indecent pictures. Also in it was evidence that the sect was international in scope with links in London, Paris and Berlin. The membership in Britain was thought to exceed 2,000.

A letter among the evidence described a meeting in which 'The place was transformed into a frenzied orgy that would surely have ranked with those reported in the Middle Ages.' There were also indications that the worldwide organization had been in existence for about five years without the authorities knowing.

The police even found mail ready to be sent to officials of the English 'branch' of the sect. These gave details of an 'international wife-swapping meeting' to be held shortly in New Orleans!

Another police sergeant who helped in the investigations said that the nudist colony apparently had screened couples for membership of the club. To be admitted to it, a man and his wife had to agree to free exchange of partners.

Quite how the 'branch' in England was started is not yet known, but the exposure in America has no doubt given the members here something to think – and worry – about.

Perhaps it will make them think carefully about the words of an eminent psychologist, who says of the sects: 'Those who join do so with the mistaken idea that the organizations can provide them with new sexual thrills. The truth of the matter is that in most cases these people are sexually immature to start with and find it difficult to have a sound relationship with their wedded partners. So they blame each other for their shortcomings, refuse to see that they might be wrong and try to find the answer in promiscuity.

'I would say these people get very little satisfaction out of their intimate relations with others – this is exemplified by the way they drink themselves almost silly before having sex – and that they are doomed to broken marriages and hopeless lives.'

The Nude Dancers

It all started harmlessly enough. They were a group of sincere people who found beauty in parading the naked body. And in their desire to understand themselves better, they filmed their activities for study and reference – a mistake which was to cost them dearly.

The Nude Dancers were, in fact, yet another of the many small cults which have developed in twentieth-century Britain. Quiet and secretive, they were for a time mistakenly thought to be black magic practitioners because they met late at night and gavotted about naked.

In fact, the group, who wallowed in a mire of gossip and innuendos for years, believed in 'a form of naturism linked with free expression'.

Today the Nude Dancers are no longer in existence. They were forced to disperse because of the films they took of their activities – films which now circulate in the depraved 'blue' film clubs of Britain and Europe.

These movies were shot by members with cine cameras while the 'dancers' were enjoying their 'free expression' sessions.

The 'performers' did not think there was anything wrong in what they did – even if society might. And besides, the films were intended for members only.

All the same, the movies came onto the 'blue' film market in 1961.

With only the slightest editing – for none of the Nude Dancers dared reveal himself to make a complaint – the films were soon being shown in backstreet clubs with titles such as *Peeping Tom*, *Call Girl* and *Night Out*.

They are among the most sought after 'blue' films and command prices from £30 to £100 for a single print.

It is still a mystery how these films were obtained, but once the fact became known, the Nude Dancers decided to disband.

The group, based in and around Liverpool, have covered their tracks well. Little is really known about them. They have been condemned as sexual perverts, and, on the other hand – which is nearer the truth – as people who wanted to remove all the taboos from sex and make it 'free' in every sense of the word.

Those who first heard about the Nude Dancers got no more than the tiniest scraps of information about them. For years, rumours about 'late night nude dancing', 'weird singing' and 'sacrifices' spread throughout Merseyside and led, not surprisingly, to the group being labelled as evil and followers of the Devil.

It was not really until their films became known to the police – following a raid on a 'blue' film club – that anything like a correct picture of the Nude Dancers was formed. But, by then, the group had disbanded.

Their history is worth relating, for they were the forerunners of several similar organizations which are known to be operating at the present time.

The sect existed for about six or seven years. Its main recruits were married couples, often with families. By all accounts not more than half a dozen single men and women were allowed to join.

Their gatherings were held in basement flats in and around Liverpool.

Though they saw nothing wrong in what they were doing, the Nude Dancers realized that outsiders might not be so broad-minded and they therefore devised special security arrangements with guards keeping watch for intruders. They also carefully blanketed and sealed all windows and burned low voltage bulbs.

The dancing never started until the early hours of the morning and only then when members were satisfied that all was quiet outside.

The activities would begin with a ceremonial disrobing, all members taking their clothes off at the same time. Then would follow the lighting of incense sticks and the pairing-off of couples.

In the early stages the dancing – usually to Latin American music – was slow and rhythmical. Then one by one the members would begin to express feelings through their bodies – pain, love, anguish and so on.

Occasionally during the activities a chant of ancient origin would be read out by one of the senior members. It was these senior members, too, who took the films of the 'dancing'.

The very high quality of the films points to the fact that only the very best and most expensive camera equipment was used – and to afford this the sect must have had considerable funds.

Investigators are convinced that because of this evidence of ample money there were probably quite a number of wealthy perverts who joined in an attempt to satisfy their jaded sensual appetites.

This may well have been so – thrill seekers would have been difficult to spot in an organization such as this which advocated complete free expression. But unquestionably the majority of the 'Dancers' were sincere people.

That the Nude Dancers ignored the accepted moral standards of today is undeniable – but they did not seek out new followers or attempt to corrupt anyone. They kept their activities as secret as possible and, but for the 'leak' of the films, would probably still be active today.

I am given to understand the police have evidence of similar groups to this Liverpool sect. These newcomers also advocate expression through sex-play and have found followings in several big cities. One or two are even believed to practise activities devised by the Nude Dancers. But anyone who considers following such principles would do well to consider one further thing about the original Nude Dancers. How dearly they must all be paying today in self-respect, knowing that they are day in and day out giving lustful pleasure to degenerate filmgoers all over the world.

The Kingdom of Hell

To those who know California it is really not surprising that it should have become the centre for diabolism and black magic in the United States. As one visitor remarked to me when I was in Los Angeles: 'There is so much more attention given to the quality of death here – to death styles, to dying the good death, to all-electric dying.'

It is a fact that despite living in perhaps the most beautiful area of America (even if there is a serious problem of air pollution in many of the major cities) the suicide rate is the highest in the country and practically in the world. Despite amazingly blue skies, miles of golden beaches with surf which is so white it hurts your eyes and a social and economic development making it the richest community in the world, California covets darkness and death. The people are bored and satiated with all they possess and have turned to the only excitement left – the ultimate excitement of dicing with the black unknown on the far frontier of life.

The upsurge of occultism in general and black magic in particular has centred itself on the coast and made Los Angeles its heart. Los Angeles, smog-shrouded, carved from the wilderness by pioneers and now basking in almost unbelievable affluence. A city on wheels, a city where anything goes – nude bars, simulated sex shows, hippies peddling drugs on Sunset Strip, Hell's Angels, and a frantic search for anything to relieve the monotony of living. A city now, to quote one authority, 'celebrating death'.

What more natural spot, then, for those who would seek a new avenue of experience through the practice of evil, to settle? Here, where no one looks surprised at anything and 'doing your own thing' was less extraordinary than not doing it; where the propagandists of drugs like Timothy Leary and Alan Watts have

60

stated that real beauty can be found only in the horrors which accompany the bad trip. If the acid vision can blend good into evil, white into black with no apparent change, they argued, why should the attraction of Satan be any different from that of Christ?

Seeking this new experience in typical California-style, the citizens of Los Angeles added their own special brand of exhibitionism to the magic, their own love of ceremonial to the practice of evil for evil's sake. The shade of Aleister Crowley looms large in the area, but his excesses pale into insignificance compared to today's Devil worshippers.

The views of observers on this scene vary, from the moderates who see it as just another symptom of California's overall sickness carrying its people headlong into perdition, to those who feel it to be part of a monstrous conspiracy. A city councillor in LA put it to me this way: 'The Second Coming has already arrived – only it was Satan that arrived not Christ. It hit Los Angeles first, naturally, we being the city of lost angels. Now there is a huge league of people, "Devilmen" I've heard them called, who have let the Devil into themselves and who work for the Devil.'

As for the world at large is concerned, this whole movement towards evil and black magic was symbolized in 1969 by the terrible butchery of the film star Sharon Tate and her friends by Charles Manson, self-proclaimed 'God and Devil', and his male and female disciples, widely referred to as 'Satan's Slaves'. The story of their hideous killings has been well documented but there are certain salient points which need repeating here.

There can be no doubt that Manson exerted complete authority over his followers and when he preached to them that evil was good and that nothing he, as their Christ/Devil, asked them to do could be wrong, they accepted it without question. Their lives were his for whatever purpose he chose.

At the time of the killings 'the Family', as the group became known, had settled on an old ranch once used for movie making and named after its owner, a former wrangler George Spahn. There they lived in commune style, sleeping together indiscriminately and foraging for food outside supermarkets and restaurants; devoting themselves to drugs, music and magic, while following the dictates of Manson.

The murders began before the Tate case. The first victim was a musician named Gary Hinman. He was killed on 6 August, 1969, when three of Manson's followers went to his house and asked for money. They were two girls and a man named Robert K. Beausoleil. The girls were holding a gun on Hinman, while Beausoleil ransacked the house. When Hinman threatened to get away from the girls, Beausoleil took over. By accident the gun went off and the half-dead Hinman was then stabbed to death. Beausoleil's fingerprints were found on the murder scene and he was arrested later in San Jose.

Drug-crazed and seemingly inspired by their first foray with death, another group of disciples then went out two days later, under orders, to strike at society again – this time against the very epitome of California wealth, its film stars. So followed the massacre of Sharon Tate and her four friends at Roman Polanski's palatial home in Bel Air.

Two days later they struck a third time, killing a Mr and Mrs Leno LaBianca in their home in the Los Feliz area of Los Angeles. The group daubed 'Death to the Pigs' and 'Rise' and 'Helter Skelter', the title of a Beatles' song, upon the walls of the house. On Mr LaBianca's stomach, one of them wrote the word 'War' with either a knife or a fork.

These scrawled words provided the police with the link between the killing of Hinman and with the deaths on the Tate estate, and in due time resulted in the arrest of the entire group.

The bizarre and gruesome trial which followed (there were ten women and three men charged in all) proved one of the most extraordinary in American legal history. It also dramatized the weird society of drug-induced obsessing, upside-down values and the adoration of the diabolical that was developing in California.

A statement made by one of the girls during cross-examination was highly significant in this context. Counsel for the prosecution asked the young woman if it was true that she regarded Manson as Satan and that she was one of his witches:

'Yes, sir, I am.'
'And you consider that witches have supernatural powers?'
'Yes.'
'Would you tell us what you thought your powers as a witch were?'

'I could do anything I wanted. I was made to believe I was a witch, right from the beginning. Charlie (Manson) said we were going to build this new culture and learn to control others by witchcraft.'

One of the men also expressed similar beliefs and devotion to Manson's cause in the witness box:

It's hard to explain. It's like nobody else counted but us and we would learn how to have all our desires fulfilled by using the same kind of magic that the witches used in ancient times. He told us that there wasn't any right or wrong. Just what was right for us. He was a strange man. He could talk four or five of the girl slaves into a circle and make each of them believe he was talking to her and the others weren't there. He was so attentive all the time, so caring that sex with him was natural. That's what he said, it was just a natural part of every day.

He was magnetic. His motions were like magic. One of the girls told me she fell under his spell the first time she heard him sing. He had this song he made up: 'There is no good, there is no bad. There is no crime, there is no sin.'

Later in the trial it was reported that Manson had made a point of speaking to one of the girls just before she left for the Tate residence and said, 'Leave a sign. The girls know what I mean – something witchy.' This, indeed, was to be his undoing.

How, though, did Manson manage to exert such influence over so many young people? One of the group giving evidence for the prosecution probably came closest when he said:

'How did he do it? Well, by the time Charlie was 35 he had done just about everything there was to be done. We were all terribly impressed by his experiences. He had been in jail a lot, bummed around the country and always had harems of young chicks. Everywhere he went he got this suicidal loyalty from everyone. He was big on black magic. It was pretty powerful stuff. He was continually hypnotising us, not the way they do in night clubs but more like mental thought transference.'

Drugs, of course, figured largely in the 'influence' as indeed they

63

do in most black magic in California. Some American psychiatrists have drawn a strong parallel between today's practitioners of the occult who take drugs and the witches of the Middle Ages who used hallucinogenic ointments and potions to give themselves a 'high' in which they believed they were flying. Manson, too, doubtless convinced his drugged disciples that they were 'flying' and could carry out his 'work' of destroying society with impunity.

A member of the US Federal Drug Abuse Control Agency to whom I spoke not long after the trial about the link between black magic and drugs was most forthcoming on the whole subject.

'You see, for a start, we just don't know how many individuals practise some form of black magic today,' he said. 'Many are members of pseudo-religious cults. These cults can be divided into several categories. Among them are those that carry orthodox religion into a psychotic realm, genuine witchcraft cults and superficial or phony cults which use black magic as a pretext for sexual orgies and other kicks.

'About six or seven years ago, while gathering data on drug abuse we estimated that there were as many as seventeen million cultists in the country, many of whom used drugs – and I do not mean addicted to them. Since then the number, from all indications, has greatly increased.

'The most dangerous type of "cult drug" is the hallucinogen, which we also call the mind-manifester or the consciousness-expander. You can readily see how a drug with these properties and psychedelic factors appeals to many modern witches, genuine and spurious.

'The most alarming in this category is LSD-25, lysergic-acid diethylamide. When a psychiatrist, the late Dr. Max Rinkel, introduced LSD clinically into the United States it could only be obtained legally from either the Federal Drug Administration or the National Institute of Mental Health by qualified medical and psychiatric research scientists.

'After studying a great many case histories, Dr Rinkel reported that under the influence of LSD the orgasm was enhanced, especially in females. Then, when Dr Timothy Leary, former Harvard psychologist, was quoted in a national magazine as saying, "LSD is the most powerful aphrodisiac ever discovered," the rush was on. I'll go as far as to say, it gave impetus to witchcraft and black magic especially in southern California where numerous new and far-out cults are created every year.'

How accurate the agent's words were soon began to manifest itself when I started my enquiries into the occult circles of Los Angeles. From my dossier I have extracted the following reports as being typical of the groups practising there:

The Order of Circe
This is a personalized cult with the members dedicated to worshipping the 'Devil Woman' who heads the group and is believed to be a reincarnation of the Greek goddess, Circe. Adepts of the order carve the so-called Star of Circe, a four-pointed star emanating from a rectangle, on to their chests, evidently as a mark of adoration of the goddess. The Circe group hold outdoor ceremonies twice a month, on the new and full moons, on the secluded beaches of Los Angeles and Ventura counties, where they sacrifice black animals such as dogs, cats, roosters and goats.

The Chingons
Another cult of animal sacrificers who meet in the Santa Ana Mountains just outside Los Angeles. Dedicated to 'the Worship of Evil' the members steal family pets and ritually disembowel them, eating the hearts as a sign of their obedience. The leader of the group is known simply as the Grand Chingon and current rumours have it that he is a very wealthy Los Angeles businessman. An unwitting and unsuspected observer of one of the cult's meetings said they assembled around an altar which was decorated with dragon symbols and slaughtered several animals on a table beside it. The witness also reported they had a portable crematorium for disposing of the bodies!

The Four P. Movement
An off-shoot of the Chingons, formed by a group of dissatisfied members who felt there was too much sacrifice and Devil worship and not enough sex. They specialize in sexual perversions carried out at night in churches and the desecration of holy buildings with the words 'Satan is the Master' scrawled in menstrual blood.

The Hollywood Cults

Innumerable groups abound in the Hollywood Hills and along Benedict, Laurel and Topanga Canyons, most practising satanism, drug-taking and attempting to utilize all the old rituals of black magic as contained in the medieval *grimoires* which are now being reprinted cheaply. The most important figure is undoubtedly the 'Princess Leda Amun Ra' now virtually a legend who lives in a castle-like home in the hills. A former Los Angeles housewife who discovered her 'status' through drugs, she is surrounded by a bevy of disciples who follow her every command and assist her when she ritually slays swans in the special temple in her home. Her followers believe that Leda can 'capture' souls and the high point of their month is the symbolic 'crucifixion' of a young male (usually high on drugs) in the gardens and the 'transplanting' of his soul into a swan.

In a house close to Leda's lives Hollywood's most famous Warlock, Samson de Brier, who professes to practise a kind of solitary white witchcraft, but says he can use his powers for evil. He calls himself the most important witch in California and the head of a dozen or so covens. A tiny man, always dressed in black, he rarely receives visitors in his huge Gothic home, but if encountered, prefers to talk more of his friends from the 'old days' such as André Gide and Anaïs Nin, than witchcraft.

In the vicinity are a dozen or more houses used for satanic ceremonies – some the particular preserve of homosexuals who practise a form of Devil worship allied to bondage in which the central figures are bound with leather thongs, wear crowns of thorns and are beaten by other men dressed as nuns. Others cater for lesbians and their fantasies while among the traditional 'open' groups, drugs and perversion are thinly disguised beneath the ceremonial rites and chants.

And so on. Even as I write, some Californian high on drugs will see himself as the new messiah and band together more bored people into a new cult of evil. It was all put very neatly in an article by Hollywood observer Tom Burke, who quoted a long-time Los Angeles resident on the new scene:

'If you sense an evil here, you are right, and I'll tell you what it is: too many people turned on to acid. If you make a habit of tripping – well acid is so metaphysical – you are going to be forced into making a choice, between opting for good, staying on a goodness or Christian trip, and tripping with the Lord Satan. That's the whole heavy thing about too many people turned on to acid: to most of them, the Devil just looks groovier. And that's one of the reasons I wear a cross, too, I believe in powers you can't explain. And if these sick Hollywood heads *are* into these powers – well, I want some protection. It freaks them to see a cross, if they're wearing a cross upside down. They just can't touch you, wearing the mark of the Lord Jesus.'

And if that sounds to you a little like the old medieval superstition of being afraid of the unknown reappearing, it does to me, too. But with a real difference – today fears of those who dabble with the deadly powers of evil are in the main fully justified. Gary Hinman, Mr and Mrs LaBianca and Sharon Tate and her friends found that out – tragically and shockingly.

* * *

Of all the witchcraft cults in California, whatever their shades of white, grey or black, there is perhaps none quite so strange, or developing as quickly, as the Church of Satan based in suburban San Francisco. The cult proclaims openly to practise black magic, put curses on all opponents, preaches a philosophy of 'indulgence instead of abstinence' and conducts a vigorous campaign of ridicule against white witchcraft in general and Wicca in particular. At the head of these people is Anton Sandor La Vey 'High Priest of the ineffable Kingdom of Hell' and the 'Black Pope of America'. A tall, fearsome-looking man with shaved, glistening head and dark goatee beard, he is a self-publicizer par excellence, and an occultist of considerable skill. All this he has devoted to creating his new world of satanic power.

San Francisco, the beautiful city on a hill with its cable cars and dramatic Golden Gate Bridge, is a most unlikely place to find a cult such as La Vey's. And indeed the house where he lives and works stands out prominently from the picturesque pastel-coloured frame and stucco buildings which cover the rest of the Bay Area of the town. It is Victorian in appearance, three stolid brick storeys high and painted black all over. The shutters remain tightly shut day and night and a notice on the door warns casual enquirers, 'Do Not Ring Unless You Have An Appointment'. For those who are invited, Diana La Vey, the small, pretty, blonde wife of the High Priest, will open the door and show them courteously into the 'Ritual Chamber' as the main lounge is called. Dominating the room are a tombstone with legs (serving as a coffee table), an old operating table, a skeleton and a vast array of occult books – primarily on black magic.

Anton La Vey, who calls himself a doctor of 'Satanic Theology', has become known as the most notorious practitioner of the black arts since Aleister Crowley and obviously delights in heightening this legend by his life style and setting. He dresses in a black suit with Roman collar and wears the satanic Pentagram of Baphomet, the Black Goat, on a silver chain around his neck. Outdoors, he strides along in a flowing black cloak.

Born in 1930 of Russian parents (who brought him up on tales of vampires and the supernatural, he says) La Vey was a circus artist, animal trainer and police photographer before founding his cult on Walpurgisnacht, 30 April, 1966.

'In effect I started the church even before 1966,' he recalls, 'because I had set up a magical circle in the Bay Area of San Francisco for people who were already students of the black arts. We had about 50 members with a hard core group of 25 or so meeting once a week for seminars of practise. I had developed a synthesis that I was putting into practice and I found that it worked.

'Basically the principles of satanism are contained in the first words of Faust's *Homunculus,* "I live, therefore I must act." We're here, and we'd damned well better make the best of it and not look beyond this life. There is a demon inside man and it must be exercised, not exorcized – channelled into ritualized hatred.'

The impact of the cult was not long in being felt and today La Vey claims to have a membership of around 10,000 people in the United States and 'branches' in most major countries of the world, including several European nations, Great Britain and even Australia. According to him, these people are aged between 25 and 45 and practise a 'controlled form of hedonism'. In this they acknowledge Satan as a symbolic personal saviour who advocates sexual freedom. They make a great point, too, of informing everyone that the word traditionally associated with their master, EVIL, is actually LIVE spelt backwards. Their ceremonials, as we shall see later, are designed to eliminate all inhibitions and include a naked woman as the 'altar' and the use of phallic symbols for benediction.

La Vey encourages his members to indulge in the seven deadly sins because they are the things we do naturally, he says. They hurt no one; besides, they were invented by the Catholic Church to instil guilt in the faithful. Actually, the seven deadly sins are virtues, he reasons, because they all lead to physical or mental gratification, and how can you be good to anyone else if you aren't good to yourself?

'If we didn't have pride, we wouldn't have any self-respect. Anger? If people exploded, there might not be ulcers. Lust? If it weren't for that we wouldn't be here. Envy? How could one get ahead if he didn't envy? It's the same for gluttony, greed, slothfulness.'

He practises what he preaches, too, and points to what happened to attorney Sam Brody as proof. Brody was the boyfriend of actress Jayne Mansfield, who was a member of La Vey's church.

'Jayne and I were very close,' the satanist leader says, 'but she had strong masochistic tendencies, a self-destructive urge.

'Sam Brody hated my group. He threatened to make trouble, all kinds of scandal for me. I told him I would see him dead within the year, and I went through a ritual satanic curse, conjuring up forces to destroy him. I told Jayne that he was under a dark cloud and that it was foolish for her to be with him. I urged her to stay out of cars with him and not be alone with him. I made it clear to her that it would happen within a year.'

Within a year, in June 1967, Brody was killed in a car crash on the road to New Orleans. Jayne Mansfield, who had been named co-respondent by Brody's wife in a court suit, was decapitated in the same accident.

'She was the victim of her own frivolity,' pronounces La Vey.

If this statement gives the impression that the High Priest has a certain lack of compassion, he can be heard at his most disparaging when it comes to discussing white witchcraft.

'Satanism differs greatly from all self-righteous and super-cilious religions who protest that *their* members use the powers of magic only for altruistic purposes. Satanists look with disdain upon "white" witchcraft groups because they feel that altruism is sinning on the lay-away plan. It is unnatural not to have the desire to gain things for yourself.

'Satanism advocates practising a modified form of the Golden Rule,' he goes on. 'Our interpretation of this rule is: "Do unto others as they do unto you"; because if you "Do unto others as you would have them do unto you", and they, in turn, treat you badly, it goes against human nature to continue to treat them with consideration.

'White witchcraft groups say that if you curse a person, it will return to you three-fold, come home to roost, or in some way boomerang back to the sender. This is yet another indication of the guilt-ridden philosophy which is held by these neo-Pagan, pseudo-Christian groups. White witches want to delve into witch-craft, but cannot divorce themselves from the stigma attached to it. Therefore, they call themselves white magicians and base 75 per cent of their philosophy on the trite and hackneyed tenets of Christianity.

'Anyone who pretends to be interested in magic or the occult for reasons other than gaining personal power,' he maintains, 'is the worst kind of hypocrite. The satanist respects Christianity for at least being consistent in its guilt-ridden philosophy but can only feel contempt for people who attempt to appear emancipated from guilt by joining a witchcraft group, and then practise the same basic philosophy as Christianity.

'White magic is supposedly utilized only for good or unselfish purposes, and black magic, we are told, is used only for selfish or "evil" reasons. Satanism draws no such dividing line. Magic is magic, be it used to help or hinder. The satanist, being the magician, should have the ability to decide what is just and then apply the powers of magic to attain his goals.'

To summarize all his beliefs, the High Priest of Satanism recently wrote a book titled characteristically *The Satanic Bible*. In this he propounds his tenets which, simplified, read:

1. Satan represents indulgence, instead of abstinence!
2. Satan represents vital existence, instead of spiritual pipe dreams!
3. Satan represents undefiled wisdom, instead of hypocritical self-deceit!

4. Satan represents kindness to those who deserve it, instead of love wasted on ingrates!
5. Satan represents vengeance, instead of turning the other cheek!
6. Satan represents responsibility to the responsible, instead of concern for psychic vampires!
7. Satan represents man as just another animal, sometimes better, more often worse than those that walk on all fours and who, because of 'his divine spiritual and intellectual development', has become the most vicious animal of all!
8. Satan represents all of the so-called sins, as they all lead to physical, mental, or emotional gratification!
9. Satan has been the best friend the church has ever had, as he has kept it in business all these years!

And so on. The book is a history not so much of blasphemy as complete opposition to all the teachings of Christianity. La Vey claims, 'What we advocate is what most Americans practise whether they call it Satanism or not. We are the new establishment and ours is the way for the future.'

It is perhaps only in the state of California, that La Vey could report truthfully that his 'Church' is recognized by the government and the state as a religion. 'We have all the advantages from the point of view of taxes and our weddings (in the name of Lord Satan) funerals and baptism (also held over the body of a nude woman) are recognized and registered.'

La Vey has carried out these rites in the full glare of publicity and, not surprisingly, has received a great deal of abuse and condemnation – particularly when he 'baptized' one of his own two daughters, Zeena, aged six. All this he accepts cheerfully and indeed the new visitor to the house (or 'Devil's Chapel' as he prefers to call it) will invariably be shown his bulging scrapbook. A conducted tour of the house is also reminiscent of a guided tour of occult history, crammed as it is with horned masks, crystal balls (La Vey is also an accomplished hypnotist and this does give a pointer to the basis of some of his skills), a black coffin, an organ and the Master's study which bears a headboard 'the Den of Iniquity'. As if this were not enough, there is also a bed of nails which La Vey claims to use regularly.

During the week, apart from being regularly consulted by would-be members of the Church (admission fee $10), Anton La Vey answers voluminous mail, writes for magazines and shows private clients how to cast their own spells. Friday he gives over to the preparation of his weekly 'Satanic Mass' which takes place in the evening and draws a dozen or so followers from around the San Francisco area. My schedule in the town did not permit me to stay on for this ceremony, but the following graphic report was specially prepared by a young and perceptive journalist Judith Rascoe. It describes, as Miss Rascoe puts it, 'just exactly what goes on in a quiet backwater of San Francisco every week.'

'Late on Friday evening I drove to San Francisco to attend a Satanic High Mass. A heavy fog, like the background of a Flemish hell, smothered the city; the streets were empty. I knocked on the door of the Church of Satan – it was so dark and misty I could not find the bell – and a young security guard in a black uniform admitted me cautiously.

'Several young warlocks, wizards, and priests were lounging and chatting in their black robes in the little hallway. In the hyacinth parlour half a dozen more people were waiting for the service to begin. Two elderly fellows sat on the sofa, dismayed or pleased by the fact that the other satanists were a youthful lot.

'Looking around, I saw that everybody except me and the old fellows and a young girl in the corner wore the familiar satanic medallion: a ram's head in the centre of an inverted five-pointed star.

'The light dimmed. Wagner filled the room, and soon we sat in warm, voiceless darkness, submerged beneath waves of the "Ring Cycle". After a long, long time, Wagner subsided, giving way to organ music from another room.

'Suddenly the door opens and a priestess carrying a candle beckons us to follow her to the Ritual Chamber, where we grope our way on to folding chairs and are plunged into impenetrable darkness once again. The organ booms on and on, making me wonder how the organist can find the keys.

'Finally the lights flicker a little at the other end of the room, flare up, and reveal half a dozen ministers of Satan, some with their heads covered with pointed black hoods, gathered before the altar. On the altar-fireplace the red-haired girl lies nude and

72

artfully disposed on a fur rug, so that her nudity is more suggested than explicit, especially to the obliquely seated congregation.

'A very tall hooded figure steps forward and rings the bell, and then Anton La Vey, who has been standing in the shadows, his robed arm lifted before his face, begins the "Satanic Solemn High Mass".

'Tonight he is wearing a horned satin cap and heavy satin robes. He seems seven feet tall rather than six; his gestures are slow and lordly; his voice is full, cold and dramatic. From one book he reads a Gospel of Satan; from another he recites the Enochian invocations. He chants the names of Satan in litany with the congregation: *"Abaddon, Apollyon, Asmodeus . . . Demo-gorgon . . . Moloch . . . Typhon!"* Priests and congregation respond smartly with: *"Shemhamforash! Hail Satan!"*

'Members of the congregation are invited to come forward and make their wishes known to Satan. A talkative wizard steps forward and heaps curses on the name of his enemy "A snivelling swine, a rotten churl, a crawling, contemptible cur." . . . "May slimy shapes rise from brackish pits and vomit forth their pustulence into his puny brain." The ministers chant, the organ music rises to a crescendo, and a blast of sound and a rifle crack of "Hail Satan" hurl the curse towards the victim's doorstep.

'Then a sexy young Frenchwoman steps forward and – we cannot hear her. Is she cursing somebody or using the conjuration of lust? ("Send forth that messenger of voluptuous delights!") Another enthusiastic *"Shemhamforash! Hail Satan!"* sends her wishes on their way. The horned salute is given, the bell rings, the service ends, and the congregation wanders back to the hyacinth parlour.

'Perhaps it was the late hour, but after it was all over it occurred to me that, as Tolstoi might have said, all happy churches are alike. Frank smiles and firm handshakes welcomed me to the congregation. And one of the elderly fellows even asked me how I liked the service . . .'

Explanation of this ritual is hardly necessary although a few comments on certain specifics may be enlightening. All the participants wear black robes (symbolic of the powers of darkness) with cowls, so that the participant is free to 'express emotion in the face without concern' to quote the 'satanic bible'.

The females are, however, urged to wear garments which are 'sexually suggestive' to stimulate the male participants 'and thereby intensify the outpouring of bio-electrical energy which will ensure a powerful working'.

The reason for the nude girl forming the altar is that satanism is a 'religion of the flesh' and apart from serving as a focal point, 'woman is the natural passive receptor and represents the earth mother' – to paraphrase from the 'satanic bible' again.

The bell-ringing also plays a significant role in the ceremony. The priest rings the bell nine times, turning counter-clockwise and directing the tolling towards the four cardinal points of the compass. This is done once at the beginning of the ritual to clear and purify the air of all external sounds and once again at the end of the ritual to intensify the working and act as a 'pollutionary' indicating finality.

A phallic symbol is usually displayed at these rites (although it was not noted by our young reporter) and, in the words of the 'satanic bible' represents 'generation, virility and aggression'. It is held in both hands by one of the assistants and shaken twice towards each of the four points of the compass, for the benediction of the house.

Further items which may be employed are candles – both black and white, representing the Light of Lucifer, bringer of enlightenment – a chalice made of silver from which is drunk the 'Elixir of Life' (a strong wine) 'to intensify the emotions' and a ritual sword occasionally used during the invocation of Satan. The use of this sword has led to charges against La Vey that, in the tradition of satanism over the ages, he continues the practice of human sacrifice.

This he denies – in *actuality*. But he does say it can occur symbolically in a satanic ritual. Someone who has unjustly wronged a diabolist or his loved ones can be destroyed by ritual curse. The curse destroys the 'sacrifice' in ways not attributable to the magician. The police never come knocking at the door, adds La Vey, but the one who has pronounced the curse *knows*.

Part Two

Paths to the Holocaust

The Jonestown Massacre

Jim Jones wanted to create an agricultural utopia in the jungle for his followers – but instead was responsible for a mass suicide that still reverberates in the public imagination almost thirty years after it occurred. The events surrounding the cult founded by the American Jones have also entered popular speech as a kind of code for the dangers of cults and cult leaders. The over 900 people who died in Guyana in November 1978 after drinking a fruit punch laced with cyanide and tranquillizers unwittingly gave birth to the expression, 'Drinking the Kool-Aid,' which has come to mean heedlessly jumping on a bandwagon.

The story of James Jones and his project for a 'People's Temple' was already starting to take shape in the late sixties when I made my first trip to San Francisco, the famous city on a hill with its 'Golden Gate' and fortress-like Alcatraz Prison on a an island in the middle of the Bay Area. The whole town was a mecca for hippies and writers – the famous City Lights Bookshop on Haight-Asbury was busy publishing the ground-breaking works of the 'Beat Generation' including Jack Kerouac, William Burroughs and Alan Ginsburg – and the city already had a reputation as a haven for radical views, outspoken organizations and controversial groups. It was little wonder that it should have attracted a man like Jones.

The ultimate suicide of James Jones's followers, which for years had the unenviable reputation of being the largest mass murder/suicide in American history, would have seemed like an impossible final scenario for the cult that looked to the Bible for inspiration, its charismatic leader for guidance and dreamed of an idyllic lifestyle far from the pressures of contemporary life in the United States. Along the way, the motives of the founder turned from holiness to faith-healing fakery, questionable finances, physical abuse of some of those in his care and a mounting obsession with a coming nuclear holocaust.

Because the first reports of the mass death at the 'People's Temple' came from the Central Intelligence Agency – and because the radical stand of Jones's group had contributed to its decision to leave America – a number of conspiracy theories have also attached themselves to the events. It has been claimed, for example, that Jones was actually a rogue CIA agent who was involved in mind control experiments. Other sources have claimed that the US government was responsible for killing the 900 people because it was afraid they might move to the Soviet Union and generate a propaganda coup for the Russians. An even more controversial later suggestion maintained that the group represented a right-wing conspiracy to perpetrate genocide on black Americans.

How the group – sometimes referred to by sceptics as 'made in San Francisco' – could have inspired such stories and come to such a finale begins in the Deep South of America with the life of Jim Jones. From there it follows an arduous and almost incredible route, certainly unlike that of any other of the group in this book, to a remote encampment known as 'Jonestown' deep in the jungles of South America.

* * *

James Warren Jones was born on 13 May 1931 during the height of the Great Depression in America in the small town of Crete, Indiana. His father, James Thurman Jones, was a disabled First World War veteran whose bitterness towards life was evidenced in his membership of the Ku Klux Klan and long absences away from his family. The boy Jim grew up close to his mother, Lynette, who was apparently sceptical of organized religion and believed strongly in spiritualism – convictions that she passed on to him along with the importance of social justice and equality.

According to neighbours of the Warrens, young Jim was taken to a Pentecostal church as a child. He found the experience very emotional and while he was graduating from high school in Richmond, Indiana, also began to study theology and social idealism. The bedrock of the doctrine which would guide and motivate his later cult was evidently formed at this time.

Soon the young man was fired with a desire to be a preacher and in September 1954 he began giving sermons at the Laurel Street Tabernacle in Indianapolis. His charismatic style soon began to attract new members to the congregation, but also upset some of the more senior members of the church who disliked his inclusion of black Americans in his sermons. Jones was told to change his message or leave the church. He chose the latter and determined to form his own church with those who had most keenly appreciated his appeal for social justice.

A popular version of the next few months of Jim Jones's life claims that he 'sold pet monkeys door to door' around Indianapolis to raise the money for his new church. This he named the 'Wings of Deliverance' in April 1955, renaming the group a year later as the 'People's Temple'.

In the next few years, Jones developed the themes that would promote his ideas to an ever-increasing congregation. He was convinced that religion and politics could mix and fashioned together Pentecostalism, the Christian Social Gospel, socialism, utopianism and Communism. As time passed, his message grew increasingly diverse – and to some, alarming.

He practised the ability to discern spirits, read the thoughts of others and see the future. Faith healing also began to pay an important part in his worship and he claimed to be able to heal with the touch of his hand. Most dramatically of all, Jones took from Pentecostalism the belief in the imminent Second Coming of Christ and pronounced himself to be the Second Coming. He was, he said, an incarnation of Jesus, Akhenaten, Buddha, Father Divine and Lenin and – so other reports state – 'performed supposed miracles to attract new members'.

In 1960, the 'People's Temple' was admitted into the Disciples of Christ denomination in Indianapolis and, despite his lack of theological training, Jones was ordained as a minister. Although his church was now officially under the banner of a mainstream Christian group, he retained his independence and continued to increase his congregation and win over admirers. In 1964, at the height of the American Civil Rights Movement, he was ordained as a minister despite the fact he had no formal theological

training. His 'People's Temple' was regarded as being excep-
tional because of its equal treatment of African Americans in
what was a largely segregated city.

However, the intransigence of the local authorities to his plans
for racial equality and social justice – which he referred to as
'apostolic socialism' – made him decide to move to the more
liberal west coast of America. He was also becoming increasingly
paranoiac about the possibility of a thermo-nuclear war. He
wanted to find somewhere he, his wife, Marceline, their growing
family and his eighty-strong band of followers – divided almost
equally black and white – would be safe from danger and free to
practise their beliefs. After considering several options, Jones
selected the Redwood Valley in northern California, a wine-
growing district where views were also more openly inclined to
new ideas, and erected a church building and several office buildings in an idyllic location.

This situation and Jones's dedication to social justice and racial
equality made the cult attractive to the increasing number of
young college-educated men and woman who were anxious to
turn their backs on the 'American Dream' and follow a route to
peace and harmony. With these vibrant souls moving in to the
community, the leader again began to change the direction of his
cult and the way its members lived and worked. He also increasingly replaced religious rhetoric with political statements.

The 'People's Temple' now became a community with the
members sharing accommodation. Everyone was to hand over his
or her money and income to the cult and any other items of value
had to be sold to raise funds to support the group. Fund raising
appeals were also launched and a number of social programmes
put into operation to help the elderly, the disadvantaged and the
mentally ill. A number of care homes were also set up for senior
citizens who were promised they could spend their retirement
years in the Redwood Valley cared for by Jones's disciples.

Now evidently feeling secure in this environment, Jones turned
his thoughts to 'reading' the future. He had also reached some
very startling conclusions which he outlined in an extraordinary
booklet he called *The Letter Killeth*. In this he pointed out what
he had discovered were contradictions, absurdities and even
atrocities in the Bible – though there were, he conceded, 'some

great truths' in it. He also maintained that the only God his followers had ever known was himself.

Unbeknown to all except those closest to him, Jones was now subscribing to *Pravda,* the Russian daily newspaper and mouthpiece of the Communist Party in the Soviet Union, interjecting his 'sacred texts' with ideas he had found in the journal's pages. He had also become intrigued by a number of the radical and underground texts then circulating in California. Soon, he would be rejecting the Bible that had been the starting point of his conversion as 'full of lies and contradictions'.

Whatever reservations Jim Jones may have felt, the appeal of his cult continued to grow. In 1972, the 'People's Temple' opened a new church in San Francisco in the black ghetto of Fillimore District, and this was soon packed with converts. Cultists bussed in from the Redwood Valley community were soon helping the people with their financial and housing problems – not forgetting to promote the lessons of their great leader. Local politicians and city officials sensing the growing power of Jim Jones's group were quick to get on the bandwagon and offer support – in return, it would transpire, for the cult's votes, promised by Jones. George Moscone, the mayor of San Francisco, even gratefully appointed Jones to the city's Housing Authority Commission.

But all was not well with the 'People's Temple'. A few voices were beginning to question the cult's beneficiaries and increasing influence over certain vulnerable groups. Even a man much less smart than Jim Jones would have realized that he might have to look again for a new home to further his movement. When events conspired to show a completely different side to the cult leader just before Christmas 1973, the need became rather more urgent.

* * *

The residents of California awoke on the morning of 13 December 1973 to read a headline story that the Reverend James Warren Jones had been arrested and charged with soliciting a man for sex. The arrest had taken place in the toilets of a cinema in MacArthur Park in Los Angeles, which was well known for homosexual activity. The media had a field day with the story until it was revealed that the man was actually an undercover LA Police Department vice officer who had been keeping observation on the theatre for some time. The case against Jones was quietly dropped after pressure from a 'People's Temple' lawyer.

Whatever the truth of the matter, Jones sensed his hold on the cult could be weakened unless he took action. He decided to look for another location for the 'People's Temple'. In the spring of the following year he discovered just what he was looking for – an area of 4,000 acres in the north-west of Guyana. The country had the added attraction of being a socialist republic, a multi-racial state and the only area of South America where English was spoken. As one of the group's spokesmen was later to put it, the request to purchase the land had been welcomed by the government:

'They were delighted at the idea of the place serving as a refuge for Americans fleeing a racist and oppressive regime.'

But after this bit of good news, bad was soon piling up on the cult. Shortly after purchasing the land in Guyana which Jones had already decided to name after himself, the US Internal Revenue Service began an investigation into the finances of the 'People's Temple'. The church, of course, was tax exempt, but it was the income from the group's business activities that had caught the eye. The inquiry, which began in March 1974, threatened to close down the entire organization if irregularities were uncovered.

A group of disaffected members of the 'People's Temple' who had found some of Jim Jones's claims absurd and his attitude to vulnerable members unacceptable, formed a group calling itself 'Concerned Relatives'. They began a campaign urging the authorities to investigate just what was going on behind the church doors. Attempts by journalists to gain entry to the community in Redwood Valley and the church in the Fillimore District were rigorously denied by a group of the leader's lieutenants.

Matters came to a head, though, when the outspoken weekly magazine *New West* published a damning article in February 1977 on the 'People's Temple' and its leader. Charging him with 'faith-healing fakery, physical abuse of his congregation and questionable finances', the publication demanded that the various government agencies investigate. Other elements of the news media followed suit with articles and broadcasts also criticizing the cult. In one particularly strong attack in the 12 June issue of the *San Francisco Chronicle* a former member of the cult told the paper of 'brutal beatings, sexual perversions and murder'.

Convincing his faithful that these persecutors could bring an end to his mission, he encouraged more followers to move to Guyana and prepare the ground for the 'People's Temple'. Although the land had been bought three years earlier, only a trickle of the strongest men and women – all understandably concerned about the conditions and workload that faced them in the barren countryside half a world away – had left California. When the bombshells of the newspaper headlines and tax investigation dropped on the cult, just 50 people were living in Jonestown.

Such, though, was the charisma and plausibility of Jim Jones that within a few months during the summer and autumn of 1977, over a thousand more cultists had set off for a new life in the unknown. Most had been swayed by their leader's talk of life in this new 'Promised Land' where communal living and a sense of purpose in an agricultural environment would soon make the world of California seem dull and prosaic. Jones said little about the months of back-breaking work that would be required to turn the open space into a community complete with houses, community buildings and a church. It is said that during the first months of occupation, men and women worked for eleven hours a day, six days a week, with only a break on Sundays for meetings. The 250 children were included in this work programme, though they were also given time off for lessons.

Everyone lived in dormitories – the children separated from their parents – and existed on a very basic diet consisting mostly of beans and rice, with meat and vegetables a rare treat. Apart from the normal requirements of any collection of human beings in such a situation – cooking, washing, building and tending the fields – the cult members had also to find time to make items for sale in Georgetown, the capital of Guyana, in order to raise money for requirements the group could not themselves make.

There were also endless sermons by Jim Jones and meetings, educational programmes and, increasingly, Russian language lessons. These were to enable members to read and understand *Pravda*. According to later reports, Jones would read out news reports from Soviet and Eastern bloc countries over a public address system which were 'highly critical of capitalist and imperialist countries'. The great leader described the America they had left behind as 'beset by racial and economic problems' that they had escaped to a new and better life.

This 'new and better life' was not only taking its toll of the 1,000-strong community. Jones himself became increasingly dependent on drugs and would fly into rages that dissipated almost as soon as they had begun. He also came to rely more on the 'Planning Commission' he had set up in Jonestown to oversee the 'Promised Land' and an all-female 'leadership corps' to run day-to-day operations. Women and sex undoubtedly featured high in Jones's scheme of things. In his book, *A Lavender Look at the People's Temple* (2006), Michael Bellefountaine claims:

'Jones used sex to control the members of his "Planning Commission". He accused everyone of being gay, but forced men and women to have sex with him and frequently proclaimed himself to be the only true heterosexual. By encouraging infidelity to one's partner, Jones demanded fidelity to himself alone. At the same time, however, in an effort to create a new, multi-racial society, Jones promoted bi-racial partnerships and the adoption or birth of bi-racial children. A Relationship Committee run by the "Planning Commission" oversaw the partnerships between a variety of people.'

It is evident from this that loyalty to Jim Jones and the community was considered of paramount importance. Before being allowed to serve on the 'Planning Commission', candidates were introduced to less religious ideals to test their trustworthiness. To show just *how* loyal they were to the leader, it is believed some 'People's Temple' members were made to sign incriminating documents in which they admitted to performing homosexual acts and even child molestation.

To promote what he described as a 'selfless, populist communalism', Jones also demanded confession and punishment for those who transgressed. A youngster who was heard being rude to an older person, for instance, would have to apologize in public and then be severely spanked by Jones. One young man who made sexist remarks about a woman was forced to fight a boxing match with her. A report of the event given by a disaffected member who left the cult in 1978 says the girl 'knocked out the man to the delight of the crowd in attendance'.

But the combination of James Jones's physical and mental deterioration coupled with his inability to hide his drug addiction from rank and file cult members and loss of support by some of his inner-circle members saw his authority diminishing. Several leading members had also defected, notably Tim Stoen, who had been the 'People's Temple' lawyer and Jones's right-hand man and was now actively campaigning against the cult. The loss of men like him made life increasingly difficult in the 'Promised Land': not helped by the steady stream of enquiries that were now being received about cult members from relatives and friends in America. All of this contributed to the leader's increasing paranoia as autumn turned to winter in the year 1978.

The string of complaints now being levelled at the cult – including complaints that Jonestown was being run 'like a concentration camp' and men and women were being brain-washed in Guyana 'to keep them there against their will' – began to be make people in the US take notice. Calls were made for US embassy officials in Guyana to visit the compound and see for themselves what was going on.

In November 1978, the California congressman, Leo J. Ryan, who had been deluged with a letter-writing campaign to investigate 'Jonestown', agreed to go on a fact-finding mission accompanied by a number of concerned relatives and representatives of the media. It would cost him his life – and also write the last, appalling chapter in the story of Jim Jones and his 'People's Temple'.

* * *

Although it is generally believed that the mass-suicide of Jim Jones's followers on 18 November 1978 was an unpremeditated action, the facts are that such a possibility had been in the leader's mind for some years before the event took place. For one thing, he had written about the rhetoric of suicide in an article for his newspaper, *People's Forum,* published in San Francisco long before the cult had left for Guyana. And it seems undeniable that members of the cult had for some time been conditioned to accept the necessity of giving their lives for the cause – as is evident in several letters written home from Jonestown. 'We would rather die than be hounded from one continent to the next,' a woman wrote in a letter to her mother in March 1978 that was later quoted to members of congress in Washington.

Documents seized in Guyana from among the dead refer to members of the 'Planning Commission' actually taking part in a mock suicide in 1976. With Jones looking on, the participants drank some punch and were then told it was poison. As they stood there in speechless horror, a few of the leaders fell to ground, seemingly dead. While the participants waited for the poison to take effect on them, Jones suddenly announced that it was actually a 'loyalty test' to see if they were willing to die for the cause!

On another occasion, in October 1977, Jones called out the faithful to defend the 'Promised Land' from an attack he said was expected by some enemies approaching them from the jungle. According to a tape recording made at the time, the cult members fully expected to die, as they had no means of protecting themselves against the marauders. They were, though, quite prepared to die, the terrified voices were heard to cry to their leader before he again told them he was testing their dedication and loyalty.

We can, though, be fairly certain of what actually happened after the arrival of Leo Ryan's group in Jonestown on 14 November. After lengthy negotiations with the Jonestown leadership, the congressman and his party were given permission to enter the community and interview residents on Friday 17 November. Jones himself told the party that they could 'take anyone who wanted to leave' with them when they went home. The day apparently ended happily with the community band, The Jonestown Express giving a concert for residents and guests.

The following day, however, the mood in the compound changed dramatically. A disaffected cultist appealed to Leo Ryan for help to leave Jonestown and by the end of the morning, sixteen more members had gathered to leave with him. In the agitation that resulted from a number of the cultists parting from relatives and friends, Ryan was suddenly attacked with a knife by one of the members, Don Sly, but escaped serious injury. With the mood now turning nasty, Ryan and the others hurriedly left the compound and drove quickly to the airfield six miles away at Port Kaituma, where two planes were waiting to take them all back to the capital, Georgetown.

In the wake of the vehicle, a group of Jim Jones's armed guards followed. As soon as the party attempted to board the aircraft, their pursuers opened fire. When the gunfire ceased and the guards drove off, five people lay dead. Sprawled in the dust were the bodies of Congressman Ryan, a reporter and cameraman from NBC, a newspaper photographer and one of the defectors from the 'People's Temple'. The dozen or so survivors who could only look on in horror included Jackie Speier, a member of Ryan's staff, CIA officer Richard Dwyer and NBC news producer, Bob Flick, who would later tell their stories to the world's media.

But the news of the murders did not even have time to reach America before the 'revolutionary suicide' that Jones had threatened took place in Jonestown. Assembling his followers, the leader proclaimed that the end had come. In a final rambling, occasionally incoherent speech, he told the cult members:

'Please, for God's sake let's get on with it. We've lived, we've lived as no other people have lived and loved. We've had as much of this world are you're gonna get. Let's just be done with it. Let's just be done with the agony of it – this revolutionary suicide. This is not a self-destructive suicide. So they'll pay for this. They've brought this upon us. And they'll pay for that.'

According to the evidence found at Jonestown, a large vat of purple Flavor Aid, a version of Kool-Aid, mixed with potassium cyanide and various sedatives and tranquillizers – including Valium, Penegram and chloral hydrate – was placed in front of the cult members who formed themselves into lines. Parents first gave the mixture to their babies and children before pouring the poison down their own throats. A few of the older adults are believed to have been forced or injected.

In all, 914 people died on Saturday, 18 November in Jonestown – 276 of them children. The man who had brought them to this terrible end did not drink the poison like all the rest, however, but sat himself down in a deckchair and shot himself in the head. There he remained in the bright sunshine surrounded by the hundreds of bodies until the authorities reached Jonestown.

What those who first entered the compound saw would haunt them for the rest of their lives. For here was not the 'agricultural utopia' that Jim Jones had promised, but a holocaust unimaginable since the end of the Second World War. The meaning of evil cults would never be the same again.

The Mormon Mafia

The town of Galeana on the west coast of Mexico was bathed in early morning July sunshine as a large vehicle bumped its way across acres of agricultural land, causing small eddies of dust to rise in its wake. From a distance it was hard to tell just what kind of motor was raising the dirty plumes, but every so often a flash of light glinted off the roof and bonnet giving it a golden hue. A stranger might have been puzzled at such an unusual sight in a dirt farming area, but those in the fields who raised their tired bodies and weary heads from their tasks as the vehicle grew nearer, knew precisely what to expect.

It was, in fact, a gold-coloured Ford Impala referred to as the 'Golden Calf' by those who lived in the surrounding neighbourhood. They also knew that behind the wheel of the speeding roadster was the hulking figure of Ervil LeBaron, a religious cult leader, declared by his followers to be the 'the Prophet of God', the 'One Might and Strong' and, at religious assemblies, as the 'Lord Anointed'. Others, however, viewed LeBaron in a very different light. To those outside his influence, he was the brutal leader of a 'Mormon Mafia' and would ultimately be labelled as 'the Mormon Manson' after his followers left a bloodbath of between 25 and 30 murders across Mexico and the American Southwest.

The progress of the gleaming gold vehicle and its occupant across the acres of agricultural land that had belonged to the fundamentalist Church of the Lamb of God since 1924, bore more than a passing resemblance to that of an old-time plantation owner overseeing his slaves. Indeed, the spread was exotically known as 'Colonia LeBaron' and Ervil had for years insisted that his labouring flock should remove their hats or raise their hands in supplication as he passed. Anyone who failed to acknowledge the appearance of the 'Anointed One' would be in a whole heap of trouble at nightfall.

LeBaron declared his colony to the world as an 'agricultural paradise' to which he said he had recruited dozens of poor Mexican converts with promises of a heaven on earth. Unknown to these cultists, though, he nursed an ambition to turn the coastal region where it stood into a paradise for tourists whose visits would line his pockets. Indeed it was these men, women and children who laboured around the clock in the fields as he sped about the dirt roads in the 'Golden Calf' who would turn this dream into a reality by producing varieties of crops to generate the necessary income. Plus, of course, the investors he hoped to attract from over the border in the US.

But when the profits failed to materialize in 'Colonia LeBaron,' LeBaron turned from cult leader to gangster, trans-forming once tranquil Galeana – named after a famous nineteenth-century Mexican liberal Hermenegildo Galeana – into his own personal fiefdom. A fiefdom that would soon be riven by family disputes, violence and, ultimately, deaths.

All this, though, lay in the future for the handsome, 6-feet 4-inch tall Ervil LeBaron, with his thick, sandy brown hair, square jaw and penetrating blue eyes, as he drove across the Chihuahua province on that summer morning, visions of his empire filling his mind. His demeanour showed that he was a man full of confidence, with a certainty about his mission, and the possessor of a profound knowledge of the Book of Mormon and the Bible, which he utilized at every opportunity.

LeBaron was also very conscious of his physical charms. His evident masculinity had for years been turning female heads and his appetite for sex drove him to seduce – and on occasions marry – dozens of women, varying in age and attractiveness from adolescent girls to middle-aged matrons. Married or single was no problem for the prophet: it seemed he had very little difficulty convincing all the women who crossed his path that God had told him they must submit to his demands.

This same God also apparently ordered him to carry out a lot of other tasks apart from those to satisfy his personal gratifi-cation. Together his actions as sexual predator, messianic figure and ruthless cultist would write his name large in the history of evil cults.

Yet, as Ervil LeBaron motored in his golden car on that bright summer morning in the late sixties – just as he had done before on other hot, luxuriant Mexican days with the sun on his face, and would do again many times – he must have reflected on just how he had come to be in this position of supreme authority, after coming from a bizarre and troubled background.

* * *

Ervil LeBaron had been born in the municipality of Galeana in 1924. His father, Alma Dayer LeBaron, was a fervent Mormon who had emigrated there from America following the decision by the mainstream Mormon church, the Church of Jesus Christ of Later-day Saints, to officially abandon the practice of polygamy in 1890. LeBaron Sr had apparently made the transition after years of 'hearing voices' and receiving 'revelations' from God, according to Ben Bradlee Jr and Dale Van Atta in their book, *Prophet of Blood* (1981). In fact, he was one of a number of polygamous Mormons who still wanted to have more than one wife and moved south to Mexico to put themselves beyond the reach of the American law enforcement agencies.

Alma and his two wives set up home in the libertarian freedom of Galeana where they were able to purchase farmland cheaply in what was then – as it is today – one of the poorest areas of Mexico, with less than a quarter of the people having an electricity supply. They had, though, been attracted to the area by its agricultural land, reputed to be good for growing maize and wheat, and the striking mountain range to the east known locally as the 'Eastern Mother'. The Mormons also liked the isolation and saw in a famous local geological formation that had been formed by the action of water a symbol of their search for a new life: the *Puente de Dios*, 'the Bridge of God'. Once ensconced, Alma named his settlement 'Colonia LeBaron'.

Eight children were born to Alma and his two wives, of which Ervil was the second. The evidence gathered by Bradlee and Van Atta suggests that despite the congeniality of life in Galeana, the family was deeply unstable and Ervil and his older brother, Joel, grew up in an atmosphere where religious fervency was an everyday fact and harsh punishments were meted out to both the male and female siblings at the slightest misdemeanours. By his early teens, Ervil LeBaron was a hyper-masculine young man – committed to the Mormon religion and eager to exploit his undoubted sex appeal. Bradlee Jr and Van Atta explain:

'In addition to his physical charms, Ervil projected an air of confidence. He leaned into people as he spoke to them, his eyes boring into theirs as he quoted at length from both the Book of Mormon and the Bible. His masculinity made women desire him and he began to desire them back.'

Life for the LeBaron family at 'Colonia LeBaron' passed uneventfully as far as neighbours and the rest of the world was concerned, however, until the death of the patriarch, Alma, in 1951. A few other polygamous Mormons had in the meantime joined the settlement from America and several of the Mexican families working on the land had also taken up the faith. But after the death of the old man, leadership of the community passed to Joel LeBaron – and everything began to change.

Joel's first action was to incorporate the group as the 'Church of the Firstborn of the Fulness [sic] of Times' in Salt Lake City. They would become known later as simply, 'the Firstborners'. His second was to appoint Ervil as an elder and his second in command. After years of repression under the iron rule of his father, the strapping, handsome younger brother seized the opportunity as a chance to realize his dreams – religiously, sexually and financially. He intended to make the most of his position in Galeana, as investigative journalist John Makeig wrote in the *Houston Chronicle* in June 1997:

'Among Ervil's many twisted beliefs was one that the Virgin Mary had become the mother of Christ at the age of fourteen. It was therefore acceptable for him to take adolescent girls as wives. The colony supported their leader's paedophilia by giving him their young daughters. "If you're going to raise up a generation in a plural marriage, it is very important not to let young girls get romanticized in the worldly sense," a woman who married her 13-year-old daughter to Ervil told this reporter.'

Makeig discovered that the parents of several of Ervil's

subsequent thirteen wives went to considerable lengths to convince their adolescent girls of the validity of their groom's claim that 'great rewards awaited them in heaven' if they consented to marriage. The journalist continues:

'Ervil was an ardent suitor, but a coolly indifferent husband and father. In "Colonia LeBaron" women were baby makers and caretakers, banished to the periphery while men made the important decisions. More often than not, he acted as if his wives were a necessary nuisance. Their wombs served to produce the children – over 50 in number – who would later become his foot soldiers. Some of Ervil's thirteen wives eventually grew weary of living in the Mormon harem and left him, taking their children back to the United States. Others stayed by his side to the biter end. Two killed for him. And two died because of him.'

* * *

It wasn't only some of his wives who proved a nuisance to Ervil LeBaron. Older brother Joel and he became increasingly involved in disputes about the running of 'Colonia LeBaron'. Wooing women into his bed and converts into the polygamous community was all very well – but Ervil had very different ideas to those of his brother about making the best of their plot facing the Pacific Ocean with the alluring surfer's paradise of Baja California Peninsula on the horizon.

Joel LeBaron wanted to turn the community into an 'agricultural paradise' where poor Mormon converts could work the land as a communal farm. Ervil wanted 'Colonia LeBaron' to be turned into a paradise for rich visitors. Ben Bradlee Jr and Dale Van Atta take up the story:

'Despite Joel's opposition, Ervil wooed investors with his millionaire's dream, meeting with money men from the States and flying them down to tour the oceanfront, pointing out where the resorts and yacht club would go.'

It was also becoming evident as the sixties progressed, that the fulsomely named 'Church of the First-Born of the Fulness of Time' was in dire financial straits. The number of converts from among the poverty-stricken Mexicans who flooded into 'Colonia LeBarron' was now such that it was difficult to even feed and clothe them. How many families saw the cult as a means of religious salvation or threw in their lot with the Lebarons out of sheer desperation in their deprived region, it is now impossible to ascertain. The main source of revenue seems to have been from those members of the cult who had outside jobs and handed a large part of their wages as a 'tithe' to the ministry. Invariably, it was Ervil LeBaron who collected these payments.

Scott Anderson in his investigative work, *The 4 O'Clock Murders* (1993), says that Ervil LeBaron tried out several methods to raise money for the church that were every bit as bizarre as some of his ideas about sex and religion. On one occasion he took a trip to Las Vegas armed with money from the church's coffers. He returned without a dime. The younger LeBaron also tried to raise finance for a fishmongery with the same lack of success as he enjoyed when proposing to harvest and sell pine nuts from the national forests of California.

These ill-fated ventures also caught the interest of Ben Bradlee Jr and Dale Van Atta who recount an even more extraordinary tale of the man from 'Colonia LeBaron':

'Once, when a potential deal was going sour in Utah, Ervil told a man that he would "throw in a couple of nubile women from his flock" if the businessman would join with him. The offer apparently deeply offended the man who was a mainstream Mormon and he walked out of the meeting in disgust."

While these schemes were being put forward – and rejected – Ervil LeBaron continued to live the life of an elder of the church. Apparently unmoved by the fact that many of the cult members were now dressed in rags, worked from dawn to sunset in the fields, and existed on a diet largely consisting of maize, he dressed in fine suits and bought himself the gold Impala in which he drove about the Galeana countryside checking on his workforce.

The car naturally raised questions among the downtrodden cultists – but few were bold enough to challenge Ervil. When one desperate old man who had supported the LeBarons since they had arrived in Galeana finally plucked up the courage to ask about the 'Golden Calf', Ervil answered dismissively that God had told him to buy it 'because it would impress potential investors'.

Trouble, though, was brewing in LeBaron's polygamous 'paradise', which by the early seventies consisted of over thirty families and their offspring living in Galeana; a second settlement in Utah; and a community known as 'Los Molinos', on the nearby peninsula of Baja California.

'Los Molinos' had been one of the family's inspired purchases, covering 8,500 acres with nine miles fronting the beach. In 1972, when the feuding between Ervil and Joel LeBaron had reached breaking point and the leadership of 'the Firstborners' was split, it became the setting for an assassination plot that would throw the entire polygamous cult into the centre of a media storm.

* * *

The relationship between the two LeBaron brothers – and in particular their different attitudes to the direction in which their 'church' should go – led to Ervil walking out of the community with a group of his wives and children in the winter of 1972. He headed across the US border to San Diego and there decided to launch his own brand of polygamous religion under the title of 'The Church of the Lamb of God'. It was a variation of what his father had established in Galeana – but with some very harsh new additions to its strictures.

Despite his luxurious lifestyle and success at seducing women, Ervil had been studying the Bible with even keener attention to detail in order to strengthen his hold on his followers. It was in the Old Testament that he found the dark story that would be his guiding principle in the years to follow. As a prophet, it told him he had to 'strike down' those who disobeyed his orders.

LeBaron read that during Moses' time, breaking the Ten Commandments was punishable by death. According to John Makeig, Ervil saw himself in the same light and believed that the same should apply to all those 'Firstborners' in Galeana, at 'Los Molinos' and in San Diego. Makeig writes:

'Ervil devised a series of decrees based on the Ten Commandments which he called the "Civil Law". He appointed himself as the law's chief enforcer and announced that people who broke this law would die. He also said that the transgressors

95

would die by the ancient death rituals that were permitted in the days of Moses.'

The list LeBarron issued made chilling reading. Among the deaths sentences that he proposed were stoning, beheading and even disembowelment. If anyone had reason to doubt his sincerity, they only had to look into those penetrating blue eyes when he leaned towards them and declared that God was his advocate to believe him. What was even more alarming was his announcement that he was going to kill his brother, Joel. His hatred of the man who had initially made him an elder of the church had now become an obsession.

The events that occurred in August 1973 at the town of Ensenada on the Baja peninsula are confused and occasionally contradictory: but the one undeniable fact is that Joel LeBaron was shot and killed. He had apparently gone with his teenage son, Ivan, to the house of one of his followers to collect a car. The boy, just fourteen years old, stayed outside the house, according to the facts later gathered by Scott Anderson:

'While Ivan waited outside the residence, Ervil's thugs jumped his father inside. Irvin heard someone yell, "Kill him!" and this was followed by gunshots. The hit men then sped off in a station wagon parked nearby. The boy ran inside to find his father lying face up on the floor. Blood was spilling across his chest and onto the floor from two bullet holes in his heart.'

Anderson is in no doubt that the death was a revenge killing ordered by Ervil LeBaron. He suggests that the younger brother believed that with Joel out of the way, the rest of the 'Firstborners' in Mexico and California would join his church. However, Joel LeBaron had already put his succession plans into place, giving instructions that in the event of his death the leadership should pass to the youngest brother, Verlan, who had been devoted to him ever since they had grown up at 'Colonia LeBaron'.

The elders of the 'Church of the Firstborn of the Fulness of Time' decided to file murder charges against Ervil LeBaron even as plans were made for the funeral of their leader, as Scott Anderson has written:

'After Joel's funeral, which was attended by his seven widows and 44 children, Verlan reluctantly took up the reins of the church, Like Joel, Verlan had a quiet demeanour and preferred to work on the farmland or spend time with his nine wives and 50 children rather than sermonize or try to gather new converts to their already sizeable family.'

One obvious reason why Verlan LeBaron was reluctant to take up his role was because he feared his mad, bad brother would mark him down next for execution. The younger man decided to maintain a low profile, changing his homes and cars regularly, and making a number of trips abroad, in particular to Nicaragua where he had friends outside the ranks of polygamous Mormons. He had good reason to be afraid – very afraid. For during the next decade Ervil would try to have him killed on several occasions.

* * *

The self-assurance that surrounded Ervil LeBaron was probably no more dramatically revealed than in December 1973 when he walked into the police headquarters in Ensenada. He was accompanied by two lawyers and asked to see the police chief. Describing the event later, Marianne Funk of the *Desert News* wrote:

'Ervil demanded that the murder charges which had been filed against him by the elders at "Los Morino" should be dropped. He said he was tired of being pursued by the police and wanted to have the time to travel and seek more converts for the "Church of the Lamb of God" without any harassment. When the police chief recovered from his amazement at the sudden appearance of the suspect they had been seeking for months, Ervil was arrested. Despite the protests of his two lawyers, he was placed in prison to await trial.'

Despite his fury at being imprisoned, LeBaron continued to exert authority over the cult from inside jail and used the time to write a curious manifesto he had been planning for some time. Grandly entitled *Hour of Crisis – Day of Vengeance*, it was written in the old English style of the King James Bible and proved to be a diatribe against all those who denied his authority. It was especially vindictive to all polygamous Mormons in America and Mexico. Claiming his 'authority' came from God, he wrote:

97

'It is a criminal offence, punishable by death, for an enlightened people to pay tithes and offerings to thieves and robbers. The sword of vengeance will hang over the heads of all those who should fail to hear the word of the Lord. Wilful failure to comply with the minimum requirements constitutes the crime of rebellion against God.'

By 'thieves and robbers', Ervil meant the 'Firstborners' and other rival polygamous and fundamentalist leaders who were all seeking converts from the same human pool of downtrodden and impoverished men and women across the continent. He vowed to carry out a string of executions of these men as soon as he was free from prison.

Ervil LeBaron was forced to fume away nine months behind bars before he was brought to trial in September 1974. Scott Anderson has described this trial at which the bizarre facts of LeBaron's 'Church of the Lamb of God' and its mixture of polygamy and religious insanity was revealed to the public for the first time:

'Ervil was found guilty of homicide. But he was only sentenced to twelve years in prison because the prosecution were unable to place Ervil at the scene of the crime. He served just one day of his sentence, however, when the Mexican Supreme Court overturned the verdict on a technicality. The co-defendants – the men who had actually killed Joel LeBaron – had not been present for the trial.'

The decision must have seemed like another revelation to the 'Prophet of God' when he walked free again on 14 February 1974. Greeted by his wives and almost two dozen of his children, Ervil was now ready for some serious proselytising – and revenge.

However, his days inside had added a new paranoia to his list. He was convinced that Verlan and the 'Firstborners' would now try and kill *him*. He decided it would be best to move away from San Diego and headed east to Yuma in Arizona. Here, surrounded by his family and his closest supporters, he began preparations for his own counter-attack. Ervil began to carry a gun and ordered his wives and their oldest children to learn marksmanship. To ensure they knew how to handle guns expertly, LeBaron put one of his cult members who had served in Vietnam in charge of the classes.

John Makeig has described these uneasy days in the desert town close to the Mexican border:

'As Ervil paced back and forth in front of his people, telling them they could all be slaughtered at any moment, the group started to act more like a Mormon Mafia than a church. They took aliases and had drivers' licences and birth certificates drawn up in their new names. They only made calls from pay phones that couldn't be traced to their location. Ervil LeBaron's intention was clear: he would get even with Verlan and then turn on his rival fundamentalists.'

There was no sense of Christmas spirit in LeBaron when he summoned his people together on Christmas Day 1974. He had received another 'revelation'. Because the 'Firstborners' on the Baja peninsula would not accept his authority as 'Lord Anointed' they must be punished. The community of 'Los Molinos' was to be destroyed the following day.

On 26 December, a group of Ervil's cult members drove across the border in a pick-up truck and Fiat car and headed south down the Baja peninsula. Darkness had fallen by the time the two vehicles drove up the dirt road leading to the little settlement near Ensenada. Inside 'Los Molinos', the thirty polygamous families were either having their evening meal or putting their younger children to bed. It was a scene of utter tranquillity about to be ripped apart in the most brutal and heartless way according to the description given by Scott Anderson:

'The vehicles cut their headlights as they neared the quiet farming community and slowed to a crawl. The temperature was hovering near freezing that night and smoke rose from the chimneys of the cosy homes into the dark blue sky. A Molotov cocktail crashing through the window of the town's largest house shattered the peaceful tableau. Within seconds, the wood-framed house was engulfed in fire. The occupants ran outside, and in the confusion that followed, Ervil's apostates sprayed bullets over the people racing to form a water brigade, their figures silhouetted against the dancing orange flames.'

The slaughter of the 'Firstborners' at 'Los Molinos' was to last for twenty minutes more as the attackers drove through the community throwing firebombs into homes. Their main target, though, was Verlan's property, a sturdy but simple farmhouse on the outskirts. When the occupants saw the pick-up truck driving towards them with five men aboard shooting and firebombing everything they passed, they fled outside and hid in the large orchard at the rear. The seven people could only watch in horror as their home, too, was burned to the ground.

The scene of devastation that greeted the terrified inhabitants as they gathered together in the first light of dawn was something they could not have imagined in their worst nightmares. 'Los Molinos' had been laid to waste. Two men had been killed and thirteen others wounded, some quite badly.

But the news that Ervil LeBaron waited to be told about the attack was not what he wanted to hear. The seven people who had fled from Verlan's home were his wife, Charlotte, and their six children. The leader of the 'Firstborners' had been far away on a visit to California at the time...

* * *

The failure to kill Verlan did not distract Ervil from his other mission to rid the world of 'thieves and robbers' – as he saw them – his fundamentalist rivals. In April 1975, for instance, he ordered the killing of Bob Simons, a polygamous Mormon whose ministry was directed at converting Native Americans. The evidence also shows that he was involving members of his extended family in these missions, particularly Vonda White, his tenth wife.

Vonda, a dark-haired, pretty but very intense and devoted young woman, is believed to have carried out several murders on her husband's instructions. It is said she killed Naomi Zarate, the wife of one of Ervil's closest associates, after she had dared to question his practices. When another member of the cult, Dean Grover Vest, attempted to leave in the autumn of 1975, Vonda also killed him. She would later be arrested for the murder of Vest and sentenced to life imprisonment on 13 May 1979.

By this time, Ervil's cruelty seemed to know no bounds. He is even believed to have ordered the death of his seventeen-year-old wife, Rebecca, after she had 'spoken out against the group'. The attractive young girl was also pregnant when her body was found in the boot of a car, her neck still bearing the marks of the rope that had been used to strangle her. According to Deborah Tedford, writing later in the *Houston Chronicle,* the killers were associates of Ervil who had been told by him that 'God has revealed to me she must die'.

When Ervil LeBaron decided to take yet another wife – one even younger than Rebecca – he seems to have overlooked the ill omen attached to the number thhireen. For Rena Chynoweth, a sweet-faced beauty with beguiling eyes, whom he married as a sixteen-year-old child bride in February 1975 was to be the thirteenth and last to enter his polygamous world. She was destined to serve not only on his terrible killing mission but would later reveal the truth about life inside the 'Church of the Lamb of God'.

Rena had not long turned sixteen and Ervil was already over 50 when they were married in the Mormon church. But unlike the generations of women who had fallen for Ervil's masculine good looks in the past, she found herself looking at a much less appealing man, as she has revealed in her book, *The Blood Covenant* (1990):

'When I was with him, I had to close my eyes and pretend I was somewhere else or he was someone else. I would often turn my head away or hold my breath so I wouldn't have to smell his breath. It always reeked of something awful, usually coffee. He kissed like a fish, very stiff-lipped, in a way that really disgusted me.'

If this was no life for a lovely young adolescent who should have been discovering love with boys of her own age, Rena could not ignore the rule of Ervil LeBaron which her parents had taught her to accept without question. In her book she also revealed how he used mind control and fear to enforce his rule:

'Ervil used many classic cult techniques to keep his followers in line. He isolated them by limiting their contact with people outside the church. He exhausted them with his hour-long sermons that broke down their resistance. He scared them by telling them that they were being hunted by religious and govern-ment assassins and they would only survive by banding together.'

Rena explained that most of the cult's children like her had been taken out of school when they reached fifth or sixth grade because Ervil was afraid they might be 'contaminated' by contact with secular playmates who could cause them to question their peculiar, isolated lifestyle. He believed – with good reason from his point of view – that knowledge of the outside world was a dangerous thing.

The whole emphasis of Ervil's plan was to make these children dependent on the cult. The boys were not being trained with any skills and the girls simply groomed to work in the home – as well as become brides for the polygamous older men as soon as they reached puberty.

They were all so brainwashed, said Rena, that being ordered to kill was no different from being ordered to go shopping. It was a task that Ervil told them God had ordered and they could not refuse. As she explains, it was not long before her new husband was involving her in yet another scheme to try and murder his brother, Verlan. It would involve another fundamentalist cult leader and, if successful, enable him to be rid of two rivals at one stroke.

The man was Rulon C. Allred, the head of the Apostolic United Brethren, also a polygamous Mormon group based near Salt Lake City. Allred had apparently refused to acknowledge Ervil's authority and pay a tithe, which sealed his fate in LeBaron's mind. Rulon was a legendary figure in Utah polygamist circles and, if he died, Ervil felt sure Verlan would be compelled to attend the funeral out of respect. *Then* his killers could finally achieve what they had so singularly failed to do ever since 1972.

Rena was sent to Salt Lake City with another member of the cult, Ramona Marston, an attractive blonde with an open, smiling face. On 10 May 1977 the two young women, wearing wigs and fake glasses, walked into the homeopathic clinic that Allred ran on the outskirts of the city. Chynoweth describes what happened next:

'I saw Rulon as soon as he stepped from a back room. I walked towards him and he nodded at me. He was exactly as he had been described to me. Tall, slender, grey-haired – a nice, pleasant-looking man. He was no more than three to five feet from me. I knew the moment had come to do what I was sent there to do.'

According to a statement later read out in court, Rena took another step and without saying a word pulled a .25 pistol from her jacket. She fired all seven shots into the old man's chest as he slumped to the ground. He was said to have been dead before he hit the floor of the clinic.

Yet despite the success of this mission, fate once again conspired against Ervil's evil plan. The funeral for Rulon Allred draw almost 3,000 people, along with the police and a large contingent of press and television reporters. Verlan, as expected, turned up, but such was the throng of people that the assassins in the crowd knew it would be extremely difficult to kill their leader's brother and impossible to escape. They had no alternative but to return and face the wrath of the 'One Might and Strong'.

The trial of Rena Chynoweth was a sensational affair with the young girl testifying about her life in the cult and the orders she had received from her husband to kill. Her revelations astounded the jury who nonetheless voted for acquittal. As Rena walked free from the courthouse, she vowed to have nothing more to do with her husband. In any event, he had fled to Mexico once again.

Now that the full horror of the cult had been revealed, the authorities on both sides of the border pursued the arrest of Ervil LeBaron with even greater determination. On 1 June 1979, after a massive manhunt, he was apprehended hiding in the mountains just to the south of Mexico City. He was taken by the Mexican police to the international bridge at Laredo and handed over to FBI agents waiting on the other side.

It would be almost exactly a year before the polygamous cult leader accused of masterminding the murder of Rulon Allred was brought to court. In the interim he was held in Salt Lake County jail while evidence was gathered about the man the media was now referring to as a serial killer who justified his actions through a doctrine of 'blood atonement'. At the trial, a number of men and women, no longer afraid of the once strapping and authoritarian 'Prophet of God', now standing bald and shrunken in the dock, testified about life under his evil regime.

Ervil LeBaron was found guilty and sentenced to life imprisonment at the Point of the Mountains Prison in Draper, Utah. Once again behind bars, he took up his pen and began writing another diatribe that would run to over 500 pages under the title of the *Book of New Covenants*. The work contained a list of over 50 people who the author believed should be killed by 'blood atonement' – including defectors from the 'Church of the Lamb of God', police investigators and prison officials. All had evidently not shown him enough respect. The final chapter of the work provided a list of succession of the men in the cult – mostly his own offspring – who were to continue his 'ministry' after his death.

This, in fact, was not long in coming. On the afternoon of 16, August 1981, the 'Lord Anointed' was found lying on the floor of his cell clutching his chest. He had apparently died of a heart attack. And in a bizarre twist of fate, Verlan LeBaron, the brother he had vainly been trying to kill for almost a decade, had died just a few hours earlier – in a car crash in Mexico not far from 'Colonia LeBaron' where the whole terrible saga had begun.

The Ripper Crew

Lorraine Borowski was a pretty, hard-working real estate agent's secretary. Not long past her twenty-first birthday, 'Lori', as she was known to her family and friends in Elmhurst in the suburbs of Chicago, was determined not to be labelled a dumb blonde because of her golden tresses and invariably put in long hours at her office to help drum up business and make every effort to sell the mixture of flats and houses on the agency's books.

It was just after sunrise on the morning of 15 May 1982 when Lorraine pulled up in her estate car at the front of her office. As she was getting out of the vehicle, she paused for just a moment to admire the rose-tinted sky overhead and hoped it would prove a good omen for the day. There were several clients coming in look at the prospectuses for a number of properties and she was hoping to be given the chance to work on the sale of a palatial house in one of the most fashionable streets in Elmhurst. It was the kind of place that would enhance the agency and her prospects if a good sale were completed.

But the young secretary had no time to dwell on the beautiful dawn, she told herself, her horizon had to be contracts and possible bonuses in order to become a full-time agent. She walked purposefully away from the car, her smart shoes clicking across the pavement and her neat, power-suited figure enhanced by the swing of her hips.

Lorraine Borowski put her key into the door of the office and was about to turn it when a disturbance behind made her stop and turn around. The good feelings she had been engendering ever since she had got up disappeared in a moment of realization . . .

and fright. It would be her last normal action and almost the last time anyone saw her alive . . .

* * *

Chicago in the early eighties was a city undergoing another chapter in the dark side of its history. The town that had become famous in the twenties as the turf of the gang leader Al Capone, and the battleground of 'the Untouchables', the police force dedicated to breaking the stranglehold that organized crime had on the citizens during Prohibition, was now suffering a new wave of violence. But this was far more vicious and unspeakable than anything the mobsters had inflicted.

A fad was sweeping the area – especially among teenagers – for conducting occult rituals. Some were esoteric, curious rather than dangerous; others were satanic in purpose and dedicated to the furtherance of evil in all its forms. Some of those following this dark path were sacrificing animals and indulging in perverted sex; a few were taking lives and preying on innocent victims in a manner that had not been seen since the troubled witchcraft era in Europe in the Middle Ages. The same streets of Chicago which had once echoed to the sound of machine-gun bullets were now prey to the almost silent swish of cut-throat knives and torture of a kind that society believed – hoped – had died with the abolition of red-hot pincers and the horrendous rack.

One aspect of this fad was particularly worrying the Chicago police force in the spring of 1982. An increasing number of prostitutes – most of them young girls from the slums or simple young females from the Illinois countryside hoping to find better lives in the city – had been disappearing from the streets. Such disappearances were not unusual: but the numbers that had occurred in the two counties of Cook and Du Page were already in double figures in less than two years.

When the bodies of these girls were discovered, all were found to have been raped, tortured and mutilated. But a particular distinctive feature was found on each corpse that marked them as victims of *someone* – perhaps a band of cultists – whose like had not been seen before. As the governor of Illinois George Ryan would say later as the story began to unravel, 'Some crimes are so horrendous and heinous that society has a right to demand the ultimate penalty when those who commit these crimes are caught.'

At first, the crimes had not seemed much different from the hundreds of stabbings that occur in what one Chicago journalist referred to 'a city full of blades'. Soon, though, as the police struggled to identify the victims, public concern grew that a serial killer was at work in the area. Almost daily, stories of a suspected maniac running loose took up acres of news space in the daily papers.

Then, in June 1981, yet another unidentified female body was found in an isolated area of Du Page County. But this mutilation, which detectives investigating the murder had seen before but managed to keep from the media, could no longer be kept silent.

The girl was named only as 'Molly'. She was described as nineteen, weighed 170 pounds and was just five foot six inches tall. She was a petite brunette with deep blue eyes and had been reported missing from the trailer park where she had lived with her parents. The pathologist, who attended the crime scene by the canal where a passing walker had found the girl's body, reported to the county coroner that the victim had been slashed repeatedly by a sharp instrument, raped and sodomized. This had evidently occurred before the corpse had been dumped at the waterside – but it was not the most disturbing feature of the murder, the expert reported.

Her left breast had been sliced from her body.

That night, a Du Page County detective working in the Special Equipment Division gave a statement to the local television station that 'Molly' appeared to have been sexually assaulted and 'her breasts amputated'. It was not the precise truth, but enough to prompt hundreds of phone calls from alarmed viewers to the station and initiate a feeding frenzy among the media that soon spread nationwide.

Across both counties and in Chicago itself, teams of detectives were set to work to try and find the killer based on the little information they had. A number of known perverts and sexual deviants were taken in for questioning, but without any success. House to house searches were instituted in the areas where the bodies had been found, but there was still no sign of a clue as to *who* the killer – or killers – might be.

That winter of 1981 two more young prostitutes were found mutilated and killed. The two county police forces had to concede there was a similarity, without going into details, and called for assistance from the FBI. In particular to make use of the service's state-of-the-art medical laboratories in Washington DC to examine samples from the victims' bodies, including semen and pubic hairs. Still, though, nothing conclusive came to light.

In the early hours of 12 February 1982, a 35-year-old cocktail waitress in Cook County was reported missing on her way home after she had left her job in a local bar. It seemed she had left work with the petrol in her car running low, but as it was raining heavily she had decided there was enough fuel in the tank to get home and she would fill up in the morning. She never completed the journey.

Shortly after dawn, her car was found at the side of the road by a passing police patrol car. The driver's door was open and there was no sign of anyone behind the wheel. It was evident to the police officer from the needle of the petrol gauge what must have happened. But what puzzled them was the fact the keys were still in the ignition and a female handbag lay on the front seat. Picking it up, the man saw that no money or identification papers had been taken. So where had the driver – obviously a woman – gone? Had she been robbed – and if so, was she still alive?

A photograph of the car shown on television that night was seen by the waitress's boss who promptly reported her missing to the police. A full-scale search swung into operation and, less than two miles from the abandoned car, her body was found, naked, on a bank running parallel to the road. Once again the victim had been raped, tortured, mutilated and one of her breasts dismembered. There was evidence, too, that it had been cut off by piano wire and someone had masturbated over the body.

Now the detectives of Du Page and Cook Counties were sure they were dealing with the same killer, or, more likely, killers. The weird mutilation was also pointing more definitely to cultists. The media, press, TV and wire services were asked not to report this fact as it was increasingly being viewed as a vital piece of evidence in tracking down those responsible and an invaluable piece of evidence in any confession.

Ten days later and the body of another victim, a Spanish

woman about forty years of age, was discovered in Cook County. The body was in an advanced state of rigor mortis and it seemed likely had been lying there for two days. She had been strangled and stabbed in much the same manner as the earlier victims, but with one notable difference. Neither of her breasts had been removed, but both bore the marks of having been extensively bitten.

Theories abounded in the media after the discovery of this – by later estimation – sixteenth victim. Gaining credibility was the idea that the killer was perhaps 'the man next door': someone living an outwardly normal life in one of the Chicago suburbs. Maybe a family man doing an ordinary job by day – but by night a psychopath driven to kidnap women, rape and kill them, and then tear off one of the symbols of femininty from her still warm corpse as a kind of grisly souvenir of his blood lust.

The truth would prove to be even stranger and more horrific.

*   *   *

Although the disappearance of Lorraine Borowski from in front of the real estate agency on the morning of 15 May would not be known until an office cleaner arrived an hour later and found the young woman's key in the door and her car on the forecourt, her going was not completely unobserved. A woman also on her way to work in the still quiet streets of Elmhurst had her attention drawn to a car, which raced past her heading out of town.

The vehicle seemed to be full of people, their heads and arms moving about restlessly. The woman thought she caught sight of two men in the front and another couple in the back. In between these two was a woman. She didn't recognize any of them, she explained later, but got the distinct impression that the woman 'was being held against her will'. When she later heard of the disappearance of 'Lori' Borowski, and when and where it had occurred, she went straight to the Cook County police.

The cleaner's report opened up a whole new line of possibilities for the Chicago investigators. Although fearing the worst, they set about trying to find the young estate agent's secretary, with a certain renewed optimism that they might at last be near to tracking down not a lone killer, but perhaps a group of killers.

Five months passed – days and weeks of searches, questions and laborious procedures – but without any new information on the missing Elmhurst girl. Then in the first week of September, the remains of a female body were found in a corner of the Clarendon Hills Cemetery. It was that of Lorraine Borowski and although her corpse was badly decomposed, extensive pathological testing established that she had been raped before being stabbed to death. There was unmistakable evidence, too, that her left breast had been removed. Clearly she had been another victim of the same hand.

The detectives scarcely had time to absorb this information before another murder was reported on 8 September. The location was the city's fabled Gold Coast and the victim was a pretty teenager, Rose Beck Davis. She had been beaten, raped, stabbed and her breasts mutilated before being dumped on a beach like a piece of discarded packaging. The police and medical team who examined Rose Beck felt the same mixture of horror and frustration that such appalling savagery could be perpetrated in such a lovely district.

Two months later, almost to the day, four young men in a car were arrested in a car in Du Page County. Chance had brought them to the attention of an officer who had never forgotten the cleaning lady's statement about the abduction of 'Lori' Borowski. When they were taken into custody a Pandora's box of horror was opened and light thrown onto one of the smallest but most vile cults of the late twentieth century.

The four young men were Gecht, Edward Spreitzer and two brothers, Andrew and Thomas Kokoraleis from the Villa Park district. They were united under the leadership of Gecht in practising an ancient ritual devoted to worship of Satan. After being taken into custody and details of their arrest and *modus operandi* in selecting their victims were revealed to the media, the cult quartet immediately became known in popular parlance as 'the Chicago Rippers' or, more commonly, 'the Ripper Crew'.

It was Thomas Kokoraleis who gave the most detailed account of the cult in his initial confession and later appearance in court. He it was, too, who provided the information about their leader, Gecht, who, he said, had the power to make all three of them do whatever he wanted. No one dared defy him.

Gecht, who maintained a silence during his arrest and adamantly refused to plead to any of the charges, had a truly extraordinary background for a cultist. A married builder with one son, he lived unobtrusively in a Northwest Side home – just as the criminologist's profile had predicted – but had a number of dark secrets in his life.

He had, apparently, developed an unhealthy interest in sexual perversions in adolescence and had molested his sister until he was sent away to live with his grandparents. It was in his teens that he developed an interest in satanism and particularly its secret rituals. During the 1970s, he had worked as a subcontractor for the building contractor John Wayne Gacy (1942–94) who was subsequently revealed as a serial killer. Gacy, who lived in the Norwood Park Township, had become notorious as the 'Killer Clown' for the many parties he attended entertaining children in a clown suit, until his blood lust was revealed. He had raped and murdered 33 boys and young men between the ages of 9 and 20, 29 of whom he had buried in the 'crawl space' beneath his home.

In an interview with a psychologist while he was awaiting trial, Gecht is alleged to have told the man of his former employer, 'Gacy's single mistake was not killing those guys, but keeping most of their bodies under his house.' According to the psychologist's report, the prisoner seemed to be quite unaware that Gacy had done anything wrong, it was just that he had gone about it the wrong way.

Robin Gecht was also a man who liked concealment. Unbeknown his wife, he had erected an altar in the attic of his home and covered this with a red cloth. On the walls he had painted six red and black crosses. A leather-bound Bible was used in the rituals, which he would conduct with the three younger men kneeling in front of him. In a blasphemous parody of Holy Communion, he would use the body parts of the cult's female victims to try and contact 'the Dark One' and continue the cult's reign of slaughter. All of these ceremonies were conducted during the evenings when Mrs Gecht was at work.

According to the statement of Andrew Kokoraleis, Gecht and his followers would drive around the streets of Chicago in a car or van looking for prostitutes who they would lure into the vehicle or snatch from the pavement. They would then rape, torture and kill these victims, using a variety of weapons such as knives, razor blades, ice picks, can openers, or even the serrated edges of tin can lids if they could find nothing else. A few of their eighteen victims were actually sacrified in Gecht's attic, he claimed, before their bodies were taken away and dumped. But from every girl a breast would be removed for the highlight of their devilish communion.

Kokoraleis told Du Page County detective Warren Wilcosz during an interview at the Chicago police station that Gecht made him and his brother and their friend, Edward Spreitzer, kneel together in front of the altar. He would then take the breast, still warm from its victim, out of the wrapping in which it had been preserved since removal earlier in the night and begin reading passages from the Bible. Each cultist masturbated into the fleshy organ. When this was completed, Gecht would cut up the breast and hand a piece to each of them. The ceremony ended with everyone consuming his portion.

During this same interview, Kokoraleis was shown a photograph of Lorraine Borowski and asked if he recognized her. He replied, 'That's the girl Eddie Spreitzer and I killed in the cemetery.' Asked if he could explain the reason for the extreme brutality and nastiness of the killings, he told the officer:

'Robin had the power to make us do whatever he wanted. You just have to do it. He had some supernatural connection and I was afraid of what he would do to me if I did not do as he told me.'

During the course of separate investigations in Chicago into 'the Ripper Crew,' police officers discovered that there were other people apart from the three followers who were afraid of Robin Gecht and believed he had supernatural powers. Some claimed he had an ability to attract people to him and make them do whatever he wanted. It was clear that no matter how sick or disgusting a suggestion he might make, his demands were impossible to refuse. One women who was interviewed even warned the detectives, 'Never look into his eyes.'

The possibility of anyone falling into that trap diminished with the subsequent lengthy trial and eventual sentencing of Gecht and the members of his cult. Andrew Kokoraleis and Edward Spreitzer were both sentenced to death, with Thomas given life imprisonment.

Despite the statements of his three followers and various other

112

witnesses implicating him in the deaths, the investigators were not able to find enough evidence to charge Robin Gecht with murder. He would admit to nothing, he said. He was, though, found guilty of raping and mutilating an eighteen-year-old prostitute, the only person to survive 'the Ripper Crew' and sentenced to serve 120 years in the Menard Correctional Center in Southern Illinois. However, Gecht's evil influence on those near to him does not seem to have quite ended there.

On 7 March 1999, his son, David, and two other men were charged with first-degree murder in connection with the shooting to death of a man in Northwest Side – the self-same neighbourhood where Gecht had run his satanic order and orchestrated a gruesome routine of kidnap, torture, rape, murder and mutilation in its name. But before the fear of a reprise could alarm Chicago, the police – so circumspect with information about the cult murders – came up with an answer. The killings, they said, were 'believed to be gang-related'.

The Judgement Pit

It was a warm spring day in 1987. On the fifteen-acre farm on the Chardin Road just to the south of the town of Kirtland in Ohio, members of the community of men, women and children who lived there, in what their neighbours believed to be 'a kind of weird extended family', were all occupied with various tasks.

In the weather-boarded farmhouse with its two-storey central section and patio, a greying, gentle lady was busy in the kitchen preparing the lunch, while upstairs a mother and daughter were cleaning the rooms and making the beds. At the back of the farmhouse, a man and boy were weeding a new crop of vegetables while out in the fields a tractor with an older man driving was systematically ploughing a field. It was the kind of scene that could have been duplicated in many states across the Midwest. But what was occurring in a little copse of trees on the edge of the property was certainly very much out of the ordinary.

A little earlier, a tall man in military fatigues strode out of the farmhouse and headed to the west of the property where a small stand of trees was being grown to provide logs for the residents during the winter months. Behind the man a small, pretty blonde woman walked in his shadow, her eyes firmly fixed on the ground and her hands clasped tightly together.

The pair walked in silence for ten minutes. The sun was growing warmer now; the signs were it would be another good day for life on the farm. As the man and women neared the trees, the female began to pray quietly under her breath. Momentarily, the man turned to see what she was doing, his dark eyes glowering under heavy eyebrows. When he realized, he quickly made the sign of the Cross and urged her on.

Inside the little copse, shafts of sunlight turned the darkness into a kind of dancing fairy world. The couple's shoes crunched over leaves and twigs as they headed deeper into the stand. In a few moments they reached a small opening where a rudimentary tent made from a white sheet had been slung up between a couple of trees.

In front of the makeshift construction, the man turned and faced the women. He indicated for her to come closer. With her eyes still averted, she moved in closer. The knuckles of her hands were showing white under the skin as she pressed her hands together. She was shivering slightly and as the man looked down he could see the shape of her full breasts under her thin shirt. When he spoke, his voice was firm and commanding.

'Now is the time, Susan,' he said. 'It is the way of God.'

For the first time since they had left the house, the blonde looked at the man. His eyes seemed to mesmerize her and, unclasping her hands, she raised her fingers to the top buttons and her blouse and began to undress. Slipping the garment off her shoulders, she undid her brassiere and let it fall to the ground. She eased her skirt down over her thighs and then eased her panties off her full thighs. The man's eyes moved from her pink-tipped nipples to the blonde hair of her pudenda and then he, too, began to undress.

The woman stood mute and naked, her hands pressed to her sides, waiting for his command. Now that he was naked himself, the man did not take her in his arms and have sex as she had half expected, but sat down behind the sheet. The sun illuminated his crouching figure and she could tell he was looking intently at her. He spoke again.

'Dance for me, Susan!'

Slowly at first and then with a growing intensity as the warmth of the sunlight stimulated her naked body, she whirled and twisted around the clearing. It is the will of God, she told herself, abandoning her emotions to the excitement of dance. She was hardly aware of her watcher until she heard him begin to moan. She knew what he was doing, but could hardly bring herself to look. He was *her* God, after all, and one did not question the divine one.

The little tableau in the woods continued for several minutes as the girl danced and the man in the tent masturbated himself until he climaxed with a shuddering cry that disturbed some birds high up in the trees. As they fluttered upwards into the spring air, the founder of what would become known as the Reorganized Church of Jesus Christ of the Latter Day Saints – or, more infamously, 'the Kirtland Cult' – sank back on the turf with a satisfied groan. He had never expected his life to bring him to this place and to such pleasure.

* * *

Kirtland is a quaint, quiet city in Lake County in the north-eastern hills of Ohio with a population of nearly 7,000 people, almost entirely white. Located just east of the large city of Cleveland, it is widely known as the 'City of Faith and Beauty' and its history is inextricably linked with the Church of the Latter Day Saints, the Mormons. The meticulously restored and reconstructed nineteenth-century 'Historic Kirtland' showcases life on the early American frontier as well as providing a glimpse into the 'Second Great Awakening' when it was home to the controversial sect.

The founder of the order, Joseph Smith, received a 'revelation' in 1843 concerning polygamy in which he was told that a man could possess ten virgins or more as wives. According to the 'new and everlasting covenant' obedience to the law of polygamy 'was accounted as righteousness' and those who were obedient to this rule and the others drawn from the Bible would 'enter into exaltation and became Gods'. Smith said that Jesus had spoken and this was to be 'an everlasting covenant and if ye abide not that covenant then are ye dammed'.

It was in Kirtland that Smith's followers – who were initially known as the Church of Christ but changed their name to the Church of Jesus Christ of the Latter Day Saints in 1834 – built their first temple. The sturdy, white-walled, two-storey building made of local berea sandstone from the Stannard quarry and timber from the surrounding forests is fitted with dormers and a tower surmounted by a large cross, visible for miles. Thousands visit it every year as a symbol of the sacrifice and dedication of Smith and his Mormons.

Begun in 1833 and dedicated three years later, the temple is a combination of Greek, Gothic, Georgian and Federalist architecture. The inside is also distinctive for the two sets of pulpits on the main floor and another two on the second floor. The seats are benches that can be shifted from the back to the front thereby enabling the congregation to face either the front or rear pulpits. On the third floor is the office once used by the founder. Today the imposing building in its picturesque gardens is regarded as representing 'the eternal principle that human efforts can be directed by the will of God'.

This self-same building was also to play a significant role in the life of Jeffrey Lundgren, the man who took the young woman Susan – and others like her – into the fields just a few miles from the Kirtland Temple. Believing himself to be the 'Third Great Awakening', he also founded his own cult on ideals not that different from those of Joseph Smith and the Mormons.

* * *

Jeffrey Don Lundgren was born on 3 May 1950 in Missouri. Accounts of his early life state that his parents were members of the Reorganized Church of Jesus Christ of the Latter Day Saints (RLDS) – an offshoot of the Mormons – and from childhood they punished him brutally for any misdemeanours. Neighbours were later to tell investigators that he was severely abused by his father and his mother stood by and let the thrashings occur without making any attempt to intervene.

These same reports indicate that Lundgren was a withdrawn and uncertain child in both middle and high school, making few friends and keeping himself to himself. His father was a keen hunter, however, and started taking him on trips when he became a teenager. He is believed to have killed his first animal at thirteen – and within a couple of years was an expert shot and proficient at maintaining guns and rifles.

Despite his shyness, Lundgren enrolled at the Central Missouri State University. Here he lived in a fraternity house that had been specially built for children of RLDS members and made the first real friendships of his life with another man not unlike himself, Keith Johnson, and the striking, dark-haired Alice Keeler. Subsequent reports of Keeler's life indicate that her father had also abused her and when the pair found they had other things from their life in common, they became lovers. In 1969, Alice found she was pregnant and the couple married the following year.

That same year, Lundgren joined the US Navy. He and Alice were able to see each other regularly during his service and by the time he was given an honourable discharge in 1974, the couple had two sons. For a time the Lundgrens lived in San Diego where they had a third child, a daughter. However, the couple were always short of money and around this time Jeffrey began to show the same traits as his father, abusing his wife and children and, on one occasion, pushing Alice down the stairs, causing her to rupture her spleen which required her to be hospitalized for several days.

In the hope of finding better-paid work, Lundgren moved back to Missouri in 1979 and settled in the town of Independence. Here, a year later, a fourth child, another boy, was born. To escape what he regarded as the drudgery of home life, Jeffrey became involved with the local church of the Reorganized Church of Jesus Christ of the Latter Day Saints. His dedicated proselytizing for the movement impressed his superiors and he was invited to become a priest.

The evidence suggests that Lundgren had become increasingly disenchanted by what he – and some of his friends in the RLDS – saw as the 'liberal drift' of the church. In particular the 1985 doctrinal change that would allow women to become priests. Lundgren believed himself to be one of the only true followers of the founder, Joseph Smith, and the *Book of Mormon*, which did not allow the elevation of females. He refused the offer of the priesthood. The next step on his road to Kirtland and a terrible date with murder has been summarized by James Walker in *Mind Control in Kirtland* (1990):

'This desire to return to the fundamentals of the Mormon faith led Lundgren and his group to break from the RLDS Church and adopt a number of discontinued early Mormon teachings including communal living, blood atonement and polygamy.'

Jeffrey Lundgren believed he had been called to teach the Bible in *his* way. He began to offer Bible study at home and soon had a membership of a dozen followers. This number would vary considerably during the next few years as some people embraced his ideals, while others found his overbearing and demanding manner too much for them. At its peak, though, the cult would consist of six families and a group of single men and women.

With the passing months, Lundgren became more confident of his mission. He told those who came to study that he was 'God's Last Prophet' and his word was law. He also began to ask his followers for money to support his ministry. What were initially gifts of a few hundred dollars would later become cultists' life savings, running into thousands of dollars. At one cathartic meeting in the Lundgrens' little house in Independence, he announced to his followers:

'I have received a call from God. We must move to Kirtland, which is, of course, the historic centre of the Reorganized Church of Jesus Christ of the Latter Day Saints. There we must do His work. God has also told me that if we move to Kirtland we shall witness the Second Coming of Christ.'

Apart from the importance of the town to Mormons, it had a tradition of prophets and prophecy that also made it attractive to a man like Jeffrey Lundgren. There was the John Johnson House at Hiram where the prophet had delivered many moving sermons on the front steps and indoors where 'heartrending events had taken place'; and also Isaac Morley's farm where the religious group called 'the Family' had set up home before joining the established church in the early 1800s. There were probably things to be learned from both, he told himself.

Lundgren urged the group to sell up their homes in Independence for the move to Kirtland. The Luff family, Ronald and Susan, with their two children, did not hesitate. The couple were both members of the RLDS, but had been 'deeply smitten' with Lundgren's teachings. Susan was later to tell the story of her life in the small Ohio community, still surprised at how she had been drawn into the cult:

'I still don't know how it happened. We were supposed to help the hungry. We were supposed to help the poor. Of course, none of that happened and then something went terribly wrong.'

The Avery family, Dennis Leroy, born in 1940, his wife, Cheryl Lynn, a schoolteacher seven years his junior, with their three teenage daughters, Trina Denise, Rebecca Lynn and Karen Diane, also agreed to move – although neither adult was completely happy about giving all the proceeds of the sale of their Missouri home to Lundgren. Instead, Dennis handed over $10,000 dollars, but put the remaining $9,000 in a bank account for the use of his family if the need should arise.

With that simple act – which Lundgren would condemn as a sin for being withheld from him – the meek and bespectacled Avery inadvertently began the process that would ultimately put a death sentence on him and his family. As a friend of the family, Marlene Jennings, explained to a UPI reporter:

'They broke away from the RLDS when the group decided to ordain women as ministers. I know that Cheryl had a tense relationship with her mother, who was a staunch supporter of the church, because of the break from the church. Dennis moved to Kirtland at Lundgren's command, selling his home and giving up a job that involved transferring cheques. The whole family looked to Lundgren as a spiritual leader, but they had reservations. They soon began to make comments that things weren't going as expected.'

In 1984, after briefly occupying a small house in Kirtland, the cult members all moved together to a communal home in the fifteen-acre farmhouse to the south of the town that Jeffrey Lundgren had bought. And although officials knew Jeffrey Lundgren's attitude towards the RLDS, this did not prevent him from getting a job as a tour guide at the Kirtland Temple. Here he took advantage of his position to expound his own views to anyone who would listen. Subsequent evidence also shows that over the next two years he stole about $20,000 from gifts made to the temple.

By September 1986, church officials had grown suspicious about the extent of his unorthodox teachings and revoked his position. Furious at this, Lundgren also withdraw his membership of the RLDS, provoking this comment from Dale Luffman, the president of the north-east chapter of the church: 'He was silenced for ethical reasons. He would have been expelled from the church on the basis of unchristian conduct had he not withdrawn his membership.'

Jeffrey Lundgren was now a very angry man with retribution on his mind. His teachings became more violent in tone and his attitude towards his cult followers more demanding. His word to the faithful became odder: often including references to sexual acts. He convinced them that he was in the same line of succession as Joseph Smith and he demanded their unquestioning loyalty. He was their ultimate authority.

By the following spring, Lundgren's obsessions were getting out of hand. He was telling the group living in the farmhouse that nearly anything could be a sin: from adding too much garlic to a meal and – with a meaningful glare at Dennis Avery which apparently turned the poor man white – keeping money to yourself. Jeffrey also announced that he had begun receiving 'revelations' that named two specific dates for the return of Jesus Christ. When the Messiah came, Lundgren said, He would cause a holocaust destroying everyone except those 'deemed righteous'.

Throughout the remainder of 1987 Lundgren piled one indignity after another on his followers. Anyone he deemed to have misbehaved, he beat with poles, and he demanded that the younger women should dance around him naked while he masturbated. A later account says that he also enjoyed having excrement rubbed all over his body by his wife while he preached about the coming Armageddon.

Taking a leaf out of the Joseph Smith book that he held in such high regard, Lundgren took a second wife from the ranks of the cult, 36-year-old Kathryn Johnson. He also 'matched' three couples that were attracted to the community, claiming he had been instructed to do so by 'visions'.

Lundgren had, of course, been handy with a gun since he was a teenager and now decided that the men in his group should be trained to use firearms. He would appear on designated days for firing practice wearing his military fatigues and carrying one or other of the guns and rifles that he had gathered in his arsenal – paid for, naturally, by cult members. His favourite was a .45 Combat Elite, which was never far from his side.

Jeff's eldest son, Damon, was put in charge of training the male members of the cult in combat tactics and marksmanship. Aided by his father, Damon also put the men through mock scenarios defending the farm from imagined attackers or planning attacks against suspected enemies. The significance of the latter became evident when Lundgren announced early in 1988 that he had received another 'vision' from Christ.

Conveniently ignoring the fact that both the dates he had

earlier given for the Second Coming had expired, Lundgren said he had been told the cult must seize the Kirtland Temple from the 'unbelievers'. The date, he said, had extreme religious significance to the cult. It was 3 May 1988 – which was also, of course, Jeffrey's birthday.

The cult leader had already drawn up a 'hit list' of ten senior churchmen attached to the church would be executed in what was termed 'a cleansing'. Anyone who got in his or her way was also to be killed. Damon Lundgren was ordered to increase the tempo of the training and according to reports, the cultists were regularly seen, 'marching in uniform, training to load and unload quickly' and they 'studied military tactics and watched violent war movies in preparation for combat'.

Despite all this frantic activity the plans to capture the temple went no further. It seems evident that whispers about the unusual activities at the farm on the Kirtland-Chardin Road had reached the ears of the local police chief, Dennis Yarborough. He had been informed by the leaders of the RLDS about Lundgren's heretical teaching and decided to keep an eye on the group. Each day a patrol car would pass the property every so often looking for any signs of untoward activity.

In fact, Lundgren was already having second thoughts about his plan. As 1998 dawned, he was contemplating a far more brutal plan. A death sentence for disloyalty.

* * *

Since the 'heinous crime' in April 1989, which thrust the Kirtland cult into the headlines, there has been much discussion about the motivations of Jeffrey Don Lundgren in killing the entire Avery family. To all intents and purposes they were the most malleable and obedient to his wishes. This, indeed, may have been the very reason for their slaughter.

An archetypal American couple with their steady jobs and three pretty daughters, Dennis and Cheryl Avery had first met Lundgren when he began holding scripture classes at his home in Independence. It was this very 'ordinariness' that brought about their tragedy. For it would later be discovered that Lundgren just did not like the clerk and his schoolteacher wife.

At the Bible study meetings, Lundgren would take every opportunity to make fun of them both, ridiculing them when they failed to understand one of his sermons or chastising them for being uncertain about the purpose of the group. On one occasion, Lundgren snarled at Dennis Avery and said that he was weak and should not let his wife make all their decisions.

Later, in court, it would be revealed that shortly after the Avery family had moved into the farmhouse in Kirtland, Alice Lundgren had confronted her husband and asked him why he had allowed the couple to move in with them. 'So I can get their money,' the cult leader is alleged to have replied.

It has been suggested that there may have been other reasons than their very ordinariness and meekness that led to the Avery's deaths. These reasons are well worth looking at for the light they throw onto the motives of an all-powerful and unrestrained cult leader.

One theory is that the killings may be linked to the teachings of the early Mormon prophets that Jeffrey Lundgren absorbed into his philosophy. Certainly this was offered by the attorney, John P. O'Connor, who later defended one of the cult members against charges of murder. O'Connor stated in an interview with the Cleveland *Plain Dealer* in January 1990:

'I have learned from my client that the Averys might have been killed because they were about to leave the cult. He told me the cult believed a member who abandoned Lundgren could achieve salvation by being killed in accordance with the Mormon teachings in the "Doctrine of Blood Atonement".'

O'Connor showed the court a copy of the doctrine and explained that it had been preached by Brigham Young, the second President and Prophet of the Church of Jesus Christ of the Latter Day Saints, who believed that the penalty for abandoning the faith is 'the shedding of the sinner's blood'.

A second argument that has been advanced for the killing is that Lundgren and his followers 'scarified' the family so that they could go in search of the fabled 'Sword of Laban' mentioned in the *Book of Mormon*. This story recounts how a certain hero named Nephi was commanded by the Spirit of the Lord to kill Laban and steal the brass plates on which sacred writings are engraved. Nephi achieved this feat by using Laban's own gold and steel sword and – on God's instructions – immediately left Jerusalem with his family and travelled to America where his sword was buried after his death.

The facts of the killing on 17 April 1989 contain elements of both of these suppositions.

On the morning of 10 April, Lundgren did not take his usual walk around the property – or even take one of the women for sexual gratification. Instead he cornered two of the men and ordered them to dig a hole in the barn. It was to be the 'Judgement Pit' he muttered to one of the men.

That night, at the communal dinner, Lundgren informed the families that they were shortly going on a 'wilderness trip'. For those who had been working endless hours on the farm – the Averys and their children in particular – it sounded like a welcome respite from drudgery and all five returned to their bedrooms with lighter hearts than usual to pack.

A week later, Lundgren invited a group of his male followers to a motel in Kirtland where they all had dinner. Dennis Avery was not among the group. After eating, he took several guns and rifles from a suitcase he had brought along and handed these to the men. They were going to kill the Averys, he said in a matter-of-fact tone, for their 'disloyalty'.

The events that followed back on the farm were later revealed in court. On his return, Lundgren went into the barn and sent Ronald Luff in to the house to get Dennis Avery on the pretence of having him help collect equipment for the proposed camping trip. As the older man walked in to barn, Luff tried to knock him unconscious with a stun gun. However, the weapon malfunctioned and although a stray bullet did hit the now terrified clerk it failed to knock him out.

Luff, by his own admission, gagged his victim and dragged his leaden weight to where Lundgren was waiting beside the recently dug pit. Two shots rang out from Lundgren's .45 Combat Elite and the former clerk who had dreamed of a new and more meaningful life on the farm, died instantly. Luff was now sent to call Cheryl Avery and tell her that her husband needed help.

Thoroughly alarmed, the one-time schoolteacher ran headlong into the barn and was seized from behind by strong arms. She, too, was gagged like her husband, but her eyes were also taped.

Moments later she was manhandled to where Lundgren had reloaded one of his guns. Without hesitation he shot the unfortunate women three times: a shot in each of her breasts and one to the abdomen. Her body was dropped into the pit next to that of her husband.

Now Luff was sent back again to bring the three Avery girls to their certain death. He was later to recall these moments in a moving statement in court when he claimed he had been brainwashed into taking part in the butchery. The oldest girl, Trina, was shot twice in the head, after the first had failed to kill her. It also took two shots to kill Rebecca Avery. Then Ronald Luff went back one more time for the smallest child:

'I've been through the scenario a hundred times or more. I put her on my shoulders and carried her to the barn. I could have put them all in the car and taken off. But was that a consideration? A viable option? No.'

Six-year-old Karen Avery was also shot twice in the chest and head. Then she was lowered into the pit to lie beside her two sisters and parents. Jeffrey Lundgren got up from the crouching position where he had killed the family and methodically cleaned the .45 Combat Elite. When he returned to the farmhouse not a word was spoken between any of the cultists, although they had been part of an almost unparalleled killing in the name of religion: Lundgren's 'religion'.

The rest of the Kirtland cult story is simply told. The following day, Jeffrey Lundgren, his two wives, and their followers climbed into three camper vans and headed for Chilhowee in West Virginia. The cult leader was convinced that the 'Sword of Laben' was probably hidden there with the brass plates on which were the engraved the letters that Joseph Smith had translated for the *Book of Mormon*.

For several months, the party looked in vain for any clues around Chilhowee that might lead them to the fabled artefacts. But when nothing materialized, Lundgren began, for the first time in his life, to doubt his own perfection, and decided to move on to California. The remaining members of the Kirtland cult were left to fend for themselves.

Nine months after the massacre on the Kirtland barn, in January 1990, the police received a tip and a flurry of patrol cars raced to the deserted farm. The 'Judgement Pit' was located and five bodies found badly decomposed, though still identifiable as those of the Avery family. It was now time to bring Lundgren and his followers to judgement.

This time it was to be Jeffrey Lundgen's turn to be hunted and he was not able to outwit the combined police forces and FBI for long. One by one the cult members were found and their stories led inexorably to the man who had caused such mayhem. He continued to protest that he had a vision that God had wanted him to sacrifice the family from his arrest to when he stood awaiting sentence in the Ohio Supreme Court.

The other members of the Kirtland cult each received sentences of 100 years imprisonment or more. Alice Lundgren and the couple's son, Damon, received five consecutive life terms. Jeffrey Don Lundgren, the man who had wanted to write a new chapter in religion and had instead horrified a nation, was sentenced to death. But the public revulsion at the events was not totally directed at the leader himself. In a ringing phrase that was repeated endlessly in the media, the prosecuting counsel had declared:

'If Jeffrey Lundgren is Adolf Hitler then Alice Lundgren is the Angel of Death, Josef Mengele.'

Horror in the Temple of Love

The atmosphere in the huge converted warehouse in downtown Miami was electric as the two big men squared up to each other. The pair looked like fighters: but the open space where they were standing was not a boxing ring and the huge building in which they stood was not a sporting arena. The Temple of Love – as it was called – was the headquarters of a cult led by Yahweh Ben Yahweh, 'God, the Son of God', and the two men were both disciples who had been goaded into trading blows with one another. For one of the men, though, the contest would be, quite literary, a fight to the death.

In the autumn of 1983, the Temple of Love, in the slum section of Miami rather inappropriately named Liberty City, was the focus of enormous public interest and believed to be the heart of a cult with many thousands of members across the southern states of America and with satellite churches in forty-five cities. The old warehouse filled an entire block and had been bought by the group three years before as a virtual ruin. The 150 or so followers of Yahweh Ben Yahweh had turned into an extraordinarily vibrant hive of worship and industry in which the black messiah had said they would live 'until our exodus to Jerusalem'. The inside had to be seen to be believed.

The cavernous old warehouse had been restored, the electricity and plumbing repaired and everything inside redecorated. The walls had been hung with paintings of Bible characters, although every one was black – Noah, Moses, the Virgin Mary and the disciples celebrating the Last Supper. There was even a huge panoramic view of a futuristic-looking city populated entirely by black people. Overhead several UFOs circled, while below was inscribed the words, 'The black Christ is risen among us today to deliver us from white people.'

All around the open square where the two men were now circling each other was a miniature village that had also been built by the cultists. Alongside a sanctuary for worship stood a grocery store, cafeteria, health centre, laundry and even an ice cream parlour.

The quarters in the Temple of Love in which the cultists lived were not so spacious, however. A ten by fifteen-foot cubicle was allocated to each family, separated by an eight-foot partition. Some of these living spaces had been made more homely with mementoes from the occupants' past lives – family photographs, trinkets and the odd piece of furniture. Others had little more than a blanket or mattress on the floor. There was no such thing as privacy for anyone living here.

Life for the cultists was a round of prayer and tasks for everyone that began at 5 am. Prayers and Bible lessons also took up any time not absorbed in worship. Distractions – like the fight in the middle of the building – were a rarity and several dozen men, women and even a few children had formed a rough square around the two scrappers.

Subsequently, no one would be quite sure what had prompted the fight. One story said it had started simply because the two men had got into an argument and decided to settle the dispute with their fists. Another claimed the slightly taller of the two men was the cult leader's favourite and he had been instructed to take on the other man who was a comparative newcomer, but reckoned to be the better fighter. A third – more sinister – rumour maintained that the shorter man was an assassin who had been sent to kill the messiah. It was settled in a way, however, that answered none of these questions.

The taller man was John Lightburn, 25, a martial arts expert, who had joined the cult in its early days and become a close associate of the leader. His opponent, Leonard Dupree, was three years younger, and a black belt karate expert. Dupree was from New Orleans and had defied the opposition of his parents to travel to Miami and join the Temple of Love.

As the two men lunged and swung fists at each other it quickly became obvious that Dupree was the more expert and proficient fighter. Twice Lightburn tried to come to grips with his broad-shouldered, agile opponent. Then, getting too close, Dupree knocked him to the ground. A silence fell across the warehouse. At that moment the heavily bearded leader, Yahweh Ben Yahweh, with his white turban and flowing gown, strode up to the throng of onlookers. Sydney P. Freedberg, who made a special study of the cult for his book *Brother Love: Murder, Money and a Messiah* (1994), explains what happened next:

'Dupree had drawn the attention of several of Yahweh Ben Yahweh's closest associates for the way he kept himself to himself and often seemed to be spaced out in the Bible classes. Rumours started making the rounds that Dupree could be an assassin sent to kill the messiah. Yahweh Ben Yahweh was already quite paranoid about the activities of some of his followers and had started censoring the mail to and from the Temple, "afraid that infidels might lurk among his throng".'

According to Freedberg, when Yahweh confronted Dupree he asked him if he wanted to hurt him. No, the young men is said to have replied, 'I just want to kiss your feet.' What happened immediately afterwards is not clear, although the words in a statement gathered for the court charges against the cult is reasonably specific:

'Because Dupree was known to be a karate expert, Yahweh openly challenged him to fight Lightburn, the Temple's resident martial-arts expert. The two men squared off in front of about 30–60 Yahweh onlookers. Dupree quickly knocked Lightburn down, at which point Yahweh ordered all present, including Ingraham and Maurice [two of Yahweh Ben Yahweh's lieutenants] to attack Dupree. Ingraham struck Dupree in the face with a tire jack. During the struggle, the doors of the Temple were locked at Yahweh's request. Yahweh allowed no one to leave and made everyone, including woman and children, strike and kick Dupree's lifeless body.'

Another account of the melee says that it began when an angry crowd surrounded Dupree as he stood over the fallen Lightburn. A cry was heard, 'Kill him!' and after Dupree was struck down by the iron bar, others continued to beat him to the floor, kicking him and tearing off his clothes. The hapless young man from New Orleans was beaten to a bloody, mangled pulp.

Freedberg believes that Yahweh Ben Yahweh ordered

everyone in the crowd to hit Dupree. By involving everyone present they would be bound by blood and no one would be able to report the murder to the authorities. When the mass beating ended in death, Dupree's body was apparently rolled into a carpet and removed from the Temple of Love.

The body of Leonard Dupree was dumped in a canal and has never been found. The fight to the death had been a terrible mismatch – but it was not the first, nor would it be the last time, that there was blood on the hands of the man who called him, 'God, Son of God.'

* * *

The little town of Kingfisher in the heart of the Oklahoma wheat-growing belt was where Hulon Mitchell Jr, who would declare himself Yahweh Ben Yahweh, was born on 27 October 1935. He was the first of fifteen children born to Hulon and Pearl Mitchell, and like his mother was born with light-coloured skin and striking hazel eyes. Hulon Sr was a Pentecostal preacher whose frenetic style of worship got his congregation nick-named 'Holy Rollers' by the other local residents who were predominantly Baptists and also made a deep impression on his first-born son.

The Mitchells were, however, one of the few black families in the town and undoubtedly suffered from the racial prejudice that then blighted the United States. They could go to 'Colored Only' stores and cinemas and young Hulon, like his brothers and sisters, was only allowed to attend a segregated school. He found his escape from this oppressive lifestyle in church and Bible study.

In order for the family to survive, Hulon Mitchell worked as a salesman while his wife took jobs as a maid. The family found their release during the years of the Depression in the tiny church in Kingfisher where ecstatic dancing and speaking in tongues were regular features. In the pulpit, Preacher Mitchell promised his people that they would be free of religious racial persecution when they died and went to heaven.

Hulon Jr, however, was more of an introvert and thinker and wondered why this better life for black people could not be enjoyed on earth. He found particular inspiration in the story in the Book of Exodus about Moses leading the enslaved Israelites to freedom.

In 1941, the rapidly growing family of Mitchells moved to the town of Enid, in the north of Oklahoma, where black families were still segregated but there was more work for the parents. At school, Hulon Jr had his first taster of organizations when he joined the Boy Scouts and learned some of the resourcefulness that he would later put to great effect.

At eighteen, the young man was drafted into the United States Air Force and served at the nearby Vance Air Force Base where his quick wit and intelligence saw him promoted to the rank of instructor. He also got married, had four children in as many years – three girls and a boy – and he and the family were transferred to several air force bases in California and Texas. There is evidence that he became as keen an airman as he was a Pentecostal worshipper.

Like many young black men of his time, Hulon Mitchell Jr bridled against the segregation laws. In the early fifties he became active in the civil rights movement being led by the inspiring Baptist minister, Martin Luther King Jr. Hulon took part in two sit-ins in a restaurant in Enid and undoubtedly helped to break down the segregation in the town.

One of the immediate effects of this about-turn in racial attitudes inspired Hulon Mitchell to leave the air force and take a degree in Psychology at the Phillips University in Enid. His free-ranging intellect also led him to enquire into a number of esoteric cults, including the Rosicrucians who taught that it was possible for believers to develop special mental powers that would enable them to achieve health, wealth and happiness. If this change of interests opened up new horizons for Hulon, it equally disturbed and upset his wife and the couple separated.

According to Sydney Freeberg, the young man now began to question the objectives of the civil rights movement and felt that the Black Muslims, led by the charismatic orator Malcolm X – who, like Martin Luther King, was doomed to be gunned down – spoke more directly to him. The author has quoted Hulon as arguing at this time:

'The Civil Rights movement was not becoming free from the oppressor; it was about fighting and dying to get inside of oppression to be better oppressed. The Civil Rights movement was about being able to stop giving your money to your black brother and give it to your oppressor. You wanted to sleep in a white hotel and eat in a white restaurant so you wouldn't have to eat in the black restaurant any more.'

At meetings of the Black Muslims he found himself in sympathy with the concept that black people were genetically superior to other races and *they* were the ones who should be striving for segregation. He preferred the ideas of militancy to the acquiescence of his father's Christianity. 'Mitchell X' – as he now called himself – had found the cause to which he could dedicate his life.

Hulon's life now changed rapidly. Recently remarried to Chloe Hight, he moved with his family to Atlanta, decided to teach his children at home and found time to take a master's degree in Economics at Atlanta University. For the first time, though, doubts began to be raised about his devotion to the Black Muslims. Although he could be relied upon to raise money for the organization using his degree to run various enterprises, soon there was talk of over $50,000 being missing. There were also rumours that he had been molesting some of the children who attended the services he ran in a converted Baptist church.

Whether 'Mitchell X' feared the same fate as 'Malcolm X', he moved on to another part of Atlanta and changed his name to 'Father Michel'. Here with another minister called 'Father Jone' he began selling a 'Total Blessing Plan' that promised health, wealth and happiness in return for a donation. He also produced brochures offering to sell a 'Blessed Prayer Cloth', which would cure illness and make all 'Disorders Disappear'.

It is evident that not everyone was as gullible as the two 'Fathers' hoped. In May 1969, 'Father Jone' was shot and killed on the streets of Atlanta by assassins who left no clues. 'Father Michel' was forced to rapidly safeguard his home and hire some bodyguards – but was determined not to change his lifestyle. He felt that the time had now come to open his own church.

The 'Modern Christian Church' had a simple message: 'God wants you to be rich.' The minister once known as Hulon Mitchell Jr now took to wearing a white satin tunic, a gold crown and carried a sceptre while telling his congregation that the more money they donated, the more the Lord would reward them.

By the mid-seventies, though, it was only 'Father Michel' who appeared to be getting any richer. When he began demanding that his followers call him 'the King', named himself as minister for life and prompted a row over communal property, the 'Modern Christian Church' collapsed in disarray. Long before the dust had settled, there was no sign of the leader.

Hulon Mitchell Jr was to have one more career change before he set up the cult that would make him notorious all over America. This time he moved further afield, to Florida, and the city of Orlando where he became a street preacher, 'Brother Love'. Once more his gift for oratory and his ability to convince the city's unfortunates that he held the key to a better future enabled him to build another dedicated band of followers.

Among their number was a 29-year-old mother of three, Linda, who saw in the beguiling light-skinned man with his hazel eyes someone with a divine mission. Indeed, she would be an eye-witness to his transformation from sidewalk orator into an all-powerful cult leader who believed he was the messiah.

*   *   *

With the problems of Atlanta behind him and a new band of acolytes to support him, Hulon Mitchell Jr resumed his religious studies like a man possessed. Mike Williams of the *Atlanta Journal*, who studied the rise of the Yahweh Ben Yahweh phenomenon, wrote in January 1992:

'He read up on Buddhism, Judaism, Sikhism, Hinduism and just about every other 'ism he could find. He grew to believe the Bible contained secret messages that would reveal themselves with enough serious attention. He plucked beliefs from the different religions to cook up a new religion based on the Black Hebrew movement which taught that Africans were the "true Jews" who'd descended from the lost tribes of Israel.'

In what he would later call a 'divine revelation', Mitchell claimed that he had been chosen to lead the 'Black Hebrews' from oppression to freedom and create their own nation, rejecting the white-centred Christianity forced on their ancestors by the slave owners. This revelation also told him that he and Linda should settle in Miami as the black neighbourhoods there were crying out for a messiah to save them from the poverty, crime and drugs that ruled their lives.

Hulon Mitchell planned his campaign of recruitment carefully. He knew how to win over the hearts and minds of distressed black people with a message that was simplicity itself: 'Do you know that God is black?' he would enquire of a likely looking man or woman. 'Well, it is *true!*' He would then give the person a copy of the booklet he had written with its provocative title, *You Are Not A Nigger! Our True History – The World's Best Kept Secret*.

How could anyone resist the smartly dressed man in his black suit, Mike Williams wrote, the conviction in his words shining out of his hazel eyes? Using the skills of persuasion honed from the years in Enid and Atlanta, Hulon Mitchell soon gathered over a hundred followers. He also took a new name once again: calling himself Yahweh Ben Yahweh, meaning 'The Lord Son of the Lord' – Yahweh being a proper name for God in the Hebrew Bible, Exodus 3:16.

In his new role, he convincingly emphasized the mixture of racial supremacy and violent separatism he had formulated. As God was black, the blacks would become powerful through him, while the whites should be regarded as infidels and oppressors. But this could only be achieved, he stressed, by absolute loyalty to him. It was *he* who would lead them on an exodus to Jerusalem. In the meantime, they must work tirelessly towards the promised day.

It seems evident that not every one of the early recruits were keen on giving up their homes and possessions, quitting their jobs and taking their children out of school, to move into the dilapidated warehouse that the messiah had found for them in Liberty City. But with a mixture of honeyed words and strong-arm tactics, Yahweh Ben Yahweh got a core group of thirty followers to agree.

In the old warehouse a new world was born into which it was vowed no white man would ever be allowed to enter. Once the premises were habitable, the cult members adopted a mode of dress identical to their leader: white tunics, turbans and a Tetragrammaton pendant around their necks. They were instructed to take Israel as their surname and follow a kosher diet.

To ensure there were no challenges to his authority, Yahweh selected a group of ten burly young men who he named the

'Circle of Ten'. They would guard the warehouse from any unwelcome intruders and keep an eye on what went on inside, reporting regularly to the leader. Just in case of any trouble, they were armed with heavy wooden clubs, euphamistically named the 'Staffs of Life'.

Yahweh Ben Yahweh also used music to control and enthuse his followers. His services were always accompanied by rock music that could be heard far beyond the block on which the 'Temple of Love' was located. He was a master at rousing his audience and would get the faithful to repeat after him like a mantra: 'Yahweh Ben Yahweh is the Grand Master of the Celestial Lodge, Architect of the Universe, and the Blessed and only Potentate.'

Soon the rule of Yahweh Ben Yahweh became absolute and theocratic. He was now the living messianic ruler of his own world. Any signs of dissent – or untoward behaviour as the unfortunate Leonard Dupree found – were brutally put down. Beatings became almost commonplace. Inexorably, the leader pushed the loyalty of his members towards the ultimate test. He would demand of them from his lectern:

'How many of you would die for Yahweh? Would you kill for Yahweh?'

The enthusiastic cries in the affirmative from the packed ranks of swaying, sweating men, women and children would have been enough to send a chill up the spine of anyone within earshot.

According to documents later produced in court, Yahweh began to show more than a leader's interest in his female members. Stories that circulated for a time – inevitably to be quashed by the 'Circle of Ten' – claimed that he developed a habit of appearing suddenly in the cubicles of single young women, especially the prettiest ones, in the middle of the night. For Bible lessons, he said.

Yahweh Ben Yahweh declared that women were unclean during their menstrual cycle. They were also forbidden to use any kind of birth control and were to have as many children as possible and increase the size of the cult. For years he carefully recorded the names and dates of birth of children born in the 'Temple of Love', in a bound volume he called *Lamb's Book of Life* – apparently named after the book mentioned in the Bible in which God records the names of those believers who will be saved from hell. Reporter Mike Clary of the *Los Angeles Times* quotes a former member as saying that one of the leader's favourite rallying cries during his 'sex education classes' was:

'Get it brothers! Sisters give it up! It's not about falling in love. It's about multiplying! Have babies and let's subdue and control the earth.'

Yahweh Ben Yahweh was also keen on subduing young women for his own ends. He is said to have told females he fancied that he was God's emissary and it was his job to teach them how to have sex. It was alleged that he singled out girls as young as ten and one of the girls he abused told investigators that he had intercourse with her and another pubescent girl on the same day. To buy their silence, the messiah apparently gave them gifts of money, necklaces, dresses and even trips out of the 'Temple of Love' to fancy restaurants.

Yahweh also gave sex lessons to his male followers, taking a particular interest in the younger men. He obtained pornographic films showing white women having sex with animals to prove that all white females were 'dirty' and no one should have intercourse with them. Because of the association with the Jewish religion, Yahweh insisted that all his young men were circumcised – and actually removed the foreskins himself in the sanctuary. The screams of agony that echoed around the warehouse at these times were said to be horrifying.

Similar screams, though, were soon going to be heard beyond the confines of the warehouse when the vengeance of the man who had once been Hulon Mitchell Jr and now regarded himself as a great religious leader began to strike out into Dade County.

* * *

Friday the thirteenth is an ill-omened day in any month of the year. But it was even more so in November 1981 when a violent and truly gruesome murder was discovered that would ultimately lead to the arrest of Yahweh Ben Yahweh and fifteen of his closest lieutenants.

The setting was the edge of the Everglades in Florida, a deceptively beautiful area of swampy land that is home to vicious insect and animal life, notably fearsome twelve-foot alligators. On this particular morning, the only life stirring were mosquitoes and the occasional bird screeching high in the trees. That is until a construction worker drove along one of the narrow dirt roads to carry out a routine equipment check in a quarry.

It was not until the man had parked his truck and climbed down from his cabin that he noticed a red blanket spread over some weeds close to the road. It was an odd thing to see in the remote Everglades at any time. He bent over and lifted the blanket – and then nearly vomited with the mixture of shock and revulsion at what he saw.

Underneath the blanket was the body of a man in jeans with a T-shirt bearing the legend 'Florida Atlantic University'. *But there was no head.*

It was several minutes before the construction worker could overcome his shock and stop himself from being sick. He had to look a second time to make sure he had not been mistaken. But the corpse was undeniably headless. As the man looked closer he could see that blood was still seeping from the severed neck. There was also blood spattered on a tree beside the body.

Even through his nausea, the construction worker reckoned the victim had not been dead for long. Without touching anything he hurried back to the truck and called his office. It was to be several moments before the girl on the other end of the line realized her caller was not joking about finding a beheaded body in the Everglades.

The mutilated body would prove to be that of Aston Green, a 25-year-old Jamaican-born man who had last been reported living with a weird black cult in Liberty City. He was the first victim of Yahweh Ben Yahweh's brutal policy towards those who defied him. Especially, it seems, defectors like Aston Green, who had fled the 'Temple of Love' a few days before his headless corpse was found.

Aside from coaching his followers in their lifestyle, their diets, finances and their sex lives, Yahweh was urging his members to 'murder white devils'. He had also handpicked 'the Brotherhood', a group of tough, muscular young men to carry out his dirtiest work. But they had to prove themselves before they

137

could join this select band. To get into this select group it was necessary to kill a white man and bring the leader a finger, an ear or even the head as proof of the kill. When news of the discovery of Aston's headless body was announced on that night of Friday the thirteenth it was now clear that 'the Brotherhood' would even kill their own in the name of Yahweh.

'God, the Son of God' was now at the very height of his powers. In the next decade, it has been alleged, at least fourteen people, men and women, would be murdered by the cult. One of these intended victims, Mildred Banks, whose husband had been butchered after talking to the police, had a miraculous escape. She was shot in the chest, her throat slit and left to die but somehow managed to get to a phone and summon help.

Despite the fact that between April and October 1986 – according to evidence later given in court – a series of random murders of white people were recorded in Miami, not one could be attributed to the 'Temple of Love'. Certainly there were police officers that had their suspicions about the weird cult, but in the community at large their reputation seemed to be going from strength to strength. The numbers applying to join the cult were increasing and trusted 'missionaries' were being sent out across the state in their traditional robes handing out copies of *You Are Not A Nigger*. By 1990, it was claimed the sect had churches in forty-five cities and towns and 'tens of thousands' of members.

The warehouse itself was now packed with over 500 people. Unable to accommodate any more, Yahweh purchased a number of old buses in which groups of four men were put. The vehicles were also used for accommodation when cultists from the outlying areas of Florida travelled to the 'Temple of Love' for special gatherings.

The proceeds from Yahweh Ben Yahweh's various business enterprises in Liberty City brought him more money than he could ever have imagined possible when he thought back to his days trying to fleece the poor folk of Enid. Indeed, so high did his prestige grow in the local business community that he was invited to join the Miami Chamber of Commerce. The mayor gave the ultimate accolade to him when he declared 7 October 1990 as 'Yahweh Ben Yahweh Day'.

Yet the net was closing around the former Hulon Mitchell Jr. Suspicions had been growing in several quarters about the white-hating cult ever since the spate of murders in the summer of 1986, as Mike Clary informed his readers in January 1992:

'After the murders, plainclothes cops started patrolling the "Temple of Love" full time. Unmarked squad cars patrolled the neighbourhood, sizing up the turbaned, machete-carrying guards. The police had no proof pegging the attacks to the cult and couldn't raid the holy compound without solid evidence. All they could do was keep their frustrating watch as fourteen terrified dissidents went into hiding, carefully erasing the trail behind them.'

A tiny thread of good fortune was literally to end Yahweh Ben Yahweh's reign of terror. A keen-eyed plain-clothes policeman spotted a thread of cotton on a carpet hanging from the warehouse wall. He knew he had seen it before. A painstaking check matched it to cloth found at the scene of the murder of Aston Green in the Everglades.

With this evidence, Sergeant Frank Wesolowksi confronted the black messiah in the Liberty City warehouse. Yahweh sat unmoved at the allegations and instead of answering any questions about the cult accused the policeman of oppressing the black population. It was an unsatisfactory meeting – but Wesolowski knew the evidence against the messiah was mounting.

Several women had come forward to complain of being abused by Yahweh. One of these was his own sister who had joined the cult and then fled into hiding. Another was the daughter of Linda, the woman who had helped him to set up the cult in Miami. After enduring abuse from him for years, she had confessed to her brothers who had never liked their mother's friend. One of the brothers agreed to collect information for FBI investigators by returning to the warehouse with a concealed microphone.

The most important evidence of all, however, was to come from a man at the heart of the cult, Robert Rozier, a member of the infamous 'Brotherhood' who had actually killed for the black messiah. His testimony in the subsequent case of 'US v God, Son of God' in the District Court at Fort Lauderdale in January 1992 was to bring to an end a ten-year investigation that involved over 160 witnesses.

Rozier was a former professional grid-iron footballer who had fallen on hard times after playing for the Saint Louis Cardinals and Oakland Raiders. He had joined the 'Temple of Love' in 1982 after serving a six-month imprisonment for a series of petty crimes. Once in the cult, he told the court, he changed his name to Neariah Israel, or 'Child of God' and flung himself into all its activities.

It was on a Saturday night in April 1986 that Rozier decided he wanted to join 'the Brotherhood'. He had taken off his white robe and turban and put on some street clothes, slipped a 12-inch Japanese-style knife into his jacket pocket and went 'hunting for white devils'. In his evidence, Rozier said he went to a well-known gay area, the Coconut Grove, and looked for a victim. He told the court:

'A white guy came stumbling down the street. He looked as if he was drunk so I followed him to his apartment. As he opened the door, I forced my way inside and stabbed him in the heart. There was another white man living in the apartment so I stabbed him to death as well. I thought about chopping off their heads to take to Yahweh Ben Yahweh. But I couldn't figure out a way to take the heads in public without arousing suspicion. So I just left the bodies there.'

Rozier told the court that the messiah had praised him – but next time he must remember to bring back a body part. The former quarterback said that on another occasions he and another 'Death Angel' had walked around the streets of Miami for hours looking for 'white devils'.

'That time we came across a man passed out in a car in a bar parking lot. We stabbed him in the chest over and over again. Then we sliced off his ear. But this got lost in the dark and we couldn't find it. So we went back and cut off the other ear and took that to Yahweh.'

Robert Rozier's evidence – and that of the stream of witnesses who passed through the court – was damning, no matter how the man who had been their leader protested his innocence. Yahweh Ben Yahweh was found guilty of conspiracy to murder and sentenced to eighteen years imprisonment. Seven of his followers involved in the killings were given between fifteen and sixteen years each. The 'Temple of Love' in Miami that they all helped to create remains standing to this day – an ever-present reminder of another dark chapter in the history of modern cults.

The Magic Hunters

The teenager staggering down the street was naked except for a thong and a string of charms around his neck. Slung over his shoulder was a British-made SLR rifle that occasionally clattered against the walls as he made his way unsteadily by the solitary light of a pale moon towards home: a slum dwelling on the outskirts of Bo Town in the southern part of Sierra Leone. The boy giggled to himself once more in a ganja-dazed haze and thought about the fun he and his friends in the Kamajors – a name meaning 'hunter' in the native language, Mende – had enjoyed during the evening, baiting some of the old men who complained about the state of the country since thugs like him had been running things.

For a moment the boy stopped, remembered something that had been said to him by one wizened old guy and let out a curse that echoed between the close-packed houses on either side and down the pot-holed road. As the sound faded, he was suddenly aware of a figure in a doorway. He shook his muddled head and squinted hard through the gloom. He was just about to reach for his rifle when he realized the figure was that of a girl. Her teeth flashed white and even through the haze in his head he could tell she was smiling at him.

The boy stumbled across the road to where the girl was leaning in a doorway. He could see at once that she was naked and had full, melon-shaped breasts and a mass of bushy pubic hair. He licked his lips. Most people looked at him with fear in their eyes – the Kamajors had, after all, been accused of all kinds of pillaging, terrorizing and even killing civilians in the district – but this girl was obviously giving him the come-on. She couldn't know he was only just sixteen and hadn't yet had sex with anyone.

For a moment the boy hesitated. After all the ganja and coke he'd taken during the day while he and the other young Kamajors had been roistering around the town he wondered if it might be a trap. There were plenty of people who didn't like the men who were supposed to be keeping the law by whatever means they chose. But then he remembered what his leader, Pa Harding, had said when he had come to the town to review his forces a few days back.

The boy could still see the shirtless old man with his bulging, hard eyes looking him and the rest of his squad up and down. Then he'd patted his pot belly and pointed at the greasy paste smeared all over it from his hairy chest right down to the top of his trousers and roared, 'As long as you're wearing this *nothing* can hurt you!'

All of the boy's squad had been given some of the magic paste by one of Harding's lieutenants and rubbed it on their bodies. Momentarily he looked down and could see the mess was still there – although parts were streaked with dust and trails of sweat from his earlier exertions. It was, though, a moment too long.

Three other figures had now appeared from behind the girl whose smile had instantly changed to one of hatred. The boy did not even have a chance to cry out before a fist smashed into his face and another grabbed the rifle from his shoulders. He was unconscious even before his body struck the ground.

The girl now quickly pulled on a dress while the three men gagged and bound the boy's prostrate figure. A few moments more and the little group were back in the shadows with their ungainly load carried between them, heading out of the town for the countryside.

The Jombola cult had struck against its enemies the Kamajors once again. The 'honey trap' set up to lure unwary members of the Civil Defence Force to which the Kamajors belonged had been a success. On this occasion the sexy, teasing girl had been enough for the drunken boy they had just kidnapped. But the cult was also believed to possess extraordinary supernatural powers that could be used in more difficult situations.

*   *   *

The south of the former British West African colony of Sierra Leone – now known as the Republic of Sierra Leone – was certainly a dangerous and unruly place in the spring of 1997. Despite the agreement that had been made the previous November between the President, Ahmed Tejan Kabbah, and the Revolutionary United Front, who had been wreaking havoc in the region since 1991, there was still much unrest and other powerful factions were at work in the four districts that make up the Southern Province – in particular in the countryside around Bo Town.

The sprawling Bo District covering an area of 5,000 square miles and home to fifteen chiefdoms – their people living in some 1,300 villages – had suffered more than most areas. The RFU rebels had destroyed large portions of the administration facilities and during the worst period of their occupation in 1994–95, almost 90 per cent of the health facilities had been vandalized, damaged or burned down. Roads, homes, schools and community buildings had suffered heavy damage and it was estimated that as much as 37 per cent of the district's infrastructure had been destroyed. Two major towns, Tikonko and Bumpe, were entirely wiped out.

The population had also shrunk to just over 50,000 men, women and children who feared for their lives at the first sight of any man carrying a gun. Into this cauldron were thrust the Kamajors with a brief to restore stability. A traditional force of hunters drawn from the south and east – though mostly from Bo where the main ethnic groups are Mende and Temne – they had originally been employed by local chiefs.

Now the CDF had been put under the leadership of the ruthless Samuel Hinga Norman, a man whose brutality would later involve him and two of his lieutenants, Moinina Fofana and Allieu Kondewa, being indicted for war crimes. But at that uncertain moment in time the Kamjaors seized the oportunity with enthusiasm, recruiting assiduously, particularly among the young. Some of the boy soldiers who would serve in their ranks were barely in their teens.

Within months, the mixture of veteran hunters and half-untrained boys were 'keeping the peace', armed with a veritable arsenal of weapons from rocket launchers to rifles. To many people in the Bo District in particular it seemed that one brutal oppressor had been replaced by another. As a United Nations report published in 1997 stated:

'The major defending factor in the district were the CDF (Kamajors). The only hindrance that impacted on interventions during this period was the persistent unbridled activities of the CDF, which culminated in widespread human rights abuse and commandeering of government vehicles by the CDF. However, these excesses did not deter agencies' efforts in reaching out to areas which had previously been inaccessible. The presence of some police personnel, through their various security apparatus, acted as a counterweight to the CDF.'

As we shall see, the report might also have added that the activities of the Jombola Cultalso played a part in countering some of the Kamajors' excesses in what was to prove a bloody battle of modern tactics and traditional magic – conducted 'through the power of darkness', as one member of the cult would later explain to officers of the UN.

Bo Town is the second largest in Sierra Leone with a long history of trading activtities including the growing of rice, coffee, cacao and olive palm. But what has always made it attractive to fortune hunters ever since the capital of Freetown was founded in 1792 by the Sierra Leone Company as a home for black Britons who had fought for Britain in the American Revolutionary War, were the gold and diamond mines.

Unquestionably, the leaders of the Kamajors were motivated by thoughts of the famous 'blood diamonds' when their ranks were being swelled to a record 20,000 in 1996. But even such numbers were no guarantee of protection as the young man in Bo Town had found out. And as another party of Kamajors camping in a village would also discover in April 1997.

* * *

The group of soldiers sitting around the camp fire were in good spirits. They had spent the day hassling some farmers on the outskirts of the town of Yambama who had been complaining about the way the CDF were holding up supplies to the area. The men had said the Kamajors were up to their old tricks of siphoning off stuff for themselves: so they had to be taught a lesson. Now, though, they were enjoying the spoils of that bit of petty thieving, and laughing at the memory of the troubled, lined faces of the farmers.

This particular squad of Kamajors had been together for some years and had taken part in a number of actions against the Revolutionary United Front. The RFU had thought they were tough and for a time had certainly made life difficult in the south of Sierra Leone with operations to take control of the four districts of the province. But *not* as tough as they believed.

From some of the enemy troops who had fallen into their hands, the CDF had learned that a lot of the RUF troops had been trained in nearby Libya. Their tactics had been based on brutality, torture and rape, although they had tried to give themselves the semblance of being a real fighting force by naming their little battles with euphemistic titles like 'Operation Burn House' – actually a series of arson attacks – 'Operation Pay Yourself' – a campaign of looting and pillaging – and the brutally self-explanatory, 'Operation No Living Thing'.

The leader of the RUF, Fodah Sankoh, had actually been urging his men to use any force necessary to wrest control of the area. He turned a blind eye to the terrible beatings his troops carried out and the violent way they incapacitated rather than killed the local population by slicing off arms and legs. In the wake of this rule of fear, Sankoh had turned up at captured towns to try and pacify the people with outrageous statements, 'You who we have wronged have every human right to feel bitter and unforgiving – but we plead with you for forgiveness.'

The men around the camp fire found it impossible not to smile when remembering their leader's words. One of the soldiers even claimed he had seen Sankoh wink at a lieutenant after delivering this piece of hypocrisy in a town near the border of the province of Tonkolili, just to the north of where they were encamped.

Despite their strength, though, soldiers like these were not stupid enough to believe that they had only the local impover-ished population to deal with. Starving men, women and children – many of them missings arms and legs – were one thing. It was the Civil Defence Force who were rapidly becoming their enemies and picking off groups of them when they least expected an attack.

But such thoughts were far from the minds of the men around the blazing fire. They had eaten well, checked their rifles and supplies, and were now taking a little alcohol and ganja before going to sleep. They knew another mission was being planed for the next day. Parts of Yambama were said to be seething with unrest and there were believed to be some hotheads there who would take on anyone.

The men were lazing on the ground laughing and smoking and it was several minutes before they first heard the peculiar sounds. It was one man, less stoned than the rest, who hissed at his colleagues and pointed into the darkness. The group fell silent and pricked up their ears.

The first noise sounded like a rustling in the air. Then came the unmistakable padding of an animal's feet. A moment later and a noise that was unmistakably like a cat yowling. The soldiers looked nervously from one to another, their eyes widening in the firelight. They were all superstitious men and there was something unnerving about the sounds as they grew closer and louder. No one moved. The bravery that had been fuelled by the stimulants drained from their bodies.

What happened next in that clearing has never been completely explained.

One story of the events that left three men dead and the remainder running madly into the jungle or captured, was that a party of Kamajors broke into the clearing and fell on the men of the RUF. Another quite different version claims that it was the handiwork of the Jombola cult who utilized their magical powers to rid the area of yet another predatory force.

One man who is in no doubt is Santigie Kawa, a 60-year-old resident of the Luugbu chiefdom in Bo. He believes this is just one example of the remarkable powers of the cult to transmogrify themselves into animals and kill their victims through a mixture of fear and savagery. Kawa explained to a reporter from the *Free Republic* in August 1997:

'The Jombolas have the power to turn themselves into bats, cats, dogs and other creatures before wreaking havoc. They can attack small groups or even whole villages. Terrified residents of the troubled areas have spoken of seeing the transformed cult members when they are going on military operations. The very sight of them mesmerizes their victims.'

People in Seirra Leone who have investigated the activities of this mystical cult believe they were formed to combat the warring factions in the country. First the RUF and then the Kamajors in the Civil Defence Force who were using their cover as a stablizing force to take advantage of the local people. How the Jombolas came by their supernatural powers is as much a mystery as the cult itself – although African magic with its mixture of suggestion, voodoo ceremonies and juju rituals has a long tradition in the rural countryside.

Certainly the mixture of hunters and uneducated boys in the CDF with their superstitious fears and use of fetishes to protect themselves were ripe for auto-suggestion. Some even believed that by eating the heads and hearts of enemies killed in action they would protect themselves from danger. And just as they used superstition to whip up a frenzy against the RUF, so similar black magic could be turned on them. Santigie Kawa has explained:

'We are not exactly sure how many people have been killed by the Jombola cult, who clearly have supernatural powers. The numbers must run into dozens. We do know there are probably as many as 300 men and women in the cult and their main area of operation is in the southern region which has suffered worse during the civil war and the guerrilla fighting.'

The cult has understandably cloaked itself and its activities in secrecy. The leader is believed to be a fiery chieftain named Pa Kujah who originates from the town of Yambama. This sprawling community over a hundred miles away from the capital, Freetown, is also a world away in terms of its facilities and the sophistication of its 5,000 strong population. It has a long-standing reputation for mysticism, too.

It was near Yambama that a 25-year-old man was arrested on suspicion of being a cult member by a group of Civil Defence Force soldiers in 1998. He was spared execution in return for providing information about Pa Kujah and the Jomolas. In a confession to his captors, the man said:

'Our objective is to overthrow the government and also the Kamajors who are persecuting our people. We shall achieve this not only by force of arms, but also through the power of the dark. About 52 of us were recently initiated into the cult and this number included 25 women.'

According to the young man's statement, female members of the cult were trained to use rifles and taught how to perform a number of magic rituals – primarily those that had the greatest effect on adolescents. He said that the primary purpose of the women was to act as 'sex objects', explaining, 'We use our womenfolk to overpower male victims, often sexually.'

Desmond Williams, a political analyst at the University of Sierra Leone, who made a study of the Jambola cult at this same time, believes they operated mostly in the southern districts of Bo, Pujehun and Bonthe, where they have 'carved a path of death and destruction on their enemies'. He wrote in 1998:

'The conflict between the Jambolas and the Kamajors was initially a battle for supremacy in the wake of the weakening of the national army. The Kamajors' powers have been revered in the country, especially in their fight against the RUF rebels. I believe the vacuum created by the government army's impotence in holding the rebels at bay, the rising power of the Kamajors and, in fact, the general chaos that followed the six-year-long war, combine to explain the emergence of the Jambolas and the credit they are given for possessing mystical powers.'

Little, though, has been heard of the Jambolas since the millennium. But the continued reporting of fetishes associated with the cult in the Yambama district is believed to show they are still in existence. Indeed, several reported deaths in which the victims have been found with their bodies covered in animal marks are claimed to show that the men and women with 'the power of the dark' are still on the prowl, attacking those who they regard as the enemies of the nation.

The Vampire Clan

The community of Murray is in most outward respects like many another small town in America. A thriving little place in southwest Kentucky near the Tennessee state line, it lies in Calloway County – of which it is the county seat – and has its own Murray State University and Calloway County Court House. It is also home to the museum of the National Boy Scout Movement and for many years the citizens have prided themselves on bringing up polite and well-behaved young boys and girls.

Settled originally in 1825, Murray has been known variously as Williston, Pooltown and Pleasant Hill before the name was changed in 1844 to honour a distinguished citizen, John L. Murray. If you look it up on the map, you will see it is located on the highways US 641 and KY 94 about midway between St Louis and Memphis. Riding through it on a bus – as many people do – it remains in the memory as just another typical rural American town.

But scratch the surface and there is more to Murray than meets the eye. It is a place of notoriety in the history of cults as the centre of a group of young people – perhaps as many as thirty – whose brutal activities in 1996 ultimately brought a new meaning to the word 'bloodthirsty'. With a population of just under 15,000 people – 87 per cent of whom are white – it was an event unlike anything that had ever occurred before. Indeed, the local police felony records show that there had not been a murder in the town for a decade, and the amount of crime was minimal.

If there is anything that might be called slightly ominous about Murray it could be the famous Blood River in Calloway County, which once ran red during a settlers' battle with Indians. Plus the fact the district is known to experience tornadoes rather more

150

often than anywhere else in Kentucky. In the sixties, for example, the town was hit twice. In 1964, a wind gusting at over 200 miles per hour killed three people, injured twenty-four and caused $500,000 worth of damage. Four years later a tornado blew even harder – closer to 260 miles per hour – crossing the Murray City Centre, killing two citizens, injuring thirty and doing $5 million worth of damage.

Perhaps, though, the one visible sign that something weird was taking place in the town in the mid-nineties was an outbreak of graffiti. In one rundown area of parkland, a community facility that had been vandalized a couple of times suddenly gained a sinister new inscription added to the other signs scrawled across its façade: the names of several punk rock groups, various New Age symbols and a whole section in black with the word ACID in capital letters.

But it was none of these that might have seemed untoward to anyone passing by. It would have been the words paint-sprayed in black across the front archway reading: VAMPIRE HOTEL. Indeed, in a short space of time in 1996 these words were to become symbolic of an evil that originated in Murray and spawned a group who called themselves 'the Vampire Cult': five young people responsible for a series of bizarre rituals that made local residents afraid to go out at night and who – ultimately – wrote their names in blood with a horrendous double murder in faraway Florida.

*   *   *

The cemetery not far from Clarks River and the US 641 had been in use for many years and sections were already beginning to show signs of neglect. Many of the graves were overgrown, numbers of the headstones were broken and some had fallen over. Or perhaps knocked over and vandalized: it was difficult to tell which.

The night the group of five teenagers, three boys and two girls, climbed over the walls was a cold autumn night illuminated by a full moon. All were dressed in black, only the blood-red lipstick of the two girls providing any colour. One of the boys was wearing a black trenchcoat and carrying a large wooden stick, while one of the females had a small package under her arm.

151

Anyone looking closely would have noticed the parcel move agitatedly from time to time, followed by a plaintive wail.

The group walked purposefully to a far corner of the cemetery, stepping over the rampant undergrowth and avoiding the broken graves, with the sense of direction of those who had been that way before. Occasionally snatches of conversation would break out among the youngsters, as if they felt quite sure they would not be overheard or disturbed. In fact, they had good reasons for feeling quite secure.

The little party found the grave they were seeking – a huge, stone mausoleum covered with verdigris and grass and weeds growing all around. There were a couple of freshly carved penta-grams on one side that indicated the grave had been visited recently. The stubs of some candles also lay in the undergrowth along with some small, bloodstained glass bottles. At first glance they might have looked like drug paraphernalia. In fact, they contained traces of animal blood that had been used in an earlier ritual by this same group.

The party gathered around the grave with obvious familiarity, putting themselves in a circle around one of the men. He was Roderick J. Ferrell, six foot tall with red hair and still only sixteen years old. Yet in his direct blue eyes seemed to glow knowledge of the ways of evil that was ageless. He was about to lead the others a further step on the path to degradation: a route that had already taken him from a role-playing fan to the leader of his own vampire cult.

Like many others of his age, Roderick had found endless fasci-nation in playing a live-action role-playing game called *Vampire: The Masquerade*. Created by Mark Rein-Hagen in 1991, it had been White Wolf Game Studio's first *World of Darkness* produc-tions based on the Storyteller System and centred on vampires in a modern Gothic-Punk world. A best-seller for several years, it won the 'Origins Award' for Best Role-playing Rules of 1991, but was discontinued in 2004 and replaced by *Vampire: The Requiem* with a new setting and revised rules. The blurb of the original described the concept of the game:

'What are we? The Damned Children of Caine? The grotesque Lords of Humanity? The pitiful wretches of Eternal Hell? We are vampires and that is enough. I am a vampire and that is far more than enough. I am that which must be feared, worshipped and adored. The world is mine – now and for ever.'

According to the game, vampiric societies consist of two levels: sects and clans. These groups can be associated with one another – depending on the ideological path they are following – or, as is often the case with the minor clans, independent from one another. The vampires were said to refer to themselves as 'Caineites' because the curse that turned them into the undead had originated with Caine.

The Masquerade in the titled referred to the vampires' determination to hide vampirism from human beings, the government and, particularly, the media where they believed themselves to be misrepresented. Significantly, it was said to serve as a *double entendre* referring to the vampires' efforts to convince themselves 'they were not the monsters they had become'.

According to later newspaper enquires, Roderick Ferrell had soon grown tried of this role-playing and wanted something 'more edgy'. He wanted to *be* a vampire and live the vampire lifestyle. There were plenty of sources to which he could refer for information in books of fact and fiction and in an ever-increasing number of sites on the Internet.

Much of the recent interest in vampires has, of course. been inspired by the films with Bela Lugosi and Christopher Lee, the novels of Anne Rice, the TV series *Buffy the Vampire Slayer,* and, of course, cult symbolism. The most obvious signs of this subculture – sometimes referred to as the 'Vampyre Lifestyle' – can be seen in fashion, where those involved have combined elements of Victorian, Gothic, Glam and Punk styles. The vampire 'look' typically includes dark clothing, long, sharp fingernails painted black or blood red, a pallid complexion and prosthetic fangs. Men and women throughout Europe and North America as well as in parts of South America and Asia have adopted the style.

Some vampirists have claimed to be related to legendary vampires while others believe they have the same characteristics as the traditional vampire: citing a pale skin and sensitive night vision, both of which are affected when exposed to sunlight. In addition, a broader range of senses, quick reflexes, prescience, and the perception of auras. A few even claim to have the ability to sense other vampires, a facility known as the 'Vampire Beacon'.

Roderick Ferrell had discovered that modern vampires used vampirism as a means of practising 'magick': using rituals to increase their energy by drawing the life energy – known as *prana* – of a willing donor. Alternately by drinking blood, ideally of a human, but occasionally that of animals. Sex was also regarded as a means of revitalizing a vampire's life force.

He was particularly fascinated by stories of the self-styled sanguinarian vampires who drank blood but did not bite with their teeth in the manner of mythological vampires. They were said to draw blood by using a sharp blade or needle and drinking the blood by applying their mouths to the cut. The equivalent of one or two tablespoons was said to be sufficient. There was, though, disagreement, about animal blood: whether it was too 'dead' to be of use, although if it was fresh it did provide an adequate alternative.

Ferrell learned that there were different theories about the creation of vampires. One school of thought argued that vampirism was part of their nature: a vampire soul inside a human body. Others felt that only by a vampire passing their blood to another person would they be 'turned' and 'fledged' with the donor in vampirism. The amount of blood passed, though, was said to be critical. If the right amount were not passed, the recipient would become 'blood bound' and neither human nor vampire.

Finally – one website informed him – a biological link could also produce a vampire. Vampire parents, it claimed, could produce vampire children. Later, a story that emerged about Ferrell's mother, Sandra, would give added significance to this rather outlandish claim.

This knowledge had been the motivation for several rituals before Roderick again gathered his four friends around the mausoleum in the graveyard. Beside him stood a girl, nineteen-year-old Dana Cooper, looking older and rather like a horror film extra in the stark white light of the moon. Her pale skin and dark hair took on a vivid sheen and the pentacle around her neck glinted each time she moved her head. In her arms was the package that again began to stir.

Roderick Ferrell repeated the words he had said before and held out his hands to the girl. This time he had not gone to so much trouble to get a sacrifice. On the first occasion, a couple of months earlier, he had broken into an animal shelter. Now he was going to use a neighbourhood cat that had been captured earlier in the day.

Although he was gaining confidence in his skill as a leader and a vampire, Ferrell knew the break-in had been a close-run thing. He and the others had only just managed to get away before the alarm was raised. What they left behind, though, was a clear indication that a new evil was abroad, as Murray police sergeant Mike Jump would later explain:

'The animal shelter thing was the first sign he [Ferrell] had gone beyond game playing. They broke in the shelter and stomped one of the animals to death. Two puppies were mutilated and they pulled the legs off one. Then they took the parts away.'

The blood of one of the dogs was used in a ritual the following night. When nothing discernible happened, Ferrell and the others returned to the cemetery. There he ordered the two girls in the group to cut their arms so they could all share the blood. Sergeant Jump again commented later:

'They apparently liked to suck blood. They cut each other's arms and sucked blood. In rituals in remote graveyards they would kill a small animal and suck the blood out of it, supposedly to give them more power. They honestly believed they were vampires.'

By the time the five met again on that moonlight night in the autumn of 1996, Roderick Ferrell was more than convinced. Indeed after he had slit the throat of the cat and they had all drunk some blood, he held up his hands and ordered silence. He had something to say. It was a statement that would shape the next few weeks of the cult's life – and their fate.

'I am possessed! I have no soul! My vampire nature has made me all-powerful. I have been chosen by real vampires and they have given me the power to do anything I please. So we are going to open the gates of hell! We are going to do this by killing a lot of people so that we can consume their souls. That is our mission and we shall not fail!'

The four other teenagers listened in silence while Ferrell told

155

them about the plans he had been making. He had devised his own sign – a 'V' with dots on each side. This would be the sign of their clan. They would put the mark on their victims so that the world would know they were the victims of vampires.

It would be a reunion with an old girlfriend from Murray who was now living in Florida that would give Roderick Ferrell the chance to fulfil this horrendous ambition.

* * *

Heather Wendorf was a shy, rather plain and insecure fifteen-year-old girl who lived in a good Florida neighbourhood on Greentree Lane in Eustis, some twenty miles north-west of Orlando. Her father, Richard, was a 49-year-old banker and her mother, Ruth, 53, a devoted housewife. The family had a strong religious background; Heather's grandfather, James Wendorf, had been a lawyer in the Evangelist Billy Graham's organization.

At junior school she was a model pupil and high achiever. But when she went to Eustis High School and became friends with a boy a year older she changed completely. The boy's name was Roderick Ferrell and he was then living with his father. His parents had separated and his mother had moved back to her hometown, Murray, leaving him introverted and unhappy. The two became inseparable.

In 1995, Ferrell dropped out of high school and went back to live with his mother. The effect on Heather was devastating. A teenage friend, Joe Barrett of Eustis, later told the *Orlando Sentinel*:

'She was a really nice girl, but deep down you could tell she had some heavy problems. When she started hanging around in a different crowd last year, she went from being really nice to being quiet. She started dyeing her hair – purple mostly – and wearing all black clothes. She often wore black fishnet stockings and a dog chain around her neck. Some people said she swore she was a vampire.'

Heather was not the only one that friends and the school authority noticed had changed. Reports from Eustis High School indicate that the dropout Roderick Ferrell had gone through a similar change. He had become hostile and prone to torturing animals. He was also wearing his red hair shoulder length, usually dressed in a black trenchcoat and carried a wooden stick wherever he went. He had even boasted that he would 'become immortal as a vampire'.

Seven months of separation did nothing to break the link between the two misfits. Heather would spend hours on the telephone talking to Ferrell and writing letters about running away. He, in turn, excited her with tales of his vampirism and the cult of young followers he was creating in Murray. On numerous occasions, the calls ended in tears, Heather begging her boyfriend to 'help her'. Finally, he agreed. He would bring four of his closest friends and make her part of the cult and take her away.

On the morning of 25 November 1996, like the four horseman of the apocalypse, Ferrell and his three cult members, Dana Cooper and sixteen-year-old Charity Lynn Keesee both from Murray and seventeen-year-old Howard Scott Anderson of Mayfield, drove to Eustis. On the journey, it is said he suggested that the group should kill the Wendorfs in order to set his 'great plan' in motion.

The first thing the quartet had to do after making contact with Heather was to initiate her into the cult. That afternoon the group went out to a cemetery on the outskirts of Eustis. There Roderick performed the induction or 'cross over' making his girlfriend drink blood to become a vampire like himself. He is alleged to have said to her after they had sucked each other's blood:

'The person that gets crossed over is like a subject to whatever the sire wants. Like the sire is boss basically. They have authority over you.'

As the couple lay on the grass after the ritual surrounded by the other three cultists, Ferrell revealed his plan to go and kill Heather's parents. The young girl was apparently horrified and told him 'not to harm them'.

That evening, the latest recruit to the ranks of 'the Vampire Clan' stayed with her two female counterparts. An Associated Press report states what happened next, based on police information:

'Ferrell took Howard Scott Anderson with him to the Wendorf home, 24135 Greentree Lane, Eustis. Inside he clubbed to death the sleeping Richard Wendorf and his wife, Ruth, with attacks to the heads with a blunt instrument. On Richard's chest, Ferrell burned the shape of a "V" with a cigarette, along with two pairs of dots on each side.'

The two men left the house without a backward glance. Roderick had begun his campaign for supreme power and left his mark. The pair took the Wendorfs' 1994 blue Ford Explorer from the front of the house and drove into Eustis to collect the girls. Ferrell told the others that they were going New Orleans. But any ideas that the famous old Southern city known to be a stronghold of voodoo practices would prove a haven for the teenage killers were soon dashed.

The following day, David Keesee, the father of Charity, contacted Sheriff Stan Scott of Calloway County, telling him he believed his daughter had 'run away from home'. Scott began his investigation – but instead of tracing a runaway girl was able to write *finis* to a merciless killing. He told a Reuters correspondent:

'It was Ms Keesee's mother who helped lead us to the killers. The girl had called her mother from South Dakota and told her she was somewhere in Louisiana and needed money. We figured out that they were in Baton Rouge and when they called again we had a plan. Mrs Keesee told her daughter to go to a motel and have the clerk call her so she could arrange to pay for the room. Believe it or not they fell for it.'

On Thanksgiving Day the five were arrested in a downtown Baton Rouge motel. Farrell was taken away in handcuffs screaming that he was 'a powerful vampire' and the police would never be able to hold him. He also claimed that it was a rival vampire gang that had actually killed the Wendorfs.

When Heather Wendorf was interviewed by investigators she told them the only reason she has gone on the run was because she had nowhere to go and was 'afraid I would be blamed for the murders'. It was only when she riding in the family car that she had been told her parents had been killed. She said she had been too distraught at the news to do anything but go along with the others.

While Roderick Ferrell was awaiting the trial that would splash his name and bloody deeds across the nation's newspapers – as well as bring him a life sentence – an incident as bizarre as the case itself came to light. It concerned his mother, Sondra Gibson, who until that moment had been nothing more than a background figure in the terrible sequence of events.

That same November, she was indicted for writing sexually explicit letters to a fourteen-year-old boy urging him to have sex with her. It was not, though, the age of the boy or the suggestion that Mrs Gibson had made that sent shivers up the spine of everyone who heard about the case. It was what she said her *reasons* were – and in particular their implication with regard to her son's belief in hereditary vampires.

'*I long to be near you,*' she wrote. '*Become a vampire, a part of the family. You will then come for me and cross me over. I will be your bride for eternity and you can be my sire.*'

Part Three

Shadow of the Apocalypse

'Ranch Apocalpyse'

It looked almost like a scene from an old Wild West movie – and although the events unfolding on an October afternoon could just have been a repeat of the kind of gunfights that were once commonplace in this part of Texas, the date was 1987 and the firepower came from high-calibre weapons more accurate at a distance then than anything the gunfighters of a century before had ever known.

The afternoon had been starting to fade under a wide blue southern sky when the first bullets smacked into the walls around the small cluster of buildings. They had been followed by the clatter of an Uzi firing from the buildings and met again by the crack of semi-automatic rifles from the edge of the compound. A group of eight men could be seen closing in, ducking from tree to tree towards the line of buildings that included several houses, some barns, a storehouse and a church. The drama was being played out at the headquarters of a cult whose name would be etched onto the public consciousness just six years later, following a fiery conflagration that would be seen all over the world on television. An apocalyptic event the causes of which are still the subject of debate today.

This particular gunfight in the town of Waco – an unfortunate name in many respects that has made it the butt of jokes for years – was more of a domestic affair. The defending 'homesteaders' were the son of one of the founding fathers of the cult and one of his members – and the attackers a man bent on disputing the leadership and with a 'gang' of seven gun-toting followers. Once the firing was over and the gunsmoke had dispersed, it was to prove an afternoon of great significance for everyone involved.

Waco is the county seat of McLennan County and got its name

from a derivation of the Wichita Native Americans known as the 'Waco' or 'Hiccup' who once lived on the land just to the west of the Brazes River until they were driven off by a Cherokee invasion in 1830. The settlers who followed, and in turn forced the Cherokee west, founded their community on the river banks and began planting the corn beans, pumpkins and melons that would sustain the development of the original Indian village into a city of just over 100,000 people.

For years gunfights were nothing unusual in Waco as the battle for the west was fought out over the vast plains of Texas. The roots of the gunfight on 30 October 1987, however, had their origins half a century earlier when Victor Houteff, the founder of the Davidians, a sect who had broken away from the Seventh-Day Adventist Church, bought a 377-acre ranch about ten miles from the city for his followers. It was named Mount Carmel after the biblical Mount Carmel.

There the small group lived in seclusion on the ranch practising their fundamentalist religion until after the Second World War. Then, with the sprawl of Waco encroaching ever nearer to their isolated community, the land was gradually sold off to property developers. After Houteff's death, his widow, Florence, disposed of the remainder of the three hundred acres and bought a new property in the countryside to the north-east of the burgeoning city. This 941-acre property was not surprisingly called New Mount Carmel.

The move did not suit all of the Davidians, however, and in 1962, Florence Houteff decided to disband the group and sell the property. After a bitter dispute, the widow's founder sold most of the land to the EE Ranch, but allowed those who did not wish to go to stay on the remaining 77 acres around the administrative building. This small band would become known as the Branch Davidians under the leadership of Ben Roden and his wife, Lois. The title of the community was also changed again to the Mount Carmel Center.

But life in the Center did not go smoothly. There were disputes about interpretations of the Bible and there were still some followers who believed they should never have left the old Mount Carmel. Lois Roden also gradually took on the role of prophetess and claimed that the Holy Spirit was feminine.

After the death of Ben Roden, Lois, who was then in her late sixties, is said to have had an affair with one of her followers, Vernon Howell, a young man from Houston. The pair went to Israel on an extended 'visit' and there was a growing feeling that she was grooming Vernon to be her successor at the expense of her son, George.

The rumour seemed to have some basis in fact when, in 1983, Lois allowed her protégé to begin preaching his own lessons. The controversy ignited a power struggle between Lois Roden, her son George, another long-standing member, George Pace, and the increasingly influential Vernon Howell, who had now fallen out with his former lover and was promoting his own cause. The following year an election was held.

After the ballot, George Roden announced he had won over the majority of the Branch Davidians. He immediately ordered Pace and Howell and their followers to leave the Mount Carmel Center. In 1987, Lois Roden herself died, leaving George seemingly in total control. But forces were moving against him – both inside the Center where those who had voted for him became increasingly disillusioned with his erratic behaviour, and outside where Vernon Howell was preparing for a violent takeover.

It appeared George Roden had developed a persecution complex and by the autumn of 1987 was viewed as increasingly paranoiac. He regarded Vernon Howell as his main adversary and lost no opportunities to attack his mother's former lover – issuing increasingly bizarre challenges to the younger man. It was observed that George had also taken to wearing a .357 revolver in a holster on his hip wherever he went.

In October, in a last-ditch attempt to prevent his support in the Center diminishing still further, George Roden issued his most astonishing challenge. To prove who had the greater power, he and Howell should have a contest to see who could 'raise the dead'. Roden told his adversary that he had already dug up a body on which to practise.

The challenge was just the sign Howell had been waiting for and on the afternoon of 30 October he and his seven supporters drove out to the Center from Waco. They were dressed in camouflage suits and carrying guns. What happened next became known as 'the Shootout at the Mount Caramel Center'.

George's wife, Amo, who was in the community centre, was the first to hear gunshots outside. She was not unduly surprised, as her husband had taken to loosing off shots a lot recently, convinced that sooner or later Howell and his followers – who the couple had nicknamed the 'Palestinian Terrorists' – would come calling. Amo did not begin to worry about George's 'war games' until bullets began thudding into the woodwork of the buildings and she saw Roden running from the community centre to a large shed. He seemed calm, she recalled later:

'I accepted George's obvious assessment of the situation; he was not in real danger. Later, from personal experience with assassins, I realized this confidence was based on faith in God rather than objective reality. I did not know there were eight men with 3,000 rounds and semi-automatic rifles out there intent on killing George.'

The 'shooting war' – as Amo described the fight – started in the front yard and pursued George into the back yard with several hundred rounds of bullets being loosed off. Only later would she discover that the raiders had held three female members of the group hostage before the firing had started. Her husband had grabbed his Uzi and called for help from a fellow member, Don Williams, who happened to be working in a storehouse nearby. He was an expert shot and had received paramilitary training.

'According to Don, as soon as he came out and joined George, several men dressed in combat fatigues stepped out from behind a house and yelled at George, then began to shoot at him. They ran for cover. Don was slender and athletic and apparently being shot at inspired him. He took shelter behind a farm implement in the Roden house back yard. Don had only six bullets in his .357. He kept his head down as some of the bullets bounced off the farm implement that sheltered him. George got behind a wide tree that stood on the west end of a storage shed, about forty feet from Don. That's where they held out until the sheriff's deputies we'd called arrived.'

A line of four cars arrived in a dust cloud down the driveway. When Amo Roden next looked, eight men in camouflage suits were laying on their stomachs on the ground with lawmen standing over them. She completed her account of the afternoon in these words:

166

'George was standing next to my car holding a compress against his chest. There was blood and a gaping hole in his T-shirt. "It's not serious," he told me as the deputy sheriff's cars started pulling out. The first one went past me as I stood close to the driver's side of the car. A handsome long-haired hippy sat behind the driver. I didn't recognize him, but I had just had my first look at Vernon Howell, aka David Koresh.'

It may have been Amo Robin's first glance of the man who had led the attack on the Mount Carmel Center – but it would not be the last. For this was the man who would soon not only usurp her husband's leadership, but also bring infamy on the Branch Davidians.

* * *

The life story of Vernon Wayne Howell, who ultimately became the cult leader David Koresh is one of singular unhappiness. He was born on 17 August 1959 to a fifteen-year-old single mother in Huston, Texas. Vernon never knew his father and when his mother later remarried his stepfather regularly abused him. His childhood was spent largely alone or being teased by other children at school who nicknamed him, 'Vernie'.

By his own account, Vernon tried his best at school and it was not until he was an adolescent that he was diagnosed with dyslexia. He dropped out of high school and by the age of eighteen was making a living as a carpenter. Despite his handicap, though, he would later be remembered as intelligent, mechanically adept, a capable guitarist and the possessor of an immense store of memorized passages of scripture.

Vernon found religion at his mother's church, the Seventh Day Adventists, where he was inspired by the apocalyptic message of church-sponsored 'Revelation Seminars' that featured dramatic images of Armageddon. He was intrigued by discussions about imminent 'End Times' such as the millennium, which in the New Testament Book of Revelation is said to be mystically revealed by the 'Seven Seals'. Howell became increasingly convinced that these seals were waiting to be opened by a new messiah.

The young zealot soon began to fall out with the church elders when he started challenging them on just such points of scripture.

At the same time, he apparently became involved with a fifteen-year-old girl. When she fell pregnant, just as his mother had done, the elders had every excuse to exclude Vernon from the church. The girl's father forbade marriage and Howell was expelled from the Seventh Day Adventists for being 'a bad influence' on other young people.

Just turned twenty-two, the tall, good-looking young man with his blond hair and hippy clothes moved to Waco. He had read about the breakaway group, the Branch Davidians, who seemed to share many of his views. In the spring of 1981 he found a ready welcome at the Mount Carmel Center. He caught the eye of the ageing prophetess, Lois Roden, who became his mentor and, not long afterwards, his lover.

The couple's trips abroad antagonized other members of the cult – in particular George Roden, who managed to get the better of Howell until the gunfight in October. Part of the reason for the success of this manoeuvre was Vernon's carefully planning. During the previous two months, Sam and Danny Jones, the sons of one of his closest supporters, Perry Jones, had infiltrated the Center as potential cultists and discovered where everyone lived and worked in the community.

The Jones boys had also learned about Don Williams's firearms skills and warned Howell and his handpicked group of seven men to beware of the ex-paramilitary. All of Vernon's supporters had been amused to hear themselves described as 'terrorists'.

Following the shoot-out and the arrest of the eight men by the sheriff's deputies, Perry Jones – who had not taken part in the attack – drove up to the Mount Carmel Center in a station wagon. He told Amo Roden to be in no doubt about their intentions. 'We've come to take the property over,' he smirked, ' but don't worry, you can still stay here.'

Vernon Howell and his seven accomplices were charged with attempted murder. The subsequent trial at the McLennan County Court gave local people their first real insight into life in the Mount Carmel Center – with perhaps a hint of the troubled days that lay ahead. During the hearing, Vernon demonstrated his formidable powers of argument by portraying George Roden as an evil man who would not allow debate about the scriptures in his closed community. He accused the leader of 'corpse abuse' and said that he and the others had gone to the community to find evidence that Roden had dug up a dead body.

Howell maintained that he had come armed to the Center because Roden had 'expelled me from Carmel at gunpoint'. He said he and his followers had no intention of trying to kill anyone – certainly not Roden – and had aimed all their shots at buildings or trees. Any injury the leader had suffered had been caused by his own panic when faced by the wrath of those he had wronged, Vernon concluded.

The jury wrestled with the evidence for some hours, but could not reach a unanimous agreement about Howell's guilt. The judge declared the case a mistrial and set Howell free. His seven followers were acquitted, too.

The events undoubtedly broke the spirit of the already erratic George Roden. Two years later, in an unrelated murder case, he was committed to a mental institution. He had apparently been involved in the killing of a former Branch Davidian and was found 'innocent by reason of insanity'.

As the decade ended, the ambitious Vernon Howell made his move to take control of the cult. He raised the money that was needed to pay off taxes owing on the Mount Carmel Center and took over the leadership. In 1990 he renamed the community 'Ranch Apocalypse' and announced he had changed his name to 'David Koresh'. He was now head of the biblical house of David from which Christian and Jewish tradition had long claimed the Messiah would come.

In a statement addressed to his followers, the former Vernon Howell explained that Koresh was an adaptation of the Hebrew name of Cyrus – the Persian king who had allowed the Jews dispersed by Nebuchadnezzar throughout Babylonia to return to their homelands. He said both Cyrus and King David were known as the 'anointed one' and he had chosen his names because he believed *he* was the Messiah. This conviction had come from a vision he had received from God in 1985 during his visit to Israel. The new David Koresh said his mission was to reunify Islam, Judaism and Christianity. Theologian Thomas Robbins has explained Koresh's philosophy in his *Encyclopaedia of Religion and Society* (2004):

'In his dualistic, mid-tribulationist vision, evil was concentrated in the "Babylonians," who he identified with the US government. An arsenal was established to defend the settlement as an inevitable war with the Babylonians was seen as necessary for the advent of God's Kingdom. This arsenal was in a constant state of expansion.'

Rumours at the time suggested that Koresh had spent almost $200,000 buying guns, gun parts and other components, 'enough to build a fearsome arsenal'. Furthermore, he was believed to be breaking firearm laws by converting ordinary guns into machine guns.

The evidence suggests that stockpiling weaponry was not all that Koresh was doing behind the doors of the community in Waco. According to Jerry Schwarzt, an Associated Press reporter who made a special study of the Branch Davidians, the handsome young leader was also advocating polygamy and 'collecting' females from among his cult following:

'It is widely known that Koresh had wives as young as fourteen and had sex with others even younger. He had appropriated the wives of all the Davidian men. His children, he claimed, would rule the world. There were allegations of child abuse at Mount Carmel and that Koresh was depraved in other ways. It was also alleged that he was running an methamphetamine laboratory.'

To those who lived around the small community there seemed little doubt that the 'weirdoes' did believe the end of the world was near. In government circles, however, the threat seemed to be more localized and personal.

*　*　*

The facts about the 'Siege of Waco' on 19 April 1993 are disputed and often contradictory. What *is* certain is that 90 deaths occurred in and around the 77-acre spread as a result of an inferno – which both David Koresh and the American government have been charged with causing. Thomas Robbins suggests the events began by accident:

'The arsenal [in the Carmel Center] was expanded in response to the coincidental manoeuvres of a local SWAT team in 1992. This expansion brought Koresh and some followers to the

170

attention of the Bureau of Alcohol, Tobacco and Firearms (BATF). Koresh was also being investigated by Texas Child Protection Officers for possible child molestation and statutory rape while "spreading the seed of the Messiah".'

At 9.48 am on 28 February 1993, a team of some seventy-six agents of the BATF – some in helicopters – arrived to execute what was termed a 'dynamic entry' into Ranch Apocalypse. They possessed search and arrest warrants and were armed. Agent Roland Ballesteros approached the front door and shouted, 'Police! Lay down.' A silence fell over the compound that suggested their visit was not unexpected. Indeed, the man who had attacked the compound with his seven followers six years earlier knew the tables had been turned and *he* was to be on the receiving end. The gunfight which followed that morning was, though, far more accurate – and deadly.

Even earlier that morning – it was to transpire later – a television cameraman, James Peeler, had met a postman on the outskirts of Waco and asked for directions to the Mount Carmel Center. Peeler then told the man, 'You'd better get out of here because they're [the BATF] going to have a big shootout with the religious nuts.' The cameraman would learn that the man he had spoken to was actually a Branch Davidian, David Jones, the brother-in-law of David Koresh.

Tipped off, the cultists knew who was at the door. The ensuing 45-minute gun battle wrought havoc on both sides and resulted in a greater death toll than had ever been seen in an old Wild West gunfight in the state. Four agents, Todd McKeehan, Conway LeBleu, Robert Williams and Steve Willis were killed and twenty-eight members of the force injured. Six Branch Davidians died, and an unknown number of cult members, including David Koresh himself, were injured.

Then began a standoff with both sides claiming the other had started the shooting. In a later BATF report, agent Jim Cavanaugh would claim that the cultists fired first. 'They were throwing everything at us – their guns sounded like cannons and our guns sounded like pop guns.'

In a telephone conversation, David Koresh denied this allegation and maintained that at least two cultists made emergency 911 calls to the police stating there were women and children in the compound. 'I don't care who they are,' he said. 'Nobody is going to come into my home, with my babies around, shaking guns around, without a gun back in their face. That's just the American way.'

No sooner had the dust settled around the compound, though, than the FBI took command of the operation. Contact was established with the wounded David Koresh who had installed himself in the church. His injury caused by a gunshot would get worse as the days passed and negotiations went on daily to try to bring the siege to an end. A group of hostage negotiators were flown in to make a deal with Koresh while the elite hostage rescue team searched for ways to break the siege.

During this period, two religious scholars, Phillip Arnold and James Tabor, spoke to Koresh on a number of occasions and suggested a 'reinterpretation of the Seven Seals scenario that would postpone the final apocalypse'. All the while, bright lights and noise were being focused on the compound, according to Dick Reavis in *The Ashes of Waco: An Investigation* (1995):

'The rescue team hit them with the squeal of rabbits being slaughtered, the high-pitched tone of a phone off the hook, dentist's drills, helicopters. They turned off the Davidians' electricity and refused to deliver milk for the children. Some argue that these may not have been the best tactics to use against a group programmed to embrace the apocalypse.'

In the first week of the siege, FBI records indicate that twenty-three Davidians left the compound. But the constant arguments between Koresh and those outside convinced many of the others that the agency could not be trusted. The cult leader is said to have spent hours talking his 'Bible babble' to the negotiators. He would 'promise to end the siege on one day and then claim the next that God had made him change his mind'. To convince the FBI he was holding no one against their will, a two-hour video tape was passed out from the ranch showing a number of adults and children explaining why they wished to stay.

The 'hostage crisis' – as it was now being termed – gave rise to yet another surprise when Koresh announced that he would surrender *if* he were allowed to finish writing his magnum opus, *Commentary Upon the Book of Revelation*. A copy of this work dated 2 March 1993, which has survived, gives an indication of the state of the mind of the man in its opening paragraph:

'My name is Dave Koresh. I'm speaking to you from Mount Carmel Center. What we're trying to present today may in somewhat shed a better light in regards to my situation and my predicament here at Mount Carmel. One point I'd like to bring out before we continue is that if we look at Matthew, Mark, Luke and John we see the "burden of these ancient writers": the burden of heart, the burden of mind and spirit, to put in a scriptural record their personal experience with Christ. A record that is to be received by men, all men...'

Koresh's rambling diatribe continued with his reasons 'To Show What Must Come' and how The Book of Revelation' Seven Seals pointed the way to the ultimate fate of mankind. News of this work seems to have been the last straw for the government agencies camped around the ranch. To some of the negotiators it looked to be yet another of Koresh's ploys to buy more time and a number of the FBI officers were now convinced the cult leader would never surrender.

The decision to end the siege by force was finally taken by the US Attorney General, Janet Reno, on the recommendations of the FBI. The assault was scheduled to start at dawn on 19 April. The world's media who had been in weary attendance for weeks suddenly roused themselves to record the mayhem and confusion that followed when army tanks and FBI officers blasted their way into the community buildings. A BBC report summarizes the day with typical precision:

'At least 70 people are feared to have died in a fire at the besieged headquarters of the Branch Davidian sect near Waco, Texas. The White House said those inside had started the blaze deliberately after the FBI began a dawn assault. Tear gas canisters and stun grenades were fired into the cult's compound and an armoured vehicle moved in to demolish the walls. Three hours later they broke down the main entrance.'

According to the BBC, by the time firefighters arrived the fire – which started at around 1200 local time – had taken a firm hold on the wooden buildings inside the compound. Among those inside with the cultists were believed to be a number of children. The fire worsened when the cult's store of munitions exploded.

Eight cult members were believed to have escaped – but Koresh was not among them.

The media that covered the holocaust were soon asking questions – particularly why the FBI had used 'such heavy handed tactics' and why several of the members, including David Koresh, were found to have died of gunshot wounds. The outbreak of the fire was of particular interest to everyone – so much so, that a special inquiry, the Danforth Report, was commissioned.

When made public, the report agreed with the initial statement that the fire had been deliberately caused by some of the cultists in the church. And commenting on the death of the seventy-six Branch Davidians – including seventeen children less than twelve years of age – who had died in the barricaded building, the report said they had been 'unable or unwilling to flee'. It added that Steve Schneider, who was David Koresh's right-hand man, had probably shot the leader and killed himself. The twenty adults who had died of gunshot wounds had also shot themselves, after first shooting their children.

However, this evidence did not satisfy a lot of people, including filmmaker Michael McNulty who compiled a documentary, *Waco: Rules of Engagement,* in 1997. In this he claimed that the fire was deliberately started when two military pyrotechnic devices were fired into the building after it had been saturated with spilled kerosene and CS gas. The gas – it was stated – is highly flammable, burns the eyes and skin and gives off deadly cyanide. The programme also presented evidence that FBI marksmen had fired on and killed a number of the Branch Davidians while they were attempting to flee the blaze. Thomas Robbins has added an interesting speculation to this particular element of the argument:

'It is quite possible that Koresh and his followers, interpreting the FBI actions as the final murderous assault of the "Babylonians", chose to die in a purifying fire or mass suicide, but this has not been clearly established.'

After the siege had been lifted and the burning buildings finally extinguished, 'Ranch Apocalypse' was razed to the ground – in an attempt to remove any evidence that might incriminate the BATF or FBI, according to the conspiracy theorists. These same sources have pointed to the fact that just weeks after the bodies of those who had died in the conflagration had been given autopsies, the refrigeration system in the local morgue failed. Within a matter of hours the corpses had liquefied beyond recognition or examination.

A year after the 'fiery apocalypse' which David Koresh had promised his followers, the eleven surviving Branch Davidians were put on trial in Waco. The jury cleared all of them of murder relating to the deaths of the four BATF agents. Five were, though, convicted on the lesser charge of voluntary manslaughter.

The remains of the unmourned David Koresh were buried in the Memorial Park Cemetery at Tyler in Texas. In a footnote to his life, it is said that the leader promised his followers before he died that he would 'rise again after death'.

The initial date for this resurrection was apparently based on a verse in Daniel, Chapter 12, Verse 12, indicating 1,335 days after death. When he failed to materialize, a date from the 'Seven Seals' was picked on, suggesting 6 August 1999. Once again, nothing happened. As I write, the man once called 'Vernie' Howell who believed he was the new messiah and witnessed the destruction of his cult at 'Ranch Apocalypse', is once again being confidently expected . . . in March 2012.

The Promised Land

The Quebec police officers had witnessed some horrific sights during their careers, but nothing quite like the two charred bodies and pathetic little bundle that confronted them in one of the region's most delightful locations in the winter of 1994. The two men had seen the carnage resulting from multiple car crashes, been on the spot to see the results of gruesome suicides and investigated some truly brutal murders. The chalet complex that they entered on the morning of 4 October 1994 was usually the haunt of wealthy Canadian ski enthusiasts indulging their passion for winter sports. Now, though, one of the condominiums was the scene of a bizarre death ritual carried by a cult whose origins, doctrines and even the people who belonged to it, was surrounded by mystery and rumour.

The complex of chalets known as Morin Heights was one of the most popular winter resorts in the French-speaking province of Quebec. With its well-equipped bungalows, comfortable facilities and indoor swimming pool, it had plenty to offer visitors in terms of spectacular views, bracing air and general sense of well-being, far removed from the pressures of everyday life. Normally, the area did not attract much publicity, but in recent months rumours had started to spread about a strange cult that had bought one of the complexes and was using it as their headquarters.

However, there were no such thoughts in the minds of the two officers as they drove up the mountainside to the condominium. A fire had been reported in the facility and the local fire brigade who attended the blaze had urgently summoned the lawmen from Quebec City. What the firemen had discovered after putting out the fire pointed to this being anything but a routine incident. There were five bodies, one so small as to obviously be a child.

But they had certainly not died of asphyxiation. To the firemen – also used to dealing with death in many forms – it seemed as if the child and two of the adults found in one room could have been murdered; while the other two bodies might possibly be the outcome of a suicide pact.

The two policemen knew by the urgency of the call that it was important to view the crime scene as quickly as possible. The water hosed onto the condominium would soon obliterate vital clues and where anything untoward had occurred it was necessary to establish the facts about the victims before anything was moved. As soon as the officers saw the bodies they immediately realized why even the hardened fire fighters were glad that someone else was going to have to deal with the awful tragedy.

The two charred bodies lying close together appeared like an elderly man and woman. There were no immediate signs of any attempt to escape from the fire, which the officers would have expected. But who were they and what were they doing in Morin Heights? They might have been renting the chalet, but why had they not fled at the first sign of the blaze?

In an adjoining walk-in closet the mystery – and the horror – deepened with the discovery of two more adult bodies. Alongside them was a small plastic bag that at first glance appeared innocuous enough. When the two policemen began to carefully examine the bodies they found a far greater mystery unravelling. One was that of a man who had been stabbed at least fifty times. The other was of a woman who had also been stabbed, but in a far more precise way. There were eight stab wounds to her back, four in the throat and one in each breast.

As they were absorbing these facts, one of the officers looked closer at the black plastic bag. He could just make out the outline of a little body. There was a child inside. As he peeled back the plastic, he found himself, for all his experience, almost overcome with nausea. The child, a boy only a few months old, had also been stabbed six times. The murder weapon lay across the infant's chest.

A tiny wooden stake.

Both men were to say later that for an instant they felt as if they had walked onto the set of a horror film. It was just too incred-ible, too outlandish, to be true. The baby appeared to have been sacrificed in the kind of ritual that most people believed had disappeared in the Middle Ages and only to be found now in B-movie gore fests. Suddenly, on that October morning on Morin Heights, there were more questions than answers. A lot more.

A closer examination revealed that the bodies of the little family – if such they were – had been dead for several days. Certainly well before the fire started. Could the two corpses in the other room have been responsible before their deaths? And what had possessed them to kill in such a barbaric way, using a wooden stake on an infant? Wasn't that the way vampires were killed? one of the officers asked his colleague with a shudder. But however the deaths had occurred, *who* had set the condominium on fire?

Checking the registrations at Morin Heights provided some answers. A family named Dutoit had rented the chalet: Tony, his wife, Nicky, and their three-month-old son, Christopher-Emmanuel. The owners of the building were listed as Joseph Di Mambro and Luc Jouret and but for the fact one of the two other bodies was female, these facts might have provided a simple identification. So who were the old couple and what, if any, was the connection between the five extraordinary deaths in the smoking chalet?

The answer to all these questions would heighten the mystery still further before exposing an evil cult, the *Ordre du Temple Solaire (OTS)* – Order of the Solar Temple – founded by Di Mambro and Jouret, who were obsessed with the approaching millennium – and what they and their follows then believed to be the inevitable apocalypse.

* * *

The story of the two founders of the OTS – which is sometimes referred to as the Solar Temple – is not dissimilar to that of many of the other cult leaders in this book: a mixture of occultism, opportunism and dictatorial methods. Both men had become absorbed in the history of the Knights Templar, whose notoriety has been made an even greater focus of attention since the publication of Dan Brown's global bestseller, *The Da Vince Code*. Neither Di Mambro nor Jouret, however, would to live to see the millennium they so feared.

178

Joseph Di Mambro, who was born in 1926 at Pont Saint-Esprit in France, already had a reputation as 'a confidence trickster who made a successful career out of masquerading as a psychologist' before setting up the *Ordre du Temple Solaire.* He apparently trained to become a clock-maker and jeweller, but grew increasingly fascinating with esoteric religions. In 1972 he was arrested and charged with fraud, breach of confidence and passing dud cheques. Undeterred, the dapper little man with his engaging smile and persuasive voice crossed the border and founded the 'Centre for the Preparation for the New Age', which he liked to refer to as the 'School of Life'. Here, Di Mambro encouraged his students to hand over all their worldly goods so as to 'achieve a state of perfect meditation'.

Four years later, Di Mambro had made enough money to move his 'School for Life' into a fifteen-room mansion – also drawing the attention of the French tax authorities to his activities. Next he decided to head for fresh pastures across the Atlantic in Canada. According to a subsequent investigation of the sect by the *Sunday Times,* at some point between 1979 and 1981, he met Luc Jouret and the two men set out on their mystic journey that would ultimately lead seventy-four 'followers' to a series of bizarre mass suicide rituals.

Jouret was born in 1947 in the Belgian Congo and studied medicine at the *University Libre* in Brussels, where he graduated in 1974. He apparently quickly became disillusioned with modern medicine and spent several years travelling around the world seeking out and practising various forms of alternative healing, especially homeopathy. The *New York Times,* which also investigated the cult, takes up the story:

'In his spiritual search, Jouret drifted in and out of a veritable solar system of ancient wisdom sects – among them Solar Tradition, Templar Renewed Order, International Arcadian Club of Science and Tradition. He operated at different levels, forming the Amenta Club to serve as host to his paid lectures on topics like "Medicine and Conscience" (which he later published as a book) and "Love and Biology". Those won over by his message might then be introduced to a set of beliefs, rituals and a hierarchy by joining the Arcadia Club. Finally, a select few of those recruited into the Arcadia Club would be recruited into the secretive Order of the Solar Temple and to join they had to contribute money and accept severe discipline.'

To the two men, the Knights Templar had seemed a perfect tradition on which to build their concept of a new age cult. The ancient order of warrior monks had been set up in Jerusalem under the aegis of the Pope during the Crusades and amassed great wealth and treasures – said to include the Holy Grail, the Head of Baphomet and proof of the survival of Jesus and his subsequent marriage to Mary Magdalene. However, all of these treasures had disappeared after the leaders were branded as heretics by the Catholic Church and burned at the stake. – generating a relentless pursuit by historians, treasure hunters and neo-Templar groups ever after.

Di Mambro and Jouret knew that these groups claimed to have a connection with the original – either actual or esoteric – and claimed they knew where the fabled Templar treasures were hidden. They also realised that by forming various organizations over which they exercised authoritarian control, it would be possible to recruit followers into distinct and secretive levels of initiation – depending on the education, devotion and, not surprisingly, the wealth they were able to contribute.

It is now generally agreed that Jouret and Di Mambro founded the *Ordre du Temple Solaire* in Geneva in 1984 with the imposing title of the International Chivalric Organization of the Solar Temple, soon after shorted to OTS.The older man was already deeply involved with two other esoteric groups, the Ancient and Mystical Order Rosae Crucis, a Rosicrucian organization, and the Foundation Golden Way, a Neo-Templar sect, whose members were adroitly incorporated into the OTS. The pair also convinced their followers they both had been members of the fourteenth-century Christian Order of the Knights Templar during a previous existence.

Establishing precisely *what* the beliefs of the Jouret/Di Mabro cult were is not easy, as very few documents from the period still exist. However, I have seen a copy of a book, *Pourquoi la Resurgence de l'Ordre de Temple?* (Why A Templar Revival?) written under the pseudonym 'Peronnik' – who was actually one of the hierarchy, Robert Chabrier – published in 1975, that provides a few clues. The author declares that the organization has four primary aims. The first of these is a rallying call to 'correct notions of authority and power in the world'. Secondly, to affirm the primacy of the spiritual over the temporal. Thirdly, and rather less specific, to assist mankind through a great 'transition'. And, lastly, to 'Prepare for the Second Coming of Jesus Christ as a solar god-king to unify all races and religions'.

This same work reveals that the OTS had its headquarters in Zurich, Switzerland, and was run by the 'Synarchy of the Temple', a group of thirty-three members whose names were kept strictly secret. Each was identified as an 'Elder Brother of the Rosy Cross' – reaffirming the cult's links with the Rosicrucians – and permitted to conduct the cult's activities which mixed Christianity, new age philosophy, homeopathic medicine and a number of rituals evidently adapted by the founders from freemasonry. There was great emphasis, too, on reincarnation.

The Order established a number of lodges – allegedly in Canada, Australia, Switzerland, Martinique and a handful of other countries – each of which was run by a regional commander and three elders. To rise in the hierarchy of the OTS it was necessary to attain different levels and grades: three levels per grade. These in ascending order were 'the Brothers of Parvis', 'the Knights of the Alliance' and 'Brothers of the Ancient Times'.

Each lodge had its own altar and rituals as well as a number of exotic costumes, which explains why Jouret and Di Mambro were eager to recruit their followers from wealthy and influential backgrounds. Initiation ceremonies for each stage of advancement involved providing expensive jewellery, regalia and a 'sizable' fee. During the rituals, the members wore robes modelled on the dress of the Crusaders. At the most senior appointments, a huge sword was placed on the altar which Joseph Di Mambro claimed was, 'an authentic Templar sword that had been given to him a thousand years ago in a previous life'.

The influence of the two founders was evident in every development of the OTS, with Jouret devoting a lot of his time to recruiting affluent Europeans during his lecture tours. Rumours persist that a number of well-known people belonged to the cult, which at its peak claimed over 600 members, including several Swiss bankers, a number of Canadian politicians and businessmen, and even a leading international orchestra conductor.

The promise of a life after death was central to the message of the OTS. Followers were told that after death, they would be led to a planet near the star of Sirius. Here they would enjoy everlasting life free of the pain and suffering that troubled earthly existence – especially with the shadow of the apocalypse growing ever larger. They must also show the greatest reverence to the sun as it controlled the destiny of the world.

According to the *Montreal Gazette,* one of the major sources of contemporary information on the cult, Di Mambro and Jouret moved to Quebec and had amassed enough money to purchase the chalet complex at Morin Heights to serve as headquarters. They also bought a centre at Sainte-Ane-de-la-Perade in Quebec and had this equipped for a number of Jouret's most loyal followers brought over from Switzerland. The *Gazette* explains:

'He told them this new establishment was the Promised Land. They believed that a global catastrophe was imminent and Jouret told his followers, "The world will soon be engulfed in warfare and famine. Only Quebec will be spared".'

Jouret had also been busy raising funds from supporters to ensure them some protection if either war or pestilence arrived before their plans for going to Sirius were complete. Under conditions of some secrecy he had a giant concrete nuclear air-raid shelter built beneath the centre at Sainte-Ane-de-la-Perade. His colleague Di Mambro kept himself busy using the cult's money to purchase luxury properties, ostensibly for the use of OTS activities. He also married a local woman, Dominique Bellaton, and when she became pregnant, used the forthcoming birth to strengthen his grip on the group. The arrival of a daughter, Emmanuelle, was reported to the faithful as a 'virgin birth'. The 'cosmic child' had special powers to lead them all to a planet that revolved around the star Sirius.

As the last decade of the twentieth century dawned, however, and the countdown to the millennium began, it seemed to some members of the OTS that the journey to Sirius might be closer at hand than they had imagined. As it transpired, for over seventy their journey was to be *much* nearer indeed.

* * *

By 1990, it seems, some of the gloss on the claims of Di Mambro and Jouret was wearing thin with a section of their more sceptical followers. There seemed to be too much money being lavished on the founders, coupled with demands for obedience and increasingly erratic instructions that seemed to have little bearing on the dogma and beliefs of the OTS. Canadian journalist, Ross Laver, who made a detailed study of the Order of the Solar Temple for *MacLean's Magazine,* wrote in October 1994:

'Some of Jouret's own colleagues in the order were now starting to question his stability. They complained that his doomsday predictions about the end of the world were becoming too specific and they resented the hold he appeared to have over some of his followers.'

There was a momentary lapse in complaints when Jouret announced at an advancement ritual in Saint Ane-de-la-Perade that he had been negotiating with executives of Quebec's Hydro-Quebec to build a dam that would provide electricity for the colony that would enable them to survive after the doomsday event. But no sooner had he revealed this plan, than he was arrested and taken to the Quebec police station.

It seemed that Jouret had been illegally stockpiling firearms in the centre of Quebec. The weapons were confiscated and, after giving certain assurances, he was allowed to return to 'the promised land' – complaining about police harassment and insisting that the firearms had been bought to protect the members of the cult in case of emergency.

However, neither of these stories seem to have satisfied a group of OTS followers who promptly left the group – the first men and women to have departed since the cult was formed. But the writing was already on the wall, as Ross Laver reports in his article:

'Jouret's behaviour became ever more eccentric. He started to abuse his power and the hold he had over the cult. "Money and sex, that's all Luc Jouret was interested in," a former member related. "Before every ritual he would have sex with one of the women to give him spiritual strength for the ceremony. He wasn't married, but he had many wives – he changed women all the time."'

A personality change was also becoming increasingly evident

in Joseph Di Mambro, according to another account of the OTS by *Sunday Times* investigative journalist, Russell Miller, in January 1995. Talking to several former members, Miller learned that the co-founder had become more dictatorial:

'Whatever he told his followers to believe, they believed. Whatever he told them to do, they did. Nothing was too outlandish or degrading: if he instructed a female *chevalier* to perform a sex act, she obeyed without question. He had no hesitation in interfering in relationships and breaking up marriages if he decided the couple were not "cosmically compatible".'

Inexorably, though, dissent and turmoil were threatening the stability of the OTS and the position of the joint leaders. Whispers turned to anger and – it has since transpired – one man began to speak out. His name was Tony Dutoit, an electronics expert, who had devoted several years of his life and most of his earnings to the cult in the hope of a better life for himself and his wife, Nicky. The *Montreal Gazette* was the first to uncover Dutoit's disaffection with the order. Initially, few had been more dedicated to the cause than him, the newspaper reported, and on a number of occasions he had used his technical skills to further the cause:

'He installed electronic and mechanical gadgets in the cult's inner sanctuaries to project images that tricked members into believing they were seeing spiritual beings conjured up by Luc Jouret. Tony told some other cult members about these devices and a few of them decided to leave the sect. But when Tony discovered that Joseph Di Mambro was appropriating cult funds for his own use he was deeply shocked.'

By the time Dutoit, his wife and their three-month-old son, Christopher-Emmanuel, were settled in one of the chalets at Morin Heights in September 1994, the die was cast for the OTS and the fate of its members sealed. The little family had become the focus of Di Mambro's anger as he saw his authority and his cult threatened not from outside – which he was used to – but from *inside* and by one of his most trusted lieutenants.

The facts fitted the conspiracy theory Di Mambro had nursed for years. He believed that the Antichrist as described in the Bible would be born into the cult one day and prevent him from achieving his spiritual aims. The Dutoit baby was obviously this Antichrist and must be destroyed.

In the last week of September 1994, Joseph Di Mambro dispatched a pair of his trusted 'knights' to kill the Dutoit family. It was especially important that there should be no doubt the baby perished. It had to be stabbed with a wooden stake. Russell Miller, who pieced together the case against the cult leader, wrote later:

'Not content with relying upon the OTS practise of casting spells and hexes against their enemies, Di Mambro selected two members of the "golden circle" to carry out the ritual murder, one of whom travelled all the way from Switzerland for the assault. Tony Dutoit was stabbed 50 times. Nicky Dutoit was stabbed eight times in the back and four times in the throat – where the OTS believed conception occurred – and once in each breast. Their infant son, Emmanuel, was stabbed six times.'

After the two assassins left, two other devout OTS members came to make final arrangements at the crime scene. They wrapped the infant in a plastic bag and left a wooden stake on his chest before meticulously preparing for their own suicide and the incineration of all the bodies. Meanwhile, the assassins made their way back to Switzerland to rejoin their comrades and the two leaders who had left Quebec some months previously under increasing scrutiny.

These facts match the discovery made by the two policemen on the morning of 4 October. A pathologist's examination established the Dutoits had been dead for about four days – making 30 September the fatal date – while the other two charred bodies, one a 69-year-old man and the other a woman probably older, had been set on fire only a short while before the blaze at Morin Heights was reported. There seemed little doubt that the aged couple were members of the Order of the Solar Temple still dedicated enough to their leader to make his orders their last act on earth.

As the sun went down over the scene of sacrilege at the ski resort, warrants were issued for the arrest of Joseph Di Mambro and Luc Jouret. Before it rose again another even more terrible firestorm had broken out 3,500 miles away across the Atlantic – and the last chapter in the story of *Ordre du Temple Solaire* was about to be written.

* * *

Two picturesque little Alpine villages in the heart of Switzerland were the setting for a day of carnage unparalled in the nation's history on 5 October 1994. In one, a small family chalet, 22 bodies were incinerated in a mass suicide in the basement; while in the other, a farmhouse, twenty-five more died by their own volition, including the two men the Quebec police were so anxious to interview.

Initially, the fire at the chalet looked like a typical house fire to the Swiss fireman summonsed by a neighbour who had spotted smoke leaking out from around the front door and window frames – with a hint of flames at a lower level. The fire fighters had no idea a scene from purgatory awaited them inside, as a report from the *Sunday Times* later revealed:

'The firemen forced their way into what they thought was a basement garage. They found themselves in a mirrored chapel draped with a crimson fabric and with a Christ-like painting on one wall. On the floor, arranged in a sun-shaped circle with their feet together pointing inwards, heads outward, were twenty-two bodies: nine men, twelve women and a twelve-year-old boy. Some of the dead were wearing the coloured ceremonial robes of the Order of the Solar Temple. Nineteen of them had been shot in the head; nine were hooded with black plastic bags.'

The firemen were still in a state of shock – as their compatriots had been at Morlin Heights the previous day – when police investigators arrived to take over the inquiry in the still smouldering building. The horror did not end with the removal of the bodies from what had clearly been a secret underground chamber full of items of Templar significance, either. There was unmistakable evidence that the whole chalet had been booby-trapped to go up in flames. Nothing had been left to chance that anyone inside might survive.

The national and international media had barely time to digest this information and confirm the link to the DiMabro and Jouret cult than another building was set on fire that same day. This time it was a farmhouse that the organization had purchased some months earlier. When the alarm was raised, the firemen who broke in found no fewer than twenty-five bodies, five of which were children and one was just four years old. Yet again the bodies were laid out in a star-shaped pattern at the head of which lay the unmistakable figures of Luc Jouret, Joseph Di Mambro, his wife and their twelve-year-old 'cosmic child', Emmanuelle.'

Evidence found at the scene of the cult leaders' immolation suggested that Di Mambro had earlier performed a ritual 'Last Supper' with twelve of his closest followers. The accoutrements also suggested that the group believed they were about to make the journey to Sirius. The plastic bags tied over each head were believed to be symbolic of the ecological disaster the cultists were convinced would strike the human race after their departure. As the bags were known to have been used in OTS rituals previously, it was considered likely they were put on voluntarily.

Among the dead at the two incidents were a mayor, a civil servant, a sales manager and a journalist – striking indication of the influence of Di Mambro and Jouet. The Quebec police also found documents at Morin Heights that revealed that a number of the more wealthy followers had donated in excess of $1 million to Joseph Di Mambro.

Other investigators of these two incidents – and the similar ones to follow – came to the conclusion that some of the victims had been drugged either intravenously or by injection before being shot, possibly to prevent them having second thoughts. The remote-controlled devices to ensure the buildings went up in flames also seemed to have been installed to ensure the members' final 'purification'. A letter written by Di Mambro and Jouret delivered after their death declared that they were, 'leaving this earth to find a new dimension of truth and absolution far from the hypocrisies of this world'.

Those who believed that the OTS would end with the deaths of the two founders had reckoned without their continuing influence beyond the grave. Just a week before Christmas 1995, the bodies of sixteen more people were found to have taken part in a ritual suicide in France. On 23 December, gendarmes were called to a remote plateau in the French Alps. Like the rituals the previous years, the bodies were lying in a star formation, their feet pointing to the ashes of a fire. As before, they had all died by stabbing, asphyxiation, shooting or poisoning. The bodies had been burned as part of the same cleansing ritual.

It emerged after the discovery, that the French and Swiss authorities had feared another mass suicide after learning that sixteen members of the *Ordre du Temple Solaire* had suddenly left home leaving hand-written messages about their intentions. One of these quoted by the Reuters News Service read: 'Death does not exist, it is pure illusion. May we, in our inner life, find each other for ever.'

The terrible story of the OTS attracted the attention of a number of experts on new age religions, several of whom made a point that the mass suicides had occurred around the dates of the equinoxes and solstices that were held in special regard by the cult. This conclusion proved fatefully true on 23 March 1997 when five more bodies were discovered in a burned house that belonged to a known member of the order, Didier Queze, of St Casimir near Quebec City. Her body and that of her husband and another couple were found in an upstairs room lying in the shape of a cross. Didier's mother was also found in the lounge with a plastic bag over her head. Once again the house had been booby-trapped.

In an extraordinary finale to this story of the cult that took the lives of seventy-four people, Didier Queze's three teenage children actually escaped their parents' fate. According to a report in the *Chicago Tribune* of 28 March, while the firemen were fighting the blaze the children emerged from a shed in the garden and told them how they had been spared.

'Apparently the teenagers woke up the day before the suicide to discover their parents and their cultist friends had placed propane tanks, electric hot plates and fire-starters on the main floor of the two-storey house and were trying to burn down the place. Realizing what was happening, they pleaded and negotiated with their parents to be spared. Fanie Queza-Goupillot, 14, and her brothers Tom, 13, and Julien, 16, agreed to take sleeping pills before their parents' fiery death and went to sleep in a workshop near the house. The children were given medication, but they knew that when they woke up their parents and grandmother would be dead.'

The Subway Killers

The morning of Monday 20 March 1995 began like most others in Tokyo although there was a certain sense of anticipation in the air because the following day was a national holiday. Not long after sunrise, the streets of the Japanese capital were throbbing with traffic while along the pavements crowds of men and women hurried to their offices and another busy working day in the massed ranks of skyscraper buildings that had created one of the most vibrant economies in the world. On the subway beneath these hurrying feet – one of the busiest in the world carrying millions of passengers daily – the trains rumbled between the stations keeping to their usual precise timetables, the men and women packed so tightly in the carriages they could barely move and all blithely unaware that soon they would be the target of a cult about to carry out an attack of domestic terrorism.

In the darkness, five men were riding the subway on different trains to perform a coordinated attack at the peak time of the morning rush hour. Their objective was to release poison gas in the packed carriages of trains as they passed under Kasumigaseki and Nagatacho, the centre of Japanese government. Each man was carrying two plastic packets of liquid sarin wrapped in newspaper: a single drop from any one capable of killing an adult. All of them had umbrellas with sharpened tips under their arms. As the trains pulled into prearranged stations, the packets were to be dropped, punctured several times and the perpetrator make their escape to meet an accomplice in a waiting car.

The plan seemed foolproof and the five men set off on their journeys full of confidence – buoyed by their fanaticism and desire to carry out their leader's instructions to the letter. They

189

were all intelligent, well-educated men prepared to sacrifice *everything* for a cause known as 'the True Teaching'.

The first man to board a train at 7.39 am was Masato Yokoyama, a 31-year-old graduate in applied physics who had worked for an electronics firm. He took the Ikebukuro-bound Marunouchi line and dropped his sarin at Yotsuya station. Fortunately for the other passengers, the anxious Yokoyama only punctured one of his packets and the train was eventually evacuated without loss of life.

The second cultist, Yasuo Hayashi, was the oldest man of the group, a 37-year-old former student of artificial intelligence and yoga enthusiast, arguably more calculating and careful than the rest. He boarded the 7.43 Naka-meguro-bound Hibiya line train and at Akihabara station punctured his sarin bags more times than any of the others. He ambled from the scene leaving eight passengers dying.

Ikuo Hayashi boarded the Yoyogi-uehara-bound Chiyoda line service at 7.48. His appearance was different: he was the only one of the conspirators to be wearing a surgical mask of the type often worn by Japanese commuters during the season of colds and influenza. The son of a doctor and a heart and artery specialist at Keio Hospital, Hayashi would prove the hardest to trace after puncturing his packages at the Shin-ochanomizu station in the central business district – causing the death of two people.

The fourth man, Toru Toyoda, got into the first car of the Tobudobutsukoen-bound train on the Hibiya line at 7.59. The 27-year-old just starting a doctoral study in applied physics pierced his sarin at Ebisu station before making his escape. One person would die here.

The last man, Kenichi Hirose, who had earned a postgraduate degree in physics at the prestigious Waseda University, was not to be so lucky as his four colleagues. He joined the westbound Marunouchi line just after 8am, bound for Ogikubo. He dropped his packets at Ochanamizu station and jabbed the sarin repeatedly with his umbrella, causing a single fatality. After making his getaway, though, Hirose developed signs of sarin poisoning and had to inject himself with the antidote, atropine sulphate. But before the end of the day, he was in need of treatment at a hospital

– and unconsciously left the first clue that would ultimately bring the five conspirators to justice.

The gas attack on that Monday morning in Tokyo was totally without precedent in history. As news of the carnage spread across the city – with ambulances rushing through the streets transporting 688 victims to hospital while almost 6,000 people sought treatment for their injuries – the shocked and frightened population waited for any news about the perpetrators of such a terrible act in the very heart of their city. The horror of what they had undergone was still being widely felt when the toll of the poison gas attacks was announced: 12 dead, 54 seriously injured and over a thousand suffering from vision problems.

It would not be long, though, before the culprits stood revealed as the Aum Shinrikyo cult, mistakenly believed at first by police to have instigated the attack as a 'way of hastening the apocalypse'. Their leader was a truly extraordinary figure, Shoko Asahara, who admired Hitler, boasted that he could levitate and said he wanted one day to be 'king of Japan'.

* * *

The term Aum Shinrikyo which translates as 'Aum the True Teaching', derives from the Hindu symbol *Aum* representing the universe and three Japanese kanji characters, *Shin* – for truth – *ri* – for justice – and *kyo* meaning faith. And it was a short, ugly, visually impaired young man named Shoko Asahara who was then living in a one-bedroom flat in Tokyo's Shibuya district who founded the cult in 1984.

Asahara had been born Chizuo Matsumoto in 1955 to a poor family living on Kyushu, one of Japan's main islands, just south of Honshu. At birth he was sightless in one eye and purblind in the other, so he was sent to a special school for the blind at Kumamoto. There he proved the old adage that among the blind, the one-eyed man is king: bullying many of his schoolfellows while championing a number of the social outcasts in his class who followed his every word. Even then, Matsumoto is said to have nurtured ideas that one day he would be a great leader. That optimism was not shared by Tokyo University, though, when he applied for admission and he was rejected.

Putting to one side his frustration, the young man made a living selling traditional Chinese medicines and began pursuing an interest in Buddhism, eagerly studying its ideals and doctrines. The more he learned, the more Chizio Matsumoto came to see himself as a man with a mission to enlighten the world, beginning in Japan. Despite his poor sight, he still managed to travel extensively and spent a time studying in the Himalayas before returning to Japan in his late twenties.

Already by this time the principles of the cult Matsumoto planned to found were forming in his head – complete with numerous idiosyncratic ideas of his own. As a first step he changed his name to Shoko Asahara and began writing the book that would present his ideas to the world, *Supreme Initiation: An Empirical Spiritual Science for the Supreme Truth*, which he would later publish worldwide in 1988.

In the book, Asahara described his doctrine as being based on various Buddhist scriptures, certain aspects of Christianity and even a sprinkling of the writings of Nostradamus. Amidst the various deities cited as being important, however, pride of place went to Lord Shiva – a variation of the well-known Hindu deity who symbolizes the power of destruction. It was the first hint that behind the writer's belief lay an anxiety about the apocalypse. He argued that the doctrine of Aum was simply to follow the path of truth, declaring:

'While various Buddhist and yogic schools lead to the same goal by different routes, the goal remains the same and all the major religions are closely related. The true religion should not only offer the path but also lead to the final destination by its own route. It may differ considerably due to the differences of those who follow it. This way, a religion for modern Japanese will be different from a religion for ancient Indians. The more custom-tailored to the audience the religion is, the more effective it becomes.'

According to Asahara, the route to this Final Realization – as he called it – 'the state where everything is achieved and there is nothing else worth achieving', involved many small enlightenments, each of which elevated the consciousness of the believer to a higher level. In this way, a man or woman would become more intelligent and a better person by getting closer to their 'true self' or *atman*.

Supreme Initiation also recommended several of the Buddhist schools, especially tantric Vajrayan – the 'diamond vehicle' – which involves meditation, secret mantras and initiation ceremonies. Asahra seized on various other traditions and translated the old traditional Buddhist terminology into modern Japanese as well as changing the meaning of certain words and phrases to suit his own purpose. The result was a doctrine that challenged the individual and used ancient history to warn of a dire future.

The cult's methodology of setting examinations for followers to attain higher levels of consciousness tapped a deep well in the Japanese psyche. Indeed, the writing and lectures being delivered by the intense young man with his misty eyes, long hair and charismatic personality were soon attracting the interest of the very people whose ranks he had once wanted to be a part of – the students at the country's top universities. Asahara thought of his organization as a 'religion for the elite' and the youngsters who had been drawn to the ideals while still in education flocked to swell its ranks after graduation.

As these numbers grew, the cult began to change into a very different organization from the original groups who had come together to hear an earnest young man talk about meditation in his apartment or on platforms in small meeting places. Now Shoko Asahara was proclaiming a way to the 'Final Realization' – the power to directly transmit spiritual energy from a teacher to a follower – and offering the world what he described as 'the Aum Salvation Plan'. In the cult itself, changes were also taking place.

Asahara's keen young followers were divided into two primary groups, probationers and *samana* or teachers: the first living at home with their families, the latter in groups leading an ascetic lifestyle. A number of 'ministries' were also set up to deal with specific aspects of the cult's doctrine. Those with qualifications in medicine were enrolled in the 'Ministry of Healing'; those with an interest in science joined the 'Ministry of Science and Technology'; and – with a covert acknowledgement that speaking these new 'truths' might not be without its risks – those from a military background or having martial arts skills would join the 'Ministry of Intelligence'. Two more rather secretive sub-groups, the 'Chemical Brigade' and the 'Automatic Light Weapon Development Scheme' were initiated soon after. There was a place for women recruits, too, said the leader: those who had any involvement with children should be part of the 'Ministry of Education'.

The cult also began to press for official recognition and in 1987 after considerable debate – and a successful legal challenge in the court – the cult was granted the status of a religious group by the Japanese government.

Ostensibly, Shoko Asahara was continuing to lead a simple and humble life, surrounded by his closest disciples. He constantly reiterated that wealth and fame were not his objective, though he did need money to take his message to more and more people. He travelled abroad again, too, and gained considerable publicity from meetings with a number of Buddhist leaders including the Dalai Lama and Kalu Rinpoche of the Tibetan Kagyupa school. His work translating Buddhist texts for an international readership was welcomed by the governments of Sri Lanka, Bhutan and India – albeit that a blind eye seemed to have been turned to some of his 'interpretations' of the ancient texts.

There were those in the media, though, who began to question the true purpose of the cult: now being described as 'the fastest growing religious group in Japan' – especially when it became known that the leader was receiving large gifts of money from grateful followers. One wealthy benefactor had apparently even provided Asahara with an armoured Mercedes to 'protect him in traffic'.

Others saw a sinister development in the pages of the increasing number of publications carrying the cult's message. Among the most curious of these were a series of comic books aimed at the young. In Japan, where the strip cartoon is regarded as an art form and the *anime* and *manga* graphic books sell by the million, this was one sure way of reaching a huge readership. In the comic books issued under the Aum Shinrikyo imprint, the cult's beliefs were cleverly interwoven in stories that mixed space missions, weapons of mass destruction and the need for conquest in order to spread the 'ultimate truth'. Robert Jay Lifton, who has studied this aspect of the cult's proselytising in his book, *Destroying the World to Save It: Aum Shinrikyo, Apocalyptic Violence and the New Global Terrorism* (1999), explains:

'One of their most extraordinary publications about ninja traced the origins of martial arts and espionage to ancient China and linked the supernatural abilities the ninja were rumoured to possess with religious spiritual practices, concluding that the true ninja was interested in preserving peace in times of military conflict. Science fiction novels by the American writer Isaac Asimov, that depicted an elite group of spiritually evolved scientists forced to go underground during an age of barbarism so as to prepare themselves for the moment when they will emerge to rebuild civilization, were referenced as basic Buddhist ideas to impress the shrewd and picky educated Japanese not attracted to boring, purely traditional sermons.'

By 1990, Asahara was so confident of his 'mission' that the cult put forward several candidates in the Japanese parliamentary elections. Despite claiming a membership of 9,000, Aum Shinrikyo failed to gain any seats although its curious message certainly registered on the population. Their existence also caught the attention of the sceptical foreign news media. The American *Time* magazine, for one, ran a piece that was less than flattering, referring to Asahara as a 'bushy, bearded figure usually pictured wearing satiny pyjamas'. The report continued:

'He admires Hitler, boasts that he can levitate and bestow superhuman powers on his disciples, Yet a look at his life reveals a rather pathetic figure at war with the world because he could not find an easy place in it. As his fortunes prospered, Asahara seems to have grown more reclusive and obsessed with danger. The religion, nominally Buddhist but really a hodgepodge of ascetic disciplines and New Age occultism, focused on supposed threats from the US, which he portrayed as a creature of Freemasons and Jews bent on destroying Japan. The conspiracy's weapons: sex and junk food. The guru's sermons predict the end of the world sometime between 1997 and 2000 and have begun citing the specific peril of poison gas-attacks.'

At the time the magazine was published, such attacks were viewed as no more than wild talk. But from 1994 onwards a series of ominous incidents in Japan would culminate in a day of almost unthinkable horror when the 'peril' of a gas attack did indeed become a reality.

*   *   *

In the early nineties, a significant shift occurred in the ideology of Aum Shinrikyo: the cult could no longer prevent an apocalypse. Shoko Asahara announced the organization would need to protect itself and prepare for the inevitable Armageddon by constructing nuclear shelters and communes where they could 'escape worldly distractions'.

This sense of isolation undoubtedly strengthened the leader's grip on his followers and their ability to think rationally. According to statements later given in court, in 1993 Asahara appointed one of his most brilliant members, Tsuchiya Masami, who had a degree in organic chemistry, to begin chemical weapons research. By the autumn of that year the cult had its own supply of sarin.

A year later, on 27 June 1994, clouds of sarin suddenly engulfed the Kita-Fukashi district of Matsumoto in central Japan. Seven people died and about 600 were injured. Initially, a local gardener was falsely accused of causing the outbreak, but suspicion was already growing in police and government circles that followers of a cult known to be living in the area might be responsible.

These suspicions were strengthened on 9 July when a serious gas leak occurred at another of the Aum Shinriko compounds and a number of cult members were reported being seen 'running in gas masks from the facility'. Trees and grass in the area suffered what was pertinently described as 'unnatural damage'. Finally, less than six months later, in January 1995, and after lot of tireless investigation, the police established a clear link between the incident and the clouds of sarin that had leaked out over Matsumoto.

Before they had completed their inquiries, however, the horrific 'Sarin Subway Incident' – as it became known in the Japanese press – occurred in Tokyo on 20 March. On that spring morning before the bank holiday, Aum Shinrikyo wrote its name indelibly into the history of evil cults. But after that events moved quickly with the detention of Shoko Asahara and 'Wanted' posters being distributed for the five members of the cult and their accomplices who had been responsible for the gas attack. They were not long in being found.

Even before these ringleaders were brought to trial, the cult lost its status as a religious organization and many of its assets were seized. An attempt by the Diet – the Japanese Parliament – to outlaw the group was rejected, though, and some followers are said to still follow Asahara's teachings today. The man himself was tried and sentenced to death along with three of the men who had released sarin in the Tokyo subway, Yasuo Hayashi, Kenichi Hirose and Toru Toyoda. The other two conspirators, Ikuo Hayashi and Masato Yokoyama, were given life imprisonment.

At the time of writing, Shoko Asahara is still awaiting execution. He is now confined to a wheelchair as lawyers continue to argue over whether he is sane enough to die by hanging. A report in September 2006 in the prominent Japanese newspaper *Sunday Mainichi* described how far the man who once dreamed of being 'king of Japan' has fallen:

'He spends his days sitting in the wheelchair, muttering and grunting. A nappy is wrapped around him and he soils himself frequently. He bursts out in meaningless laughter, or retreats into silence.'

Inferno in the Ark

Copies of the little handbook with its unequivocal yet seductive title could be seen being read in streets and homes all over Uganda as the last years of the twentieth century slipped by and the millennium grew ever closer. *A Timely Message From Heaven: The End of the Present Times* with its dramatic cover picture of a bleeding and crucified Jesus Christ offered its readers escape from their lives of poverty, uncertainty and the scourge of AIDS which was sweeping the country. In its 163 pages, the booklet promised salvation for those who joined the Movement for the Restoration of the Ten Commandments – and hell fire and damnation for eternity for those who did not.

The work, which was distributed in thousands of copies throughout the country and especially in the rural districts, was the main propaganda weapon used by the sect and its leader, Joseph Kibwetere, who had founded the organization in 1987 to recruit members to face the apocalypse – which he predicted would occur on the last day of December 1999. After the reigns of terror of the former Presidents Idi Amin and Milton Obote, the doomsday theme was one that Kibwetere knew had a natural appeal for the superstitious and oppressed population.

The text in the sixteen sections of the book was carefully worded to appeal to the poor and the abused. It made no mention, however, of the demands and punishments that would be imposed on every man, woman and child who chose to join Kibwetere's Doomsday cult. No mention they would have to hand over all their money and possessions, just a euphemistic comment that the group, 'resolves that each person should contribute'.

There was no indication, too, that cult members would be prohibited from sex, banned from conversation with nonbelievers, and women would not be allowed to wear short skirts and use cosmetics. Equally forbidden was soap and no one was allowed to read newspapers, listen to the radio or watch television. Instead, the 'faithful' would be committed to a regimen of prayers, fasting and endless hard work.

The message of the sect was clear from page one. Uganda was a country deeply afflicted and these afflictions were the handiwork of Satan. The only cure was obedience to the Ten Commandments in the Bible. According to the text, AIDS, which had been killing hundreds of thousands of Ugandans since the early 1980s, was a 'divine punishment' meted out on the population for deviant sexual practices that had 'increased the anger of Almighty God'. Beer drinking was also a contributing factor: 'All alcohol is under the control of Satan. If anyone wants to go to heaven and is drinking they should stop.'

Readers were left in no doubt that evil lurked everywhere and in the shape of many different kinds of people – from government officials to officers of the law. Herbalists, too, who many Ugandans were known to rely on for medical care in remote districts where there were no doctors, were especially to be avoided. For they were actually 'witch doctors' and consorted with the Devil.

Not only human beings were a threat in the eyes of the Movement for the Restoration of the Ten Commandments. Animals were also on the banned list: 'Cats and dogs are already possessed by the Devil. From these animals Satan is actually fighting against man, particularly those who own animals.'

As if to reassure the people of Uganda that they were not alone in the world fighting the Doomsday scenario, the *Timely Message From Heaven* stated that many other countries and their towns and cities must repent or face punishment. Among the places specified, North America was particularly admonished with a warning that, 'Heavy arms that are going to destroy five countries will be transported through your roads.'

A similarly dark picture was painted for those living on the other side of the Atlantic. The French were informed, 'Your laziness will not permit you to endure the chastisement that will be inflicted upon you until you are destroyed in lamentations.' Things looked even blacker for Londoners, claimed the text: 'Your desire for doing evil will be fulfilled.'

The contents of the booklet may have seemed like gobblede-gook to the more sophisticated readers into whose hands copies fell. Yet the mixture of homespun advice for righteous living and the threat of a terrible fate for those who did not still struck a chord with thousands across the country, who were soon being recruited into the cult. Many of these people, it seemed, were disaffected members of the Roman Catholic Church, to whom the appeal had been cleverly directed by the text. It argued that the group was actually *not* trying to set up a new faith:

'Ours is not a religion, but a movement. It endeavours to make the people aware of the fact that the Commandments of God have been abandoned. It gives what should be done for their obser-vance. Only those who obey the commandments and follow will be spared within our church which is the Ark, a ship of righteous-ness on a sea of depravity.'

In the penultimate chapter, the *Timely Message From Heaven* makes its case for being superior to the many churches and religions that have 'come and gone in Uganda as people seek answers to life questions and relief from its burdens'. Citing a striking example, the booklet said, 'In Kampala, you cannot take two steps without meeting a religion.' An additional paragraph – apparently written by Joseph Kibwetere himself for a new edition of the booklet published in 1996 – was to prove horrifically prophetic:

'The Lord told me that hurricanes of fire would rain forth from heaven and spread over those who have not have repented. This fire will also reach inside the buildings; there is no way one can escape.'

Lastly, the curious little publication provided pen portraits of the sect leaders, Joseph Kibwetere, called 'the Prophet', Credonia Mwerinde, known as 'the Programmer' and their close associate Dominic Kataribabo. Once again the publication omitted to mention some very significant facts about the trio. The first was an excommunicated bishop, the second a former prostitute and the third a fraudster and multiple murderer. Together they would ultimately be responsible for an inferno that would kill more people than had died in the Jonestown massacre.

* * *

The early life of the man who founded the Movement for the Restoration of the Ten Commandments is one of surprising piety and dedication. Joseph Kibwetere is believed to have been born near Entebbe in Uganda in 1936 to comparatively wealthy parents who were devoted Catholics. His childhood was spent in various religious pursuits at his local church and it appears that during this time he developed an interest in Catholic visionaries that would influence the rest of his life.

Kibwetere went to the university in Entebbe for three years after which he worked as an educational administrator. In 1960, he married and following the death of his parents inherited a large sum of money which he used to buy a tract of land in the small town of Kanungu in the west of Uganda. On it he built a Catholic school for local children with himself as the only teacher.

The evidence suggests that the school was completely orthodox for a number of years and its success earned Joseph Kibwetere a respected position in the local community. Then, in 1980, concerned with the increasing political and religious upheaval in the Uganda, Joseph entered politics, but soon became frustrated at his inability to change the lot of his constituents.

In 1989, it was Kibwetere's life that was changed dramatically when he visited the town of Nyamitanga to hear a lecture being given by Credonia Mwerinde, who claimed to have been receiving visions of the Virgin Mary for years. She told her audience that she first saw the Virgin while looking at a stone in the mountains. The stone was an exact image of Mary. Later she began to see visions of Mary and hearing her voice. Her message was that faith was dying and only by obeying the Bible could people hope to be saved.

Kibwetere sat entranced in the audience and after the meeting ended introduced himself to the vivacious young speaker. He invited her to return with him to Kanunga. Mwerinde, who time would reveal, was a charismatic performer and clever opportunist, did not hesitate to accept her smartly dressed admirer's invitation.

Once settled in Kanungu, Credonia is believed to have soon begun exerting an influence over her patron, convincing him that orthodox Catholicism was no answer to the country's problems. When she 'produced a vision of Our Lady for Kibwetere in the

201

winter of that same year', it is said he felt his life change for ever.

During the course of making their plans for a movement to bring the people back to the Ten Commandments, Kibwetere learned the truth about his beguiling houseguest and her history of seeing visions. Born in 1952 in the village of Ngakishenyi, Credonia had received little education and had only been in her mid-teens when she set up a shop with a common-law husband to sell banana beer and fiery local liquor, Promiscuous by nature, she also used her charms as a prostitute when times were hard.

It was on 24 August 1988, Mwerinde told Joseph Kibwetere that she had first seen a vision of the Virgin Mary in a cave near her village. This had seemed to her like history repeating itself, as back in 1960 her father had had a vision of her dead older sister, Evangelista. Credonia said she was 'deeply moved' by these experiences and had decided to 'spread the message of Jesus' touring Uganda with four of her relatives. All were present when she met Kibwetere and he later invited the family to join him in Kanungu. Credonia's former husband was not, though, included among this number.

Before the end of 1989, the couple had formalized their ideas into the Movement for the Restoration of the Ten Commandments and begun work on *A Timely Message From Heaven*. Kibwetere erected a small church and several buildings around the school building to form a compound. This, he said, would be the cult's 'Ark against adversity'. He and Credonia also gave themselves new designations. He was 'the Prophet' and equipped himself as a bishop with ornate vestments and jewellery, while she became 'the Programmer' a title that some would claim indicated her true authority in the sect.

Converts were sought all over Uganda. As the numbers grew too big to house in Kanungu, groups of followers were settled on different sites, particularly in the impoverished farming region of south-western Uganda where they could be put to work 'for the benefit of the Virgin Mary'. Large families were often separated and increasingly children were moved away from their parents. These moves occurred regularly and often quite randomly as the membership of the cult soared to its peak of as many as 5,000 men, women and children.

Orchestrating these moves was Credonia Mwerinde, who was

soon beginning to show herself in her true colours. She became increasingly autocratic and deluded, as Paul Ikazire, a former cult member, told the Africa News Service in December 2000:

'She came to dominate the group and Joseph Kibwetere was just a figurehead. Mwerinde was called the programmer, but she was a trickster obsessed with the desire to grab other people's property. The "Virgin Mary" as channelled through her provided all our rules.'

According to Ikazire, she gave long, rambling speeches to the converts telling them that personal possessions were evil:

'She encouraged new members to sell everything and give all their assets to her. She would come in and say things like, "The Virgin Mary wants you to bring more money." Eventually she became rich, owned a huge farm and several shops and vehicles and frequently travelled around Africa to evangelize and recruit new members. Those of us in the settlement had nothing.'

Joseph Kibwetere would also speak to cult members telling them he had received more visions and had actually heard conversations between the Virgin Mary and Jesus. He said the Virgin Mary had 'complained' about the world's departure from the Ten Commandments. He even claimed to one group that he had a tape recording of one of his conversations – though this was never played.

Despite the promises of salvation that were made to those living in the Kanungu compound, life there was anything but heavenly, as subsequent testimonies from people in the vicinity have born witness. The cult members rose at daybreak, prayed and sang hymns until noon and then worked in the banana and cassava fields until 10 p.m. They rarely went into town or mixed with other residents. A path to the main road that had once passed the sect's compound was suddenly redirected away from it.

Even from a distance, though, it was possible to see that a style of dress had been introduced to differentiate the hierarchy from its followers. The leaders wore expensive-looking white robes, while those cultists who had given generously to the cult when they were admitted wore green. The workers who toiled in the fields or in the workshops of the compound were provided with simple black vestments that were often ragged and always dirty from the forced labour.

The policy of isolation was strictly enforced: no one was allowed any contact with 'sinners'. Some members were sworn to a vow of silence and only allowed to speak when they were praying. Sign language became the only means by which certain families could communicate for fear of incurring the wrath of 'the Prophet' or 'the Programmer'.

Newcomers to the cult were invariably fed well until they had been sufficiently integrated and then they shared the same diet of beans the rest were forced to eat. Those who had given up their Catholic religion in the hope of a better life found they had swapped their poverty for some things even worse: isolation, estrangement from their families and a weariness and hunger that broke even the strongest spirit.

And if they thought times were hard under the iron rule of Kibwetere and Mwerinda, they became even worse when a third man, Dominic Kataribabo, arrived in Kanungu in the spring of 1988.

* * *

The early career of Dominic Kataribabo is almost a mirror reflection of the man who invited him to join the Movement for the Restoration of the Ten Commandments. Born in Kampala in 1968, he was destined like Joseph Kibwetere to progress from devout Catholic to defrocked priest and murderous cult leader in just a few short years.

Records in the Los Angeles Archdiocese show that after qualifying as a priest in Kampala, his local bishop had put him forward for a scholarship in America under a programme set up to help third world priests. Granted a 'sacramental ministry' by the clergy in Los Angeles he was sent to the Loyola Marymount University, one of the country's top Jesuit colleges.

Here the young man lived quietly in the rectory of St Anthony's parish in the idyllic coastal city of El Segundo. He worked hard and was awarded a master's degree in religious studies although his marks were never particularly outstanding, according to the records.

'He seemed to be pretty ordinary,' a spokesman of Loyola Marymount was to tell the media in April 2000 when Dominic's

part in the story of the cult was revealed. 'He seemed undistin-
guished.'

If Kataribabo was aware of this verdict it might just have been
one of the spurs that turned him from man of God to man of
blood. Returning to Uganda, there is evidence that he became
fascinated with the stories of Credonia Mwerinde and her visions.
According to AP reporter Deborah Hastings, who investigated
Kataribabo, 'He got into trouble with his diocese in Uganda for
how he used donations collected in Los Angeles and for his
interest in Mwerinde.'

Just turned thirty-two, he was excommunicated and decided to
follow 'the Programmer' to Kanungu and cast his lot in with the
burgeoning sect. He was invited to serve as second in command
to Kibwetere – who had also just been formally excommunicated
by the Bishop of Mbarara diocese with the declaration, 'He
claimed that he could talk to God, which was unacceptable' – and
completed the elite group of twelve 'apostles' who were now
running the cult. Dominic's job specification was to teach
seminars at the church compound on the coming end of the world
on 31 December 1999.

As a mark of his status, Kataribabo was given his own ten-
room house complete with spacious grounds. The property and
the sugar cane patch to the rear were both kept immaculate by
forced labour from the compound. He also used a group of male
cultists to dig a pit to install a refrigerator in his house. It would
later be discovered to have been used for anything but domestic
purposes.

Despite the best efforts of the triumvirate of Credonia,
Kibwetere and Kataribabo all was not well in the Ark as the
twentieth century drew to a close. Too many punishments
involving caning or food deprivation were causing a sense of
despair to fall over the cultists. A man who decided to try to
escape, Emmanuel Bisgye – one of twenty-five relatives who
joined the cult – later told his story to Rosalind Russell of Reuters
in March 2000. His account offers a grim picture of life in the Ark
of the Movement for the Restoration of the Ten Commandments
just before the millennium:

'They made me work until I was exhausted. They treated us all
like serfs. If we sold any food or any crafts we were not allowed

Shadow of the Apocalpyse

to keep the money. Even the children who were brought into the compound were also put to work, fetching water and firewood. For a time they ran a school, but this was closed down in 1998 by the local authorities who said in a report that the children were malnourished and made to sleep on the floor without any mattresses or blankets.'

Bisgye says that he remained so long because, 'all of us believed in the Blessed Virgin Mary':

'We though that Credonia Mwerinde would make miracles for us and save us. But when her predictions did not come true we began to have doubts. In the end I just walked away from the field where I was working one day. It was a decision that would save my life but unfortunately not those of my relatives.'

Emmanuel Bisgye's mention of the local authorities prompts the question as to why no one investigated what was going on in the church until it was too late. An answer of a kind was provided by a local police officer, James Byaruhanga:

'The sect was a registered charity and the people were very good taxpayers. They had permission to operate from the authorities, so we had no reason to stop them. We did not suspect the sect of any wrongdoing.'

One of the oldest residents of the village, 82-year-old Erneo Rwarinda, who lived only a few metres from the compound, did have reasons to be suspicious, however. His brother had joined the cult in 1994 and tried to convert him. But when Erneo refused, 'he never spoke to me again'. Even when one of his sons did agree to join along with seven relatives he was still unable to find out much about the people who lived there. He told investigative journalist Todd Pitman:

'The cult had very little success in converting people in our area and most of them seemed to come from other districts of Uganda. They lived in isolation. They were not even permitted to talk. Whenever I saw them, they could not greet me. They were just communicating with each other through signs. This was supposed to maintain discipline and prevent quarrels, but it also kept everything they were doing secret.'

Rwarinda also introduced Todd Pitman to another of his sons, Peter, who told him how his uncle who had joined the cult lured away his wife and children:

'I told my wife that I didn't want us to join the sect because we were Catholics and these people just pretended to be. But when I came back from a business trip to Kampala I found her and my five children had gone. She had just kept quiet after what I had said and joined secretly.'

As the doomsday that had been predicted arrived – and passed – without any of the awful consequences that 'the Prophet' and his elite group had predicted, the cult neared the moment of destiny which would write its name as perhaps the most evil of all evil cults. And this moment is still surrounded by mystery years afterwards.

* * *

There is no record as to just what happened in the compound at Kanungu when the dawn of the first of January 2000 broke and the world was still in place. The cultists had, of course, already suffered the disappointment of a number of prophecies by Joseph Kibwetere and Credonia Mwerinde failing to materialize. But very few had doubted that the millennium would provide a moment of truth. Instead the sun rose over the church, the row of buildings and the acres of red earth filled with crops and a day very much like any other started.

It is believed that during the day a number of cult members approached their leaders and demanded to have their money and goods returned. Others apparently decided that this was one too many prophecy unfilled and they wanted to return to the world of family and friends they had left. They had never heard or seen the Virgin Mary that 'the Programmer' was said to be in contact with almost daily and there was no sign that 'the Prophet's' statement that the year 2000 would be 'Year One of the New World' was going to come true.

Nonetheless, feverish activity was reported in the compound. A group of cultists were put to work slaughtering the movement's cattle. Long overdue repairs to the doors and windows of the church were ordered. And, strangest of all, large quantities of Coca-Cola were ordered and put in storage. Was this in preparation for yet another doomsday – or perhaps a feast for the teetotal sect? Undoubtedly *something* was going to happen.

On 15 March, Joseph Kibwetere wrote a letter to local government officials in Kanungu. A copy has never been released publicly, but it is said to have taken the form of a 'farewell' in which the writer speaks of the 'imminent end of the current generation and the world'. It was apparently similar to an earlier communication in 1999 when Kibwetere had written, 'God sent us as a movement of truth and justice to notify the people to prepare for the closing of this generation, which is at hand.'

In the light of what happened two days later, the 15 March letter has been described as 'a premeditated suicide note'. That said, there is still a lot that is unclear about the events on the morning of Friday, 17 March. It is a fact that, as usual, a large congregation of cult members gathered in the church and began a service of hymns and prayers that lasted for several hours. At noon, the stench of petrol blew across the compound and flames could be seen lapping from inside the wooden building.

The doors of the church were firmly locked – as they apparently often were for services – but the windows and doors had been nailed shut. Everyone inside – 530 people including 11 children – was incinerated. It was some hours before the horrified authorities could get into the smouldering ruin and examine the charred bodies. The evidence of a desperate struggle to survive was noticeable on the corpses of dozens of the victims.

Horror piled upon horror when the local police began a thorough search of the compound and a group of pathologists were summoned from Kampala. Dozens more bodies that had been poisoned, strangled, stabbed or had their skulls beaten in were found in shallow graves, under houses or thrown down wells and latrine pits.

Particularly grisly remains were unearthed under the big house belonging to Dominic Kataribabo. Beneath a newly laid cement floor, eight-one more bodies were exposed. And in the sugar cane plantation to the rear, which the former priest had tended with such care by cult members, the mutilated remains of another seventy-four people were dug up. The young man who had once seemed set on a good career with the church had become instead a vengeful serial killer 'in the name of his new religion'.

Weeks passed before anything like a correct estimate of the number of dead could be made. An interim total suggested 780, but there were believed to be another 144 cultists of whom no trace could be found, pushing the total up to 924. There was no doubt the number of mass deaths at Kanungu exceeded the 913 who had died in the Jonestown massacre.

Mystery also surrounds the fates of the triumvirate who led the Movement for the Restoration of the Ten Commandments. Joseph Kibwetere is believed by members of his family to have died in the fire in the church after they had identified a ring thought to be his that was found on a finger among the rubble. Rumours have, though, suggested that he escaped and could be still at large in Uganda. The local police are also convinced that Dominic Kataribabo was in the building. One of the corpses still had the remains of a clerical collar identical to his around its neck and a 1997 passport in the name of Kataribabo was found in the compound.

As to Credonia Mwerinde, there are conflicting claims as to precisely where she was on 17 March. Initially, the local police identified one of the charred corpses as hers. However, other sources believe the body was too burned for proper examination and 'the Programmer' may well have escaped the inferno. A report in the state-owned *New Vision* newspaper of 23 May reported:

'Some people speculate that Mwerinde is still alive. Cult survivors claim she killed the other leaders before fleeing. A local businessman has stated that just days before the church fire, Mwerinde talked to him about selling cult property, which included large tracts of land, vehicles and buildings.'

So did the failure of the doomsday prediction trigger the killings? Was this immolation in the church a deliberate act by the leaders of the cult or a mass suicide instigated by the members themselves?

The mystery was further compounded when a BBC report revealed that Kibwetere had been receiving private medical treatment in 1998 for a bipolar disorder that could cause manic depression. Another investigation was also launched into claims that the cult had mistreated and possibly even kidnapped children. The article in *New Vision* expounded on this aspect of the events:

'No children were ever produced by the cult because the men and women slept in separate dormitories and sex was banned. The one time a woman did become pregnant she was beaten until she miscarried. The children that lived in the compound had moved there with their families and were subjected to child labour. Some were even there without their parents' knowledge.'

The answers to all of these questions will probably never be satisfactorily resolved. The one fact that remains absolutely inescapable is that the deaths at Kanungu remain the most horrific cult tragedy in history.

The Rasputin Sect

The city of Tyumen standing beside the meandering Tura River was the first town to be founded in Siberia: that vast area of Russia that conjures up images of freezing ice and heavy snow and amounts to almost 56 per cent of the country's territory, stretching from the Ural Mountains to the Pacific Ocean and from the Arctic to the borders of China. According to some authorities, the name Siberia originated from the Turkic for 'sleeping land': an apt description for a place where the temperature can drop to below –90 degrees Fahrenheit (–68 degrees Centigrade) and where most of the coastal waters, lakes and rivers are frozen for much of the year. Yet Siberia also boasts an abundance of natural resources – including many minerals, rich forests and vast oil fields – as well as probably more orthodox religions, strange beliefs and bizarre sects than anywhere else in Asia.

Despite this hostile terrain which has limited Siberia's development and population growth – the density is reckoned to be just three people per square kilometre – the various ethnic groups who have lived in the region over the centuries have placed their beliefs very much at the centre of their lives. The Russian Orthodox Church naturally predominates; but there are also groups practising Buddhism, Islam, Judaism and Christianity, not to mention those who venerate the ancient local gods, their numbers running into dozens and including Bugady Musun, Kara Khan, Numi-Torem, Tomam and Zonget.

Many of these beliefs are to be found being practised in and around Tyumen whose population consists of just over half a million: the town dwellers living in apartment blocks and those in the surrounding areas in simple, but rather more spacious log houses. Both have to battle the long and bitter winters that last for almost six months of the year.

Yet Tyumen, which lies 2,144km to the east of Moscow, functions well as the administrative centre of the area known as Tyumen Oblast in the Urals federal districts. Founded originally as a fort post, it has since become an important trade centre for routes to Central Asia, China and Persia, and ever since 1885 has been linked to the rest of Russia by the Trans-Siberian railway.

Because of its icy fastness, Tyumen has not featured a great deal in history, beyond being taken by the Red Army during the Russian Revolution in 1918 and being used as the storage place for Lenin's body during the Second World War when there were fears that Hitler's invading forces might take Moscow. The discovery of oil in the region in 1948, however, has made the city an important centre for the gas and oil industries and raised the living standards of the inhabitants to second only to those in the capital.

But none of this has done anything to displace the unusual beliefs and practices that have been entrenched in Tyumen for centuries. If anything, the social and economic growth encouraged them – as an outbreak of what was initially described in the media as 'Satanic Cults' in the mid-1990s dramatically revealed. It was the first time that the remote and ice-clad locality had made international news for many years, too.

In fact, the bizarre events that began in Tyumen in 1996 created widespread interest for three principal reasons. The first was the idea that a modern brand of satanism had been added to the list of local practices. Secondly, a police suggestion that behind the outbreak of hangings among young people that had given rise to these stories was an underground sect that had been in existence for almost three hundred years. And, thirdly, that the notorious 'mad monk', Gregory Rasputin, who had exerted such influence in the later days of the Romanov dynasty, had not only belonged to this sect but had also predicted the coming of Satan to Tyumen – where he was born – a century after his death.

* * *

The morning of 20 April 1996 began brightly in Tyumen. There were the first signs of the great snows and ice on the Tura River beginning to thaw after a particularly hard winter. The towers of the eighteenth-century Trinity Monastery were gleaming in the pale sunlight and for the first time in weeks the ground staff of UTair Airlines at the airport had been able to clear the runways of ice in record time for the early morning flights to Moscow and the East. The plants of the three major oil companies in Tyumen, Gazprom, LUKoil and Yukos, were also giving off less steamy condensation in the welcome higher temperature.

The only bad news of that day was a small story in the local papers that a nineteen-year-old boy, Denis Abramov, had been found hanging in his room at his home in the suburban village of Roshchino. The death might not even have made the news at all, but for the fact that the investigating police officers had found the walls of his room covered with occult symbols and there were piles of books about the supernatural and fundamentalist religions around his bed. Although the boy's unusual interests puzzled the local coroner, he declared the young man's death to have been suicide 'by his own hand'.

Almost exactly a month later, on 18 May, a teenager, Dima Bronikov, was found hanging in his room in an apartment in the centre of Tyumen. There was evidence that he, too, had been very interested in the supernatural. When a third boy, Stas Buslov, was discovered hanging from a tree in the same neighbourhood on 5 July, the police and newspapers began to suspect a pattern was emerging. Could a serial killer be at work? one paper asked.

Any doubts that Tyumen was in the grip of a spate of mysterious deaths was dispelled just three days later when one of Buslov's closest friends, Sergei Sidorov, eighteen, also killed himself in his apartment just a street away.

As the brief summer in the city passed and the police were still no nearer to finding a solution to the deaths – or any reason to connect them beyond friendship – a girl was discovered hanging in her bedroom on the west side of the city on 3 October. Tanya Stankeyeva, twenty-two, had pictures of heavy metal rock groups on her bedroom walls and several books about satanism and black magic in a cupboard.

In the intervening months since the death of Abramov in April, the police had been picking up clues about the five dead young people. It had been established they all knew one another and there were suggestions that they met together regularly in some hiding place. But where?

The mother of Sergei Sidorov provided the first clue. She told the investigating officers that shortly before his death, her son had admitted to her that he belonged to an unusual cult. Mrs Sidorov said that her son confessed, 'Mama, I'm a satanist. I know it is bad, but I cannot escape. They are terribly strong.' He had given her no indication who 'they' might be, though she suspected the cult was in the city as her son was rarely away from home for any length of time.

The father of the third suicide, Stas Buslov, was far from satisfied with the speed with which the police were investigating the death of his son and his friends. He carried out his own enquiries into unexplained deaths in the Tyumen province during the past year and was horrified to find a link between them all. He discovered that as many as thirty-six young people between the ages of twelve and twenty-two had hanged themselves in circumstances very similar to those of his boy.

Mr Buslov also proved himself better at detection work than the local detectives when he found the locality where his son and his four friends had met. It was a basement in a rundown apartment block on the outskirts of Tyumen which had been vandalized so badly that much of it was now unoccupied. In the dank and dingy basement room he found a 'kind of satanic altar' and the walls painted with diabolical signs and cryptic symbols, all in black paint. He recognized the handiwork of his son who wanted to be a graphic artist and had filled books with drawings of infernal creatures.

Further painstaking searches among the belongings of the other four finally brought to light jottings and pictures which pointed to the group having been investigating a 'seven-stage initiation ceremony that culminated in ritual suffocation'. It appeared that the oldest boy, Denis Abramov, and the 22-year-old girl, Tanya, had been the male and female leaders of the group. There was a suggestion both used names of traditional religious figures in their ceremonies as a parody of orthodox worship. This would prove significant at a later stage of the search for the cult involved.

All these discoveries – and especially the basement that linked the five young people – generated demands for action from the local community. The large number of deaths discovered by Mr Buslov horrified the people of western Siberia and seemed to point to some sort of Devil-worshipping sect in their midst. One, it seemed, that demanded extreme sin and the ultimate pain.

In November 1966, Tyumen police came clean about their fears – though they were typically guarded in their comments. A spokesman for the provincial prosecutor's office told the media: 'We may be dealing with a serial killing, though it is not clear if this is murder or incitement to suicide.'

It was not until the brutal Siberian winter was almost over with the freezing conditions making inquiries even harder to carry out, that the Tyumen police announced that the deaths of the young people were probably linked to a cult operating in western Siberia. Their hand had been forced by the extraordinary news on 3 March of a siege of a building in a remote Siberian town where sixty members of a religious sect had barricaded themselves in for three days and 'asked to be shot dead', according to police sources. A report in *Izvestiya* the following day stated:

'The group of evangelical Christians locked themselves in the administrative building on Sunday evening demanding compensation for timber they had provided for local residents. But they subsequently rejected offers of money, broke off negotiations with the police and began singing and praying. The group, which earlier on Wednesday had asked police to shoot them dead saying the police would be forgiven, was not officially registered.'

The newspaper had also sought a comment on the situation from Patriarch Alexiy, head of the Orthodox Church in Moscow, whose words further emphasized the urgency for action in Siberia. Criticizing the activities of minority religious sects, he said, 'Russia has been flooded by sects of a destructive nature which often cripple people's soul.'

In Tyumen, the patriarch's words were used to push for further action from the police and local authorities. A statement two days later confirmed what many had feared. The police were now searching for 'the ring leaders of a satanic cult believed to be operating from the city'. The provincial prosecutor's office went further, clearly based on the result of inquiries:

'The leader of the cult is believed to be a man in his forties. He is assisted by two younger acolytes who together have exerted enormous influence on provincial children and teenagers. They may well have now left the area and inquiries will continue on a nationwide basis.'

The evidence suggests that these three mysterious figures had indeed left Tyumen. But in their wake was strong evidence that they belonged to one of the most mysterious sects in Russia, the Khlysty, who had a history of extremism that matched with the series of deaths in Siberia. And among their number had been the most infamous of all the city's sons, Rasputin.

* * *

The city of Tyumen lists among the famous people born there, Irvin Berlin, Tamara Toumanova and Gregory Rasputin. It mentions, too, that Rasputin was for a time a member of the Khlysty sect, which numbered the remote town as one of its secret strongholds for generations. The facts about both the mystic monk and the cult are almost equally surrounded by controversy.

The Khlysty sect is believed to have been founded in the early eighteenth-century by a peasant, Danila Filipich, in the town of Verkhoture. It was a breakaway group from the Russian Orthodox Church, which had a huge monastery nearby. Filipich's philosophy could be summed up in a few words: 'In order to be saved you must first sin.' According to his convictions, cardinal pleasure in no way tarnished the interior purity or soul of man just as dirt could did not tarnish gold.

Those who have investigated the shadowy organization down the years have compared it to some of the more extreme American Pentecostals, the Snake Handlers of the south and the Holy Rollers. Like them, the Khlysty sect believes its teachings come directly from God and as such are unknown to orthodox religion and unacceptable as 'heretical'.

The cult took its name from the Russian word for 'whip' and renounced the priesthood, all holy books and the veneration of saints. In an early message to his cultists, Filipich declared:

'Keep my laws secret, entrust them neither to your father nor to your mother. Be steadfast and silent even under the lash or the flames. Thus you will enter the kingdom of heaven and even here on earth receive the bliss of the spirit.'

Early members of the sect – including, it is claimed, monks from the Verkhoture monastery – were instructed to perform the prayers and rituals of the orthodox church with great fervency in order to dispel any suspicion and conceal their secret belief that God, or the Lord, could reincarnate in man at any time and any where. The birth at Nazareth where God became man, they were told, was not an isolated event, but was constantly being repeated.

This reincarnation could only be achieved through a process known as the 'mysterious death' in which a person died to all sensations of the flesh. After this mystical transformation, a Khylsty member would be able to heal, prophesy, 'rescue souls from hell and lead them to heaven' as well as raise the dead. Among cultists who were said to have God reincarnated in them were a peasant named Andrei Petrov, and a prophet by the name of Radaev who allegedly surrounded himself with a harem of thirteen women.

Sex was said to be play a major role in the life of the sect. Married men and women who wanted to join the Khylsty were made to abandon their partners and children as they were told the blessing of their union was considered the 'seal of the Antichrist'. Indeed, there was every chance if a person stayed married of becoming the Antichrist themselves.

However, once a person had joined the sect they could take part in the services known as the *Radenyi,* or Arks of the People of God, in which they were allowed to sleep with other partners in 'spiritual marriages'. If the women became pregnant, though, there was another ceremony in which they would be aborted.

During the heyday of the sect in the years before the Russian Revolution, dozens of groups existed in Russia – there were said to be approximately 40,000 followers – but this number dropped drastically in Soviet times, with the most active groups proselytising in Tambov, Orenvurg, the Northern Caucasus, the Ukraine and, of course, Siberia

Each group of the cult was led by a male and female who were called the 'Christ' and 'Mother of God' respectively. It was their job to encourage the 'attainment of divine grace through sin' in ecstatic rituals. These are known to have turned into mass orgies. Flagellation, torture and even mock hangings were frequently practised – elements of the Khlysty that the investigators of the 'suicides' in Tyumen were to ultimately chance upon.

Since the turn of the century, it was also learned, the sect had placed great emphasis on training its leaders in mental disciplines such as mind control, to prevent others from reading their thoughts and meditation to endure extremes and control pain. Members were trained to be able to mask any feelings that might be shown through their eyes – appearing disinterested or vacant – and perfect methods of deception and infiltration. Persuasion and seduction could also be used to achieve the sect's objectives.

It also became evident that the Khylsty had a new saint in their pantheon of men in whom God had been reincarnated: the monk Rasputin from Tyumen. One of the symbols of the cult was said to be a tiny wooden phallus with stylized crystal testicles that represented the mystic's penis, which had been cut off by one of his assassins and then preserved in a velvet container. According to some accounts, new initiates are allowed to look at the relic, but never touch it. This story, too, added to the legend surrounding Rasputin.

Few historical figures have generated more myths than Grigori Yefimovich Rasputin. The man often referred to as the 'Mad Monk' or *Icha*, a diminutive of his first Christian name – though he was never a monk and certainly not insane – became one of the most notorious and mysterious figures of the twentieth century around whom rumours circulated throughout his life and redoubled after his death. The master of strange powers, he was said to be a man whose eyes changed colour when he spoke to people and he claimed to have a link with the supernatural. To his detractors – and there were many of them, out of envy or malice – he was a charlatan and clever hypnotist who used his undoubted charisma to satisfy an immense craving for women and sex.

For years, the date of Rasputin's birth was uncertain – ranging between 1863 and 1873 – and it is only recently that documents have come to light which show he was born on 22 January 1869 in a village beside the Tura River in Tyumen Oblast. He was the son of a carter and at the age of eighteen entered the Verkhoture monastery where, of course, Danila Filipich had created the

Khylsty sect at the beginning of the century. He spent just three months in the religious establishment where he came under the influence of a holy man named Makariy, who was both feared and respected by the monks.

Makariy was, in fact, a member of the Khylsty sect. He quickly sensed the young man's dissatisfaction with the orthodox church and introduced him to the cult. There can be little doubt that that libidinous Rasputin embraced the ideas of the group with enthusiasm and modelled himself on Makariy. He is believed to have taken part in a number of the sect's orgies and it is said that he thought he would derive vitality from lots of sex.

In 1889, despite the teachings of the cult, he married Praskovia Fyodorovna, with whom he would have three children. He also had a child with another women – who may have been the 'Mother of God' in the sect, but refused to have an abortion. The young man with his long hair and beard and mesmeric eyes also held orgies in the basement of his home in 1900 under the auspices of the group, while simultaneously perfecting his techniques at faith healing, mysticism and prophecy. Both inside the cult and in the outside world he was gaining a reputation as a *starets* or elder, a title usually reserved for monk-confessors.

The following year, Rasputin left home and travelled to Greece and Jerusalem before arriving back in Russia in 1903. In 1904, while he was travelling under the guise of a *stannic* or religious pilgrim, he heard reports that Tsarevich Alexei, the only son of Tsar Nicholas II and wife, Alexandra, was suffering from haemophilia. The boy had only to fall gently or bruise himself to start internal bleeding that could go on for days.

When the Tsarina, desperate for any help, heard about the healer called Rasputin who was said to possess the ability to cure illness through prayer, she appealed to him by way of a friend, Anna Vyrubova, Miraculously, the boy got better. Rasputin was summoned to St. Petersburg and asked to oversee the boy's health. The child's health improved noticeably as a result of what the sceptics described as the *stannic*'s hypnotic powers. More probably, it was his urging of Alexandra to allow her boy to rest, when others wanted him to be more active, and enable Alexei's natural healing processes to work.

Whatever the truth of his method, Rasputin's stock in the

Russian capital grew daily. His appeal to women was enormous and there is evidence that he created a new secret Khlysty cell from among the society ladies in the city who jostled for his favours. Certainly there are numerous photographs of the mystic surrounded by adoring females – although stories that he raped a lot of women seem ludicrous in the light of how many females were more than willing to submit to his advances.

Equally lurid tales that Rasputin had an affair with the Tsarina are without foundation: although he did undoubtedly influence the royal family with his various psychic and healing powers. Notably his power of precognition – predicting events that happened just a few months later – and clairvoyance, seeing events happening elsewhere.

Particularly relevant to our story is the rumour that he predicted the coming of the Judgement Day in a hundred years time, 'when Satan will arise in Tyumen'. Whether he meant this literally or as a warning to those in his native Siberia who had become the most serious debunkers of his powers is unknown. But the events of the multiple hangings associated with the Khysty sect in 1996–7 certainly give some validity to this claim.

Rasputin is also said to have predicted his own death, although this was becoming daily more likely as some of those close to the royal family wanted to see his influence removed. It came, though, terribly and brutally and in a manner that matched the weirdness of his life. Recent evidence suggests that it was not the first time an attempt had been made on his life.

According to historian Greg King in *The Man Who Killed Rasputin* (1996), when Rasputin visited Tyumen on 29 June 1914 to see his family, he was attacked by a former prostitute, Khionia Guseva. She had become a disciple of another holy man, Idliodor – who was once a friend of Rasputin and may well have been a member of the Khysty sect – but had become outraged by his behaviour in St Petersburg. She approached the mystic as he was walking along the street with his entourage of men and women and thrust a knife into his abdomen, screaming, 'I have killed the Antichrist.'

In fact, Guseva had not struck a mortal blow and after extensive surgery Rasputin recovered, although his health was never the same and he regularly took opium to ease stomach pains. His actual death – two years later on 16 December 1916 – was equally sensational, though there are still doubts about certain aspects of the assassination.

It seems that a group of nobles, led by Prince Felix Yusupov, who believed that Rasputin's influence over the royal family made him a danger to the Russian court, agreed to kill the *stannic*. With this in mind, he invited the mystic to the Moika Palace. There he was served cakes and red wine said to have been laced with enough cyanide 'to kill ten men'. When Rasputin did not die, Yusupov took out a revolver and shot him, leaving him slumped on the floor. According to the prince's own recollection of the events, when he returned to the room later expecting to find a corpse, Rasputin opened his eyes, grabbed him by the throat and hissed in his face, 'You bad, bad boy.' He then got up and stumbled across the room.

At these sounds, the other conspirators burst through the door and seeing the dishevelled, bearded figure they expected to be dead looming before them, they shot him again, three times. Rasputin was hit several times with clubs before he finally fell dead to the floor. The killers then wrapped the body up in a sheet and quickly threw the bundle into the icy Neva River.

The body of Gregory Rasputin was not found until three days later. Even in death he was able to give his rescuers a shock they would never forget. His arms were frozen solid in an upright position as if he had been trying to claw his way out of his icy tomb. Later the body was autopsied and gave rise to another legend that has persisted to this day. The coroner decided that death was by drowning – despite the fact that the mystic's corpse had four gunshot wounds, evidence of being badly beaten and enough poison to have killed him several times over.

The last mystery concerns Rasputin's penis. The *stannic*'s maid who attended the autopsy was said to have retrieved several organs from the morgue, including his genitalia. Shortly afterwards the penis disappeared and was variously said to be jealously guarded by a group the Khysty cultists – who used the relic as a symbol of their order – or, alternately, had been purchased by a French brothel where it was kept in formaldehyde as an exhibit to show *very* special clients.

In April 2004, when the first Russian museum of erotica was

opened in St Petersburg under the auspices of the prostrate research centre of the Russian Academy of Natural Sciences, the founder, Igor Knyazkin, announced there was one exhibit of which he was especially proud: the preserved penis of Rasputin. He told a reporter from the *Nezavisimaya Gazeta*: 'Having this exhibit, we can stop envying America where Napoleon Bonaparte's penis is now kept. Napoleon's penis is but a small "pod" and cannot stand comparison to our organ of 30 centimetres.'

If that fact wasn't hard enough for the Americans to swallow, when the Rasputin penis from the French brothel turned up to be sold at auction in California – without provenance or a guarantee – the lucky purchaser, a woman, agreed to have the relic tested.

It proved to be *a sea cucumber*.

Journey to Heaven's Gate

Viewers of the latest episode of *Star Trek: Deep Space Nine* on the evening of 25 November 1998 were probably mostly too engrossed to be aware of the heavy symbolism surrounding both the day of the broadcast and the storyline about a messiah-like figure urging a group of gentle aliens to mass suicide. The story of 'Covenant' actually had a basis in fact and the night on which the religious-cult-themed drama was transmitted fell in the very same month that marked the twentieth anniversary of the Jonestown massacre when hundreds had died by their own hands in Guyana.

Probably, though, no such thoughts crossed the minds of fans of the classic science fiction serial – *Deep Space Nine* was *then* chalking up its 159th episode in its seventh season – and it was only those with a particular interest in cults who would have been aware that a number of members of the group on which the story had been based were committed fans of *Star Trek*. Indeed, there are some sources that claim the cultist believed the programme was *literally true*. What *is* a fact is that one of the group was the brother of the actress Michelle Nicholas who played the popular starship *Enterprise* crewmember, Lieutenant Uhura.

'Covent' focused on the actions of Gul Dukat, an alien Cardassian, who has become a messiah-like figure to the people of the recently occupied planet Bajor. They worship entities known as the Pah-wraiths and Dukat tries to convince them that these entities have abandoned them in their time of crisis. The Bajorans should follow him, he says, because he 'walks with the true prophets' who possess 'powers beyond our understanding'. He reminds them how prophets have already made an entire fleet of spacecraft vanish into thin air during the

223

occupation. The only course of action for the people of the planet is to take their own lives and join the prophets in the vastness of eternity.

Regular viewers of the series were already familiar with the duplicitous Dukat who had been appearing regularly in *Star Trek* since 1993. Played by Marc Alaimo, a Wisconsin-born actor who had made something of a speciality of playing villains in TV shows such as *The Bionic Woman* and *The Incredible Hulk* as well as appearing as an alien assassin in *The Last Starfighter* and a devious Martian security officer in *Total Recall*, he brought a compelling gravitas to the role of a pseudo cult leader. His methods of persuasion ranged from honeyed words to a fight in an airlock with a disbelieving Bajoran female.

A significant moment in the story occurred when a painter, Benyan (Jason Leland Adams) one of the most devoted believers in the Pah-wraiths – 'I have come to feel their love' – was seen at work on picture that closely resembled *The Last Supper* by Leonardo Da Vinci. But in this version. Christ's position in the centre of the painting with his arms outstretched and flanked on either side by his disciples was the unmistakable figure of Gul Dukat.

In fact, the *Star Trek* crew help to expose the insincere motives of Duket in trying to generate a mass suicide and reveal that the pill, which he planned to kill himself with, was actually a fake. The episode, written by Rene Echevarria, and directed by John T. Kretchmer, rated among the best in the series. But it is clear that viewers did not immediately spot the allusions in the story – or the fact the inspiration for the episode had been the real-life mass suicide of members of the Heaven's Gate cult over a year before in March 1997.

The story of this group – whose leader once said of them, 'we take the prize of being the cult of cults' – was also arguably the most extraordinary of the dozens of UFO-based organizations that developed in the run-up to the millennium. Certainly no other cult took quite the same option as a means of escaping from the cataclysm that they anticipated at the end of the twentieth century.

* * *

The couple that founded the Heaven's Gate cult, Marshall Herff Applewhite and Bonnie Lu Nettles, first met in the psychiatric ward of a hospital in Houston, Texas, where Nettles was a nurse. Their shared interests in New Age religion was to lead them to study the nature of UFOs, look for clues about the future of the world in the four gospels and the Book of Revelation, and eventually create their cult to 'open a doorway to the Kingdom of God at the end of this civilization'. Both of them had curious lives before their fateful meeting.

Herff Applewhite – he apparently dropped his first Christian name before founding Heaven's Gate and never used it again – was born in May 1931. He was the only son of a Texas Presbyterian minister who led a very peripatetic life while the boy was growing up. It seems Preacher Applewhite moved every three years or so, starting new churches wherever he went, and was noted for his charismatic sermons. Young Marshall grew up wanting to be a preacher like his father, but as he showed signs of a musical talent as well, was encouraged to take a degree in theology and music at Austin College.

His devotion to music proved the stronger of his two inclinations during his college years from 1948 to 1952. Records at Austin indicate that young Applewhite did not complete his theological course, but majored in philosophy and music, leaving with a bachelor of arts. During the fifties and sixties he pursued a career in music, starred in a number of stage musicals in Colorado and Texas and sang fifteen roles with the Houston Grand Opera. He later taught music at the University of St Thomas in Houston and in his spare time served as the director of the choir at St Mark's Episcopal Church in the city. He also married and had two children.

The first cloud to settle over the life of Marshall Applewhite occurred when he was summarily dismissed from his post at the university in 1971. The official reason for the termination of his contract given by St Thomas's, a private college, was 'health problems of an emotional nature'. The real reason is said to have been homosexual affairs with one or more of his students – a facet of his character that it has been argued affected his subsequent career as a cult leader.

A year later, when Applewhite was attending hospital for

psychiatric treatment, he met Bonnie Nettles. Their meeting was a doubly traumatic moment for him as he was also being treated for heart problems.

Bonnie Trusdale Nettles was two years older than her patient and had already developed a profound interest in the occult and New Age philosophies. Born in Houston in 1928, she had been a nurse since leaving college and raised two children. In her spare time, Bonnie was a prominent member of the local Theosophical Society, a group that had been founded in the US in 1875 by the Russian-born mystic Madame Helena Blavatsky (1831–91). Based on Egyptian occultism, it called for the 'brotherhood of man' and the study of religion and the occult. Despite various scandals and exposés, Madame Blavatsky gained a large following and wrote a number of pamphlets and books about her ideas, notably *The Secret Doctrine* (1888) – which was Bonnie's favourite reading almost a century later. To augment her salary, she also wrote a column on astrology for the local newspaper that was popular with readers.

According to contemporary accounts, while Marshall Applewhite was in hospital being treated, he had a 'near-death experience'. Bonnie Nettles convinced him that the experience was for a special reason, the meaning of which would become obvious in the fullness of time. She told him about the Theosophical Society and gave him a copy of *The Secret Doctrine* to read. The former music teacher later admitted to leaving the hospital with his mind buzzing with thoughts.

A short while later the couple met again – this time at a local theatre where Bonnie Nettles's daughter was employed and her son attended drama classes. By then, Applewhite had studied Madame Blavatsky's book and read many of his new friend's columns on astrology. He asked her to produce a chart for him. She did – and both their lives would never be the same again.

As Applewhite poured over the astrology chart that Bonnie Nettles had produced for him, he became convinced they had a 'spiritual link'. He was full of admiration for her knowledge and wisdom and the evidence suggests he regarded her as his superior and guide to what the future held. Within a matter of months they were seeing themselves as two people with a mission. A mission to inform mankind about the uncertain future as well as planning the first of several groups that would culminate in the fateful Heaven's Gate.

After intensive study of arcane and biblical sources, Nettles and Applewhite had reached the conclusion that they were 'the two witnesses' of the Book of Revelation (11.3). The earth was now in the control of evil forces and it was their destiny – as described in the Bible – to be killed, lay dead in the street for three and a half days and then be raised from the dead and taken up in a cloud (a spaceship) to enter the 'Kingdom of Heaven'.

Pumped up with fervour, the pair abandoned their respective families and took to the road like old time evangelicals travelling across the old Wild West. Initially, they referred to themselves as 'the Two Witnesses of Revelation', but soon shortened this to 'the Two'. The name chosen for this first version of the cult in 1975 was 'Human Individual Metamorphosis' (HIM) because of the two leaders' dualistic belief that the soul was a superior entity, which is only housed temporarily in a body. Marshall explained in one of his speeches:

'Our bodies are only the temporary containers of the soul. The final act of metamorphosis or separation from the human kingdom is the "disconnect" or separation from the human physical container or body in order to be released from the human environment.'

To feed and clothe themselves, Applewhite and Nettles took odd jobs, spoke in small public halls and left 'calling cards' at local churches announcing their mission. On more than one occasion they were in danger of being run out of some of the more religious little towns that had no time for what they saw as 'the madness of two vagabonds'.

But the mission was not without its successes. Soon the pair had a small coterie of followers in their wake. They also began to see themselves as like 'Bo' and 'Peep' in the old children's nursery rhyme looking for lost sheep – and for a time referred to each other by these names. Later they changed these to the more sophisticated-sounding 'Do' (pronounced 'Doe' and 'Ti':'Tee') – soubriquets that cynics would seize on to deride the pair as 'the UFO two'. But they were not to be deterred by criticism or ridicule, as Robert W. Balch and David Taylor, who investigated the cult, reported in *Salvation in a UFO* (1976):

227

'They believed that about 2000 years ago, a group of extra-terrestrials came to earth from the Kingdom of Heaven (the "Next Level"). One of these was "Do". "Ti" – his female companion – whom he referred to as his "Heavenly Father", gave him instructions. He left his body behind, transported to earth in a spaceship and incarnated (moved into) a human body, that of Jesus Christ. A second group of extra-terrestrials returned to earth, starting in the 1920s. "Do" was the captain of this expedition; "Ti" was the admiral. They each moved into a human body, but somehow became scattered. "Do" and "Ti" held public meetings to disseminate their beliefs. They were pleasantly surprised to find that most of their converts were the long-lost crew members.'

Those who fell in with the couple were told that they would only be able to reach this kingdom and a higher plane of existence if they renounced all human possessions – 'to break all attachments with earthly existence' – including their families, material assets and any money they might have. 'Ti' and 'Do' said they would be responsible for taking care of any wealth to further the mission.

According to *The Gods Have Landed: New Religions from Other Worlds,* edited by James R. Lewis (1995), the group lived for several years in isolation in the western United States:

'Members often travelled in pairs and rendezvoused with other members for meetings or presentations they gave to recruit new members. For a time some of them lived in a darkened house where they would simulate the experience they expected to have during their long journey in outer space. A group even travelled to the Colorado Desert to wait for the arrival of a UFO. None came.'

Although the members of HIM surrounded themselves with secrecy, they were occasionally challenged by religious groups to prove their beliefs. Gretchen Passantino who led a small group, 'Answers in Action' confronted the two leaders in Los Angeles in the late autumn of 1975 and accused them of being 'false prophets':

'They assured us that they were still true prophets, that the world "just wasn't ready" for the full disclosure yet. To this, the Bo-Peep followers derisively mocked, "We have the truth! Do and Ti will be a demonstration no one can deny!" However, it didn't surprise us when shortly after, Bo and Peep got a new revelation – they had been "massacred" in the press so they didn't need to be killed physically after all.'

With the benefit of hindsight, the remarks were grimly prophetic. But the next stage of the development would not take place without heartache and death.

* * *

In 1985 the first tragedy to hit the cult occurred. Bonnie Nettles, the beloved 'Ti' died. She had been in increasingly poor health after being stricken with cancer. For the next decade, the heartbroken Marshall Applewhite was rarely seen and it seems probable that many of the members of Human Individual Metamorphosis slipped back into society and ordinary lives. For his part, 'Do' apparently began a quest to find the women who had opened his mind 'on a higher spiritual level' in the hope of being reunited with her at the 'Next Level'.

By the early nineties a revitalized Applewhite was active once again. He now believed the message he and Bonnie Nettles had been trying to get across was even more urgent. He announced the formation of a new group, Total Overcomes Anonymous (TOA), and took the unprecedented decision of placing full-page advertisements in newspapers across America announcing that the earth's present civilization was 'about to be recycled'. The full page in *US Today* also warned that anyone who truly desired to enter the kingdom of heaven would have to give everything – adding ominously – 'including their human existence'.

In 1996, Applewhite began these preparations in earnest for the new appointment with fate by moving to San Diego County and renting a large house in the fashionable Rancho Sante Fe district. Here he set up a community based on a medieval monastic order in which the members would call each brother and sister and live a highly ascetic lifestyle devoid of any luxuries or indulgences. The cult would be known by the title that would go down in infamy in less than four years time – Heaven's Gate.

In the tradition for name-changing that the founders had initiated, the men and women drawn to the message of Herff Applewhite – as he was referring to himself to those outside the cult – were instructed to add the appellation '-ody' to their

Christian names. This curious fact came to light when three members took jobs in a small San Diego computer company, Advanced Development Group, to help finance the cult. The trio, Elaine-ody, Sylvie-ody and Thurston-ody, were remembered after their deaths as polite and reserved and for always keeping themselves to themselves. Behind the closed doors of the mansion house the life of the cultists was even stranger, according to the investigators Balch and Taylor:

'They looked on themselves as monks and nuns and called their community "the monastery", Most members had little contact with their families or with their neighbours. Some abandoned their children before joining. They dressed in unisex garments: shapeless black shirts with mandarin collars and black trousers. They were required to commit themselves to a celibate life. Eight of the male members, including "Do", submitted to voluntary castration. This seems to have been a form of preparation for their next level of existence: in a life that would be free of gender, sexual identity and sexual activity.'

The point about sexuality in the cult – and in particular that of Herff Applewhite – has been taken up by a number of writers because of its perceived significance. B.A. Robinson, writing on behalf of the Religious Tolerance Organization in May 1997, has this to say:

'Marshall Herff Applewhite was gay. There are rumours he had one or more affairs with male students when he was a music teacher. He is believed to have checked himself in to a hospital over two decades ago in order to overcome his homosexual feelings. This occurred when many therapists believed that a person's sexual orientation could be changed. Needless to say, the therapy was unsuccessful.'

Robinson says that one theory being proposed about the founder of Heaven's Gate was that he was unable to accept his sexual orientation because of the homophobia that he had absorbed during his youth. He goes on:

'This motivated him to live a celibate life and to create a group which also suppressed their sexual behaviour. Another theory is that among UFO groups, there is a widespread belief that extraterrestrials have no vocal cords, an atrophied digestive system and no sexual organs. This is symbolic of three common religious disciplines: silence, fasting and celibacy. Perhaps Applewhite was attempting to emulate both the UFO inhabitants and ancient Christian tradition.'

The cult made full use of the latest technological innovation, the Internet, to promulgate its beliefs on a site called the 'Higher Source' where Herff called himself the 'Present Representative' and drew parallels between himself and the spirit from heaven that had occupied the body of Jesus Christ. In an early announcement he declared:

'As was promised, the keys of Heaven's Gate are here again in "Ti" and "Do" as they were in Jesus and His Father, 2000 years ago. Our task is to work individually on our own personal shortcomings and change in preparation for entering the kingdom of heaven.'

In September 1995, Applewhite gave the first public indication that he believed that by committing suicide together 'at the correct time' the members of Heaven's Gate would leave their 'containers' (bodies) behind allowing the soul to go to sleep until 'replanted' (reborn) in another container. In the fullness of time, he said, this soul would be grafted onto a representative of the 'level above human'. All that was required now was a sign that the 'correct time' had arrived. 'Do' was not naïve enough, though, to think that everyone reading his words would accept them unreservedly:

'I am quite aware that what I am saying here will to many, if not most, sound like I should be locked up as a mental case at the least. However, that awareness cannot stand in the way of my simple acknowledgement of these facts for the sake of those who might go with us, and also for the sake of those who desire to be a contributor to our demise or exit from this world.'

Striking a more sinister note, Applewhite suggested that anyone who wanted to follow his 'guidance' should buy themselves some weapons. The statement had two immediate effects. The FBI began to monitor the website and the activities of the people in the San Diego mansion, while rumours began to spread that the cult had amassed a large cache of weapons and ammunition against fears of 'some irate individual' or from the 'powers that control this world'. Applewhite continued his diatribe:

'I would recommend that you purchase firearms, get comfortable using them (or partner with someone who can) and somehow position yourselves (separate from others enough not to be vulnerable) so that you might establish a relationship with me, protected from interference as far as possible.'

Herff insisted that 'in this day and time', the authorities made no bones about their need to protect the public from 'dangerous radicals like us'. He feared persecution, death, arrest, physical torture or psychological torture while they remained on earth. The sense of paranoia grew even more strident as he added:

'They [the authorities] will aggressively attempt to require us to abide by their values and their rules (which are of this Luciferian world and its society – as difficult as that might be to believe). They won't hesitate to trump up charges or suspicions in order to search us or to take into custody so they can "judge for themselves" whether or not we are some kind of threat.'

Before any such 'threat' – real or imaginary – could take place, however, the several dozen members of Heaven's Gate living in the big house in Rancho Sante Fe in the winter of 1996 were told that the sign they had been looking for was imminent. Appropriately, too, it would coincide with the great Christian festival of Easter.

* * *

It is impossible to know exactly when Applewhite informed his followers that they were all going to commit suicide together in order to fulfil his belief about the 'Evolutionary Level Above Human'. In statements during late 1996 and early 1997 he is still being equivocal, as these words from a video made by the cult demonstrate:

'I feel that we are at the end of the age. Now, the end of the age, I'm afraid I feel is, right upon us. It's going to come. Now, I don't want to sound like a prophet, but my gut says and everything else that I know points to, that it's going to come before the turn of the century. That it's going to come in the next few months, or the next year or two.'

In fact, 'the next few months' would prove to be correct. Reports that the closest approach to earth of the long-expected

232

Hale-Bopp comet would occur near Easter was the 'marker' that 'Do' and his late companion, 'Ti', had been waiting for. The spacecraft to take them all home could well be accompanying the comet – but this was not relevant to the overall plan, he said.

The weeks between that announcement and the dramatic events of 26 March 1997 are clouded in typical Heaven's Gate secrecy. But one thing *is* certain. A mass suicide took place and a press release was issued to the media that is probably unique in the history of journalism and certainly in cult history. The impact it had when landing on the desks of hardened news editors and veteran TV producers can only be imagined

Under the heading, HEAVEN'S GATE AWAY TEAM RETURNS TO LEVEL ABOVE HUMAN IN DISTANT SPACE, it stated by way of a preamble: 'By the time you read this, we suspect that the human bodies we were wearing have been found and the flurry of fragmented reports have begun to hit the wire services. For those who want to know the facts, the following statement has been issued.'

The *facts* the police found when they broke into 'Rancho Santo Fe' were anything but fragmented. The bodies of 39 people – 18 men and 21 women aged between 26 and 72 – all with short-cropped hair, black clothing and new, black and white Nike tennis shoes, were found lying on their backs throughout the pristine house. Each body lay with hands to the side and triangular purple shrouds covering every head. The cultists had apparently died in three groups over three successive days, starting on 23 March.

Officers who walked through the building in astonished silence noticed that each body had a form of identification as well as a $5 bill and some change. Carefully packed little suitcases stood beside every bed. One lawman told the media later that all the dead looked to him 'as if they had fallen asleep'.

A pathologist who examined the bodies found they had all died under identical circumstances. They had first drunk citrus juices to 'cleanse their bodies of impurities' and then committed suicide in shifts. Each member had then taken phenobarbitone mixed with vodka, after which plastic bags had been put on their heads to ensure that they died in their sleep. A hand-written note that was found by one of the bodies on the lower floor – believed to be the last words of Herff Applewhite – explained how everyone should leave their 'containers':

'Take the little package of pudding or applesauce and eat a couple of teaspoons. Pour the medicine in and stir it up. Eat it fairly quickly and then drink the vodka beverage. Then lay back and rest.'

The cult did not pass into history with these thirty-nine deaths, however. Two months later, two more members, Charles Humphrey and Wayne Cooke, attempted suicide in a hotel room a few miles from the Rancho Santa Fe mansion. Cooke died, but Humphrey, who was resuscitated, tried again in the Arizona desert in February 1998 and succeeded. A number of other cultists who chose not to 'graduate from the Human Evolutionary Level' have also attempted to keep the ideas of 'Do' and 'Ti' alive on the net.

The most striking memorial to Heaven's Gate remains the press release and its insight into the minds behind one of the many UFO-religion cults that sprang up in the last years of the twentieth century. As these three extracts show, it is small wonder that the creation of Herff Applewhite and Bonnie Nettles should have generated great interest in the entertainment industry, especially in hugely successful TV series like *Star Trek*. Whether it will prove a lasting phenomena only time will tell.

 # By the time you receive this, we'll be gone – several dozen of us. We came from the Level Above Human in distant space and we have now exited the bodies that we were wearing for our earthly task, to return to the world from whence we came – task completed. The distant space we refer to is what your religious literature would call the Kingdom of Heaven or the Kingdom of God. We came for the purpose of offering a doorway to the Kingdom of God at the end of civilization, the end of this age, the end of this millennium. We came from that Level, that time, that space and entered this one. And in doing so, we had to enter human bodies – which we did, for the most part, in the mid-seventies. Now it is time for us to leave these bodies (vehicles) – bodies that we borrowed for the time we were here (by previous arrangement) for this specific task. The task was not only to bring in information about that Evolutionary Kingdom Level Above Human, but also to give us the experience of working against the

forces of what the human evolutionary level, at this time, has become. And while it was a good learning experience for us, it also gave all who ever received knowledge from that Kingdom an opportunity to recognize us and this information, and to move out of the human level and into the Next Level or the Next Evolutionary Level, the 'Kingdom of Heaven' the Kingdom of God.

 # During a brief window of time, some may wish to follow us. If they do, it will not be easy. The requirement is to not only believe who the Representatives are, but to do as they and we did. You must leave everything *of your humanness behind. This includes the ultimate sacrifice and demonstration of faith – that is, the shedding of your human body. If you should choose to do this, logistically it is preferred that you make this exist somewhere in the area of the West or Southwest of the United States – but if this is not possible, it is not required. You must call on the name of 'Ti' and 'Do' to assist you. In so doing you will engage a communication of sorts, alerting a spacecraft to your location where you will be picked up after shedding your vehicle and be taken to another world by members of the Kingdom of Heaven.*

 # We know what we're saying. We know it requires a 'leap of faith'. But it's deliberate: designed for those who would rather take that leap than stay in this world. We suggest that anyone serious about considering this go into their most quiet place and ask, scream, with all their being, directing their asking to the Highest Source they can imagine (beyond earth's atmosphere) to give them guidance. Only those 'chosen' by the Next Kingdom will **know** *that this is right for them and will be given the courage required to act.*

End Times

The roads of South Korea were once again choked with traffic as millions of people headed for their homes to celebrate *Chusok* in the first week of October 1998. The annual harvest season festival – often compared to the American 'Thanksgiving Day' – which has been held for thousands of years, was once again bringing families together to thank their ancestors for providing them with another year of rice and fruits. The celebration – which traditionally falls on the fifteenth day of the eighth month reckoned by the lunar calendar – invariably brings chaos to the roads in September or October. This year, the date fell on 5 October, making it a day second only on the South Korean calendar to New Year's Day.

The exodus was usually estimated to involve more than 30 million people – half of the total population – all travelling to their hometowns or resorts for the three-day celebrations. With the festivities beginning on the day before *Chusok* and lasting until the day after, it had become traditional for workers to take three days off in order to brave the traffic jams and reach their destination in good time. Once there, they would eat the rice cakes called *Songphyun* – made of rice, beans, sesame seeds and chestnuts – and afterwards visit the tombs of their ancestors to pay their respects and leave small gifts.

This year was proving no different from any other. High spirits were evident among the vehicles loaded down with passengers even when they were slowed to a crawl. The cars and vans packed with gifts made it clear that everyone had been responding to the stores selling the traditional *Chusok* gift sets of *Songphyun,* high-quality beef, yellow corbina, honey and green tea. It was a time for everyone to look forward to being reunited with loved ones they might not have seen for months, even years.

Lots of the travellers were wearing new warm clothes: for after the scorching summer heat, these days marked the onset of the bone-chilling winter cold. Indeed, the celebration itself had been started in the first century when two teams of women in Sorabol (today's Kyongju) had taken part in a weaving contest to provide clothing for the winter. The contest lasted for an entire month – to the night of the eighth full moon – before one team was declared the winner and the losers had to acknowledge the defeat by holding a great feast of wining and dining. Within a few years the practice had become a nationwide annual festival.

Another important aspect of *Chusok* is cleanliness. When most Korean families had no baths, it was traditional for mothers to take their children to the public paths just before the celebrations to scrub them clean 'so they could attend the next morning's sacrificial rite with a clean body and mind', to quote the ancient *History of the Three Kingdoms*.

This book also instructed families that the first thing they must do at *Chusok* was to hold a 'sacrificial rite' for their ancestors. This could be either at home or at the family shrine. The family were encouraged to make offerings of soup, meat and rice cakes augmented with the season's first crop of fruits such as persimmons, nuts and dates and placed on the sacrificial table. The *History of the Three Kingdoms* added, 'It is shameful not to undertake the sacrificial rites for your ancestors at *Chusok*.'

However, unnoticed among all the millions of travellers in South Korea on 3 October 1998 were seven men in a van who also had their minds set on sacrifice. But a very different sacrifice to those being anticipated by millions of their happy fellow countrymen. The sacrifice of their own lives.

* * *

Yangyang County in Gangwon Province in the north-east of South Korea was as busy as ever in the first week of that fateful October. Once again thousands were pouring into the district to celebrate *Chusok* with their relatives: the older generation and children mostly with their elderly relatives, with teenagers heading for fun times in the coastal resorts.

The normal population of 31,000 living on the shore of the East

Sea (Sea of Japan) usually doubled at this time of year and strangers were hardly noticed in the throng of people in the streets and shops. The famous fish market was as busy as ever selling large quantities of the delicious local salmon and the nearby vegetable stalls were doing a roaring trade with the tasty mushrooms known as *song-I*.

But it was not just the local produce that brought South Koreans to Yangyang County. There was the famous sunrises – depicted in the provincial symbol – the Naksan Provincial Park and the buildings belonging to the five major religions keenly practised in the vicinity: Buddhism, Confucianism, Protestantism, Roman Catholicism and Shamanism.

The religious sites that drew pilgrims and tourists each year were the *Yangyang Hyanggyo,* a Confucian shrine built in 1340; the *Yangyang Cathedral* burned to the ground during the Korean War but now completely rebuilt; and *Seonghwangsa,* a shamanistic altar traditionally used for sacrificial rites.

Among those mingling around this altar on the eve of *Chusak* were a group of seven men. Despite their solemn faces, curiously lightweight clothes and slightly dishevelled appearance, they hardly attracted a glance from passers-by, too preoccupied with the festivities that lay ahead. Indeed, the men did not stay long in the vicinity before fading away into the crowds and returning to the mini-bus in which they had travelled the eighty-five miles east from the capital city of Seoul.

Nothing more was seen of the men that day. Their movements are unknown and their intention of remaining anonymous until their moment of destiny was evidently part of a plan to be swallowed up in the melee of *Chusok*. Indeed, their final destination would not be known until the following day. This was Naksan beach and to reach it, the men drove through the picturesque Twenty-four-km national park extending along the coastline. They might well have paused as many did at the famous multi-tiered Naksana Temple built by a group of monks in the eleventh year (671) to mark the visit of the Buddha when he had stayed at the beach. Inside hung a huge bronze bell and the mysterious artefact known as the *Hongyemun*.

It is believed the men reached the beach as the sun was setting on the evening of 4 October. It was still light enough for them to see the miles of beautiful sand that had been packed with holiday-makers for much of the summer. The pleasure boats and sea rafts now lay high up from the shore and many of the bars and restaurants were now closed and shuttered from the winter. The sea was riding a little higher than for some time and a handful of surfers were making the last of the dying light against the sound of the waves breaking on the shore.

The men admired the scenery, each lost in his own thoughts. It was here that a large 'Sunrise Festival' was held each New Year's Day and the leader of the group knew that a similar observance would take place the following morning of *Chusok*. By then, though, he planned that none of them would be looking on. They would have taken leave of life.

Woo Jong-min the leader of the *Youngsang* (Everlasting Life) Church had chosen this idyllic spot with great care. With its breathtaking sunrise and booming sea, it was the perfect place to embark on what he had described to his followers as an 'everlasting journey'.

At some point during the night, the car was driven to a more isolated part of the village. There the vehicle was swamped in petrol by the cultists who then all got back inside. A small cigarette lighter was used to ignite the car and all seven men died in the inferno.

Nothing was seen of the blazing vehicle until the following morning when the first celebrants of *Chusok* began arriving at Naksan beach to watch the sunrise. Drifts of smoke from the still smouldering wreck lead a curious couple to the scene of the incineration. They were still slumped to the ground and sick with horror when the first police cars screeched onto the beach.

It would take senior police investigator Kim Bong-yon and forensic experts several days to establish what had happened on their beach. There were enough scorched clothes and bones to establish that seven people had been inside the van in what appeared to have been a self-immolation ritual. The number plate of the vehicle was still visible and enabled the authorities to establish the owner as 27-year-old Woo Jae-hong who lived in Seoul. From Woo's grief-stricken family – who were in the middle of celebrating *Chusok* – they were able to piece together the facts about the dead and the Everlasting Church to which they all belonged.

Woo Jong-min had been a 57-year-old businessman who was convinced the world would end on the last day of the century. He formed the *Youngsang* church offering eternal life in the early nineties and documents indicate that the cult's promises attracted 'thousands of devotees' by 1996. In a statement widely quoted, he claimed that when members died they would 'achieve god-like status' and be able to lead a new, happy life in heaven.

However, these numbers had started to dwindle after the church became mired in controversy. Rumours whispered of widespread fraud and Woo Jong-min himself came under suspicion. He was briefly arrested and interrogated, but no charges made.

As support for the cult dropped still further – and there were reports that 'some of the church's followers seem to have disappeared' – Woo was seen less and less in Seoul. He also apparently began telling his closest associates that the persecution of the cult was getting him down and he was drawing up 'plans for a special journey'.

These plans did not materialize until the autumn of 1998, according to Jong-min's sister, who told the media after the discovery of her brother's body that the group had 'taken to the road to martyr themselves'. When given details of the circumstances of his death she felt sure that had 'burned themselves to death in a religious rite to obtain everlasting life in heaven'.

The news of the deaths shocked millions of South Koreans in the midst of their celebrations. It also left a mystery as to whether the date had any particular significance for the cult members who perished in the van. For the authorities, though, it was enough to write *finis* on yet another cult that believed suicide was a passport to eternity.

* * *

South Korea was not the only place in which doomsday cults proliferated in the closing years of the twentieth century, although with the Korean National Council of Churches estimating there were some 300,000 followers in over a hundred Korean cults in the year of the ritual suicide on Naksan beach, it had more than most other countries of the world.

Viewed now with the benefit of hindsight, that whole final decade can be seen to have witnessed a great surge in the number of predictions about the coming of a messiah-figure as well as a steep rise in the number of millennium cults. This phenomenon came to be known as the 'End Time' and had evidently evolved from various people's ideas that the biblical apocalypse was imminent and that various 'signs' occurring in current events were the omens of Armageddon.

Coincidentally, the wire service, Associated Press, had conducted a poll in the US which found that nearly 25 per cent of adult Christians – more than 26 million people – said they believed that Jesus Christ would return to earth during their lives and He would set in motion the apocalyptic events described in the Bible in the Book of Revelation and the Gospel of Daniel.

The fear of doomsday seemed to grip more tightly as the end of the century neared and an ABC news bulletin that heralded the final twelve months, on 5 January 1999, undoubtedly caught this mood:

'As the year 2000 creeps ever closer, millennialist cults are becoming ever more frenzied. Many of them are convinced that the world will end or transform itself soon after January 1, 2000. Israel's decision to deport eleven members of a Denver-based cult called Concerned Christians shows how seriously the authorities there take the fervour. The group, whose members were holed up in Jerusalem apartments, allegedly planned mayhem that would unleash the second coming of Christ.'

The bulletin also quoted Ted Daniels, the director of the Millennium Watch Institute, which was said to have more than 1,200 cults on file:

'People who expect the world to end soon do a lot of very strange things. They reject and even contradict the rules of common sense that keep the rest of us sane and feed our lives. They destroy the things they need to survive. They provoke fights they can't possibly win and they talk about things that obviously won't happen.'

But still the cults prospered. Among those typical of the 'End Time' groups that evolved around a series of beliefs in Christian millennialism were the Concerned Christians, Elohim City and the bizarrely named 'Outer Dimensional Forces'. These three can serve as typical of many other cults that briefly flourished in the shadow of the millennium and bring this book to a fitting conclusion.

Concerned Christians
The story of this cult is of a poacher turned gamekeeper. Founded by Denver-born Monte Kim Miller in the early 1980s, the group was originally based in his hometown and focused on combating New Age cults and the growth of anti-Christian sentiment. By the early 1990s, however, Miller had moved to Colorado and was claming that he spoke to God each morning and now believed he was the last prophet on earth before Armageddon. He told his followers that America was Satan and the government was evil. He also notoriously compared US Presidents Calvin Coolidge and Bill Clinton to Charles Manson.

In 1999, after a series of failed prophecies, the cult decided to move to Israel after Miller predicted that he would die on the streets of Jerusalem just before the millennium – rising from the dead three days later. His prediction had no chance of being proven, however, when Israeli intelligence sources became suspicious the group intended to provoke an incident at the Temple Mount in order to start a war between Arabs and Jews, generating 'the Rapture'. Miller and ten followers were immediately ordered to be deported.

The cult was next suspected of moving to Britain and planning a major incident – perhaps even a mass-suicide – in the heart of London on millennium night. David Bamber and James Langton of the *Sunday Telegraph* reported on 17 January 1999:

'Scotland Yard and the FBI are mounting a major security operation to guard against cults staging mass suicides or terrorist attacks to mark the millennium. There has been an upsurge of interest in millennial death pact bids in this country and the USA, and Monte Kim Miller, the dangerous American Millennium cult leader, is in hiding in Britain. Police on both sides of the Atlantic fear extreme religious groups will use the festival for their own ends. A key target for any cult suicide bid or terrorist attack is believed to be the Millennium Dome in Greenwich.'

Since the safe passage of the millennium, little has been heard of Miller and Concerned Christian and the security forces have downgraded its 'potential threat level'. When last reported, the remaining members were said to be living in Greece.

Elohim City
The somewhat tortuous story of this cult begins in the 1950s with a Canadian, Richard G. Miller, the founder of a charismatic church in Oklahoma. A few years later, the fiery Mennonite preacher had built up a dedicated flock of followers and decided to move to Ellicott City in Maryland. Here, near the intersection of Route 29 and Route 144 in Howard County, he established 'the Camp' on the former site of a Roman Catholic abbey. The fundamentalist Christianity that Miller combined in a dangerous mix with racialism and astrology behind the closed doors of the mansion made it the subject of repeated accusations that convinced the cult leader he would find no peace until he moved again.

In 1973, he moved to Elohim City (*Elohim* is the Hebrew word for God), a spread of 400 acres in Adair County, Oklahoma, just fifty miles across the border from President Clinton's home in Little Rock, Arkansas. It was a fortress-like place that had already seen its fair share of controversy as a base of the Christian Identity followers and supposed ties to members of the Silent Brotherhood. From the town, Richard Miller disseminated his message and turned his hundred-strong following into a para-military group who worked the land, prayed assiduously and learned how to handle pistols and rifles.

The message that Miller preached was blunt – and sinister. He dreamed of a white Christian nation in North America and was preparing Elohim City for an invasion from Asia which he believed was 'inevitable'. He told his members that Jesus Christ had been revealing himself for the last two millennia, but no one had taken any notice. The result was that a series of disasters were about to strike soon after the year 2000, 'when the unworthy and the wicked will be cleansed from the earth'.

While those inside Elohim City clung to the beliefs Miller had taught them, people outside only got a glimpse of what was going on through the occasional 'incident' that found its way into the press. One such event occurred in 1986 when a Canadian divorcee and her children sought refuge in the city to defy a court order that had awarded custody of the minors to her husband. Oklahama police officers that attempted to arrest the woman were met by a show of guns and for a few hours there were fears of a repeat of the events in 'Ranch Apocalypse'. Fortunately no violence occurred.

An equally unsettling event happened in April 1995 when the body of a former member of the cult, Richard Snell, was released to Elohim City. He had been executed in Arkansas on 19 April and had requested that his remains be given to the cult. The coffin arrived with the chilling information that Snell had taunted his jailers that 'something drastic will happen the day I'm executed'.

The prophecy came true when the Alfred P. Murrah Building, the US government federal complex at 200, NW 5th Street, in Oklahoma City, was destroyed just a couple of hours before Snell died. While the FBI were following up leads as to who might have been responsible for the explosion, statements from an earlier criminal case against Snell and some of his known associates revealed they had visited the Murrah Building to examine it as a possible bombing target in 1983.

Another persistent rumour claims the convicted Oklahoma City bomber, Timothy McVeigh, phoned some friends living in Elohim City before setting off his blast. This has now, though, been dismissed as hearsay for lack of any definite evidence.

Other Dimensional Forces

This group was certainly the most bizarre of the millennial cults I chose to investigate and was founded in 1966 by a reclusive octogenarian, Orville T. Gordon, based in a fenced-off compound in Weslaco, Texas. His inspiration was similar to that of Herff Applewhite's Heaven's Gate: he, too, believed that UFOs would come to save him and his followers from the coming apocalypse.

Like Applewhite, Gordon chose to rename himself by reversing his Christian name to 'Nodrog' by which his followers had to address him. His message was a mixture of New Age philosophy, biblical traditions and a virulent hatred of America, which he referred to as 'the Big Brother Police State to ensure that you remain in the Dark Stone Age of the Wheel'.

'Nodrog' denounced the jailors (politicians) who forced the humatons (men, women and children of the US) to 'sweat and exist in this Stone Age *juzgado* (the great American dream that has turned out to be a nightmare.) He also heaped approbation on all his rivals, 'the false prophets of the many of the End Time who are preventing you from knowing by restricting your belief and faith'. He accused the CIA of repeatedly attacking the Other Dimensional Forces, but was certain the cult's 'heavenly allies' would soon appear in the US and rescue him and his followers from persecution.

In a document issued in 1989 under the heading 'State of Time Station Earth', and date-lined 'Armageddon Time Ark Base', Orville explained the origins of his cult in equally weird jargon:

'After 6,000 years under free moral agency, ending on September 3, 1996, occupants of the Positive Birthright Territory on Time Station Earth were found, by the Outer Dimensional Forces, to be abusing themselves by still existing in the Stone Age, thereby automatically being measured as humatons. These humatons did retain some knowledge of the Circle, shown by the use of the Wheel, but have only been employing it in a negative manner by producing friction and by gathering and distributing Dump Energy for the sole purpose of debt creation against the Bond slaves. This ignorance, by self-restriction of Perfect Knowledge, has produced the end product of capitalization of costly, deadly, time-wasting experimental research, with its volumization of material and noisy pollution, man-made sickness, disease and death.'

Now, though, said Orville Gordon, the Outer Dimensional Forces had returned and would ensure that those who saw the light would survive the 'fatal Armageddon disease (AIDS II)'. He and his people would 'activate the protocol for the tapping of the Universal Time Bank for unlimited energy'. What he described as 'Seal No. 6' was now in a 'functional position for activation at 6 p.m. preceding the S. Day for the rendering of Time Station Earth safe for future habitation'.

Declaring that the Great American Dream had become, 'a nightmare of bloodsucking and terrorism', Gordon attacked industry for the 'Capitalization of Calamity' based on 'inefficiency and poor quality, short-life products'; and hospitals and healthcare organizations for becoming 'a vast industry of birth and death factories for the creation of debt claims'. He also vilified the

American government for emulating the Chinese warlord system, 'in that whichever Lord has the most tax money to hire the most burglars and gunslingers (SWAT teams and various raiders) takes the most loot and prisoners to pack the Great American Gulag Archipelago'.

The final words of Orville T. Gordon expressing his hope of seeing a new century and new world seem to me to be yet another echo of the blind faith and utter conviction in themselves and their mission that has characterized the pronouncements of so many of the cult leaders who have featured in this book:

'If you do not understand this plain English which you are trying to read, it proves that your mind is constipated by the enforced limitations of religious unreality. In such case, it is not always safe to physic your brains with too much knowledge as it may result in a fatal case of varicose brains. Use Extreme Caution!'

The verdict on them all is, I suggest, yours.

London,
November 2006.